APEX PREY

Xander Franklin

Meddleworks Publishing
Colorado

Other Books From The Author:

Absolute Zeros
Brittle Systems

Apex Prey

ISBN: 978-1-7355845-3-9

For my mother, who always took me hunting for monsters

Chapter 1

Monday

Sharon Kruschek yawned behind the leather-wrapped steering wheel, looking out on the glow of taillights stretching towards the horizon. Pop radio burbled from speakers in the dash, mingling with the light thud of princess sneakers kicking against a car seat. Reflexively, Sharon looked up, checking on her daughter in the rearview mirror. Sydney rocked against the padded belts, heels bouncing against the car seat's wide plastic base as she stared out the window, a plush purple elephant clutched in marker-stained hands. Satisfied that all was well, Sharon's pale blue eyes settled back to the road ahead. The bumper of the rusty work truck in front of her announced the candidacy of George W. Bush in peeling letters, perfectly matching the four faded NRA decals on the rear window.

In the distance, a green light flashed. The taillights dimmed as the column of cars crept forward. Sharon released the brake, inching up a few spaces before coming to another stop behind the rusty work truck. Reading the peeling bumper sticker for the fourth time, she allowed herself a momentary feeling of superiority. A proudly independent voter, no permanent politician's statement would ever lower the resale value of *her* car. Not that she'd voted in the last election. Or the one previous. She'd been busy.

The green light faded to yellow and then to red. A small sigh escaped her lips, shoulders slumping as she leaned back in her seat. Traffic was always bad after tumbling class, especially on Lincoln Street. Sharon kicked herself for not turning earlier and taking the long way home. The traffic was lighter on the neighborhood streets, even if the distance was longer, and Gregory swore it took half the time. But she needed to get gas, and the Sinclair station on Santa Fe was always five cents cheaper. Banging her head softly against the seat rest, Sharon sighed again, resigning herself to another lecture from her husband. Gregory always nagged her when he got home before she did, since it meant he had to start dinner. *Not that throwing a Swanson lasagna in the oven takes that much effort*, she mused. And tumbling class had been his idea, to give Sydney an outlet for her energy after she'd knocked the wind out of him with a flying leap from the back of the couch over New Years.

Sharon flicked her eyes back to the rearview mirror, checking in on her daughter once again. Sydney continued to watch the cars outside, blue and green dyed fingertips stroking the elephant's soft fur. Sharon made a mental note to try alcohol wipes when she got home, soap and water proving no match for the daycare's 'washable' markers.

She caught her own reflection in the mirror as her eyes dropped. Running a hand through her straight blond hair, she smoothed down the back of her side-swept bob. Her tongue clicked behind her teeth as she watched the sides and ends start to curl up. *Time for another cut*, she thought, nose wrinkling with discontent. *And another comment from Gregory about the bill*. She frowned, the edges of her thin pink lips trailing downwards into dimples that deepened the longer she looked at herself. Disapprovingly she noted the bags under her blue eyes, the perpetual worried crease in her forehead, and the sagging start to a second chin. She critiqued the woman in the three-inch mirror, picking apart her ruddy cheeks and flabby underarms, judging her against the lithe beauty who used to look back at her. That beauty was behind her now, ten years and fifty-five pounds ago. She used to turn heads whenever she walked into the *Brass Saddle*, silky blond hair trailing behind her as she stepped onto the dance floor of the crowded country bar. Now she had stretchmarks, and a hair-tie extending the button of her high-waisted jeans. Sharon felt another sigh brewing in her chest.

A horn blared behind her, yanking her violently from her thoughts. Sharon jolted forward, manicured hands scrambling back to the wheel. The horn sounded again, furious repeating notes cutting through the air.

"*Alright, alright*," Sharon stammered, jamming the gas pedal. The blue SUV lurched forward, picking up speed to match the other cars.

"I didn't realize you were Mister *fucking* Important," Sharon muttered before catching herself. Looking up sharply, she met Sydney's eyes in the rearview mirror.

"Bad word, Mommy," Sydney announced gravely, kicking her legs out as she turned back to look out the window. "Bad word."

Sharon accepted the rebuke with a shake of her head, guilt weighing down her shoulders. "I know, I'm sorry."

"Daddy says bad words too," Sydney announced loftily from the back seat, watching restaurants and strip-malls passing by.

"I know, I'm sorry." Sharon felt her jaw clench, a exhaling a thin sigh through her nose. She'd talked to Gregory about swearing in front of Sydney countless times, it was part of the reason she was so mindful about her *own* language. *Someone should be an example.*

She took her foot off the gas as the traffic slowed, drawing abreast of a red Mack truck. The big eighteen-wheeler loomed over her, battered white trailer casting a long shadow across her blue Chevy Equinox. Sharon shivered a little in her seat. Big trucks always made her a nervous, a friend of hers in high school had been sideswiped by one as it merged on a busy highway. Since then, she never quite trusted that they could see her, regardless of the mirrors sprouting around their cabs.

Something huge and white crashed to the road beside her car. Sharon cast an anxious eye towards the truck, but it was only snow sliding off the roof of the trailer. *Must have come in from the mountains,* she thought, scrutinizing the dirty frost clinging to the truck's sides. It was a decently warm day for a Colorado spring, fifty degrees and cloudy, but she'd heard on the news several feet of snow had dropped over the mountains last night. *That snow better* stay *in the mountains.* Sharon's lips pursed a little at the thought, the last thing she needed was another snow day trapping her in the house with an energetic four-year-old and day's backlog of emails.

The light at the intersection changed again, granting her a temporary reprieve from her worries as the traffic ahead began to pull away. Picking up speed, she saw billowing smoke erupt from the stacks of the Mack truck as it rumbled alongside her, keeping her in the trailer's shade. Out of habit she swerved around the manhole cover in the center of the road, guiding the compact SUV around the road's bumps from memory.

The semitruck was not so lucky, and she heard the thump as the big wheels clipped the edge of the manhole. A glimmer of self-satisfaction at her superior road knowledge was quickly extinguished as something crashed hard onto her car's roof.

"*Fuck!*" Sharon yelped, jerking the wheel left. She heard something bounce across the roof as she cranked the wheel back to the right, swerving away from the median. She straightened the Equinox out, catching her breath again as a splatter of snow trailed off the roof-mounted RocketBox and fell behind her. *Just snow, Sharon, it's just snow.* She forced herself to breathe easier as the semitruck sped past, oblivious to the chaos it had caused. Briefly, she imagined a world where all large trucks were banned, or at least kept off the town streets. Her thin lips turned ever so slightly up.

"Bad word, Mommy," Sydney chastised from the rear.

The thin lips dropped further into a scowl.

"I know," Sharon muttered. "I'm sorry."

Sharon and Sydney drove on, grateful for a spell of green lights that thinned the traffic around her. Outside the window, an early dusk set in as the sun began its descent behind the mountains. A glance at the clock told Sharon it was a quarter to eight, her pulse quickening before she remembered the clock was fast after daylight savings. She'd asked Gregory to fix it last week—cars were supposed to be his domain. Sharon tapped her fingers on the steering wheel, resolving to ask him one more time before giving up and digging through the owner's manual herself. She asked Gregory to do a lot of things around the house. Most ended in the same way.

Sydney mumbled something from the back.

"What, sweetie?" Sharon asked, eyes flicking up to the rearview mirror.

"Monster, mommy," Sydney repeated calmly, big brown eyes looking out from a nest of curly hair.

"What monster, sweetie?" Sharon asked, voice lilting up as she feigned interest. Imagination was important to a child's development—all the experts said so—and Sharon strove to be encouraging.

"Back there," Sydney said, twisting in her seat and pointing out the rear window.

Sharon's eyes followed her daughter's pointing before returning to the road.

"Oh, yes," Sharon nodded. "And is it a funny monster or a friendly one?"

"Scary monster," Sydney giggled, turning back to the front.

"A *scary* monster?" Sharon asked, exaggerating the words as she watched for the next green light. "With *big* eyes and *big* teeth?"

"Noooo," Sydney giggled. "Shiny monster. Like the movie."

"Like the movie," Sharon repeated absentmindedly, forehead creasing with worry as the words settled into place. It'd been nearly two months since she and Gregory had settled in for a movie night—her pick, for a change. Halfway through the sci-fi flick they'd heard a small cough behind them, Sydney's eyes wide and staring from around the hallway corner. Sharon blamed herself in the moment—she should have heard her get out of bed, and she should've known to pick a different movie. It took nearly a week of careful cajoling and distraction to get Sydney to forget what she'd seen; all she'd wanted to talk about were the glossy black aliens stalking hapless colonists from the shadows. Sharon sighed, steeling herself for another long week.

She pulled into the Sinclair station on the right, coasting to a stop beside an empty pump. As she put the SUV in park she heard a faint scraping on the roof. *Must be the RocketBox, knocked loose by the snow.* She made a mental note to ask Gregory to check it out when she got home, then thought better of it. She'd might as well do it herself.

She swung the door shut behind her, pawing through a cavernous paisley purse for her credit card and Sinclair Rewards card. Retrieving them, she stepped forward to the pump, frowning at a strip of tape pinned over the card reader. 'Card Reeder Broke,' announced a sign taped to the pump, 'Pay inside.'

Sharon looked hopefully to the pump behind her, frown deepening as a dented green Jeep pulled in instead. A man in plaid and a yellow trucker hat hopping out, scattering flakes of rust as he slammed the door. She sighed, slinging her purse over one shoulder as she walked into the storefront, clicking her key fob to lock the Equinox behind her.

"Hey, lady."

Sharon stopped mid-step, turning to face the man in plaid. "Yes?"

The man pointed to her roof. "I think there's something on your car."

Sharon's brow furrowed.

"It's the RocketBox," she replied, stepping quickly to position herself between him and the SUV. "It's just loose."

"You sure?" he asked, removing his hat to scratch his head. "Coulda sworn I saw somethin' else."

He squinted at the roof before turning back to her. "You wan' me to take a look?"

"It's fine," she said curtly. "My *husband* will take care of it when we get ho—"

"There it is again!" he blurted out.

Sharon turned to follow his point, squinting hard in the glare of the sunset. He walked around to the back of the SUV, staring up at the roof rack and RocketBox. Seeing her chance, Sharon stole past him to the driver's door. *On second thought, I'll fill up tomorrow.* Unlocking just her door, she looked back at the man, still staring quizzically at her roof.

"It's fine," she called back to him, swinging open her door and preparing to hop in. "Thank you."

"S'alright," he drawled in reply, touching a finger to the brim of his hat

Sharon let out a small breath as he turned to head back to the Jeep. She slid one leg up on the leather seat, stopping short as she heard something scrape along her roof, skittering towards the back. Half in the cab, she watched the man stop and turn towards the source of the noise. A moment of confusion passed over his face, thick brows knitting together. Taking a few steps forward, he rested a leather boot on the rear wheel.

"You got a cat up there or somethin'?" he asked, hands outstretched towards something on the roof.

Sharon opened her mouth to answer, but stopped short. A blur of green movement arced downwards from the roof of the blue SUV. It whirred by the man in plaid, opening up his throat as it passed. Sharon eyes went wide as he stumbled back, arterial blood spurting from his neck. She jumped into the seat, slamming the door behind her as she fumbled for her keys in the ignition. The engine caught and turned on, radio blaring to life over the cheap plastic speakers. Sharon punched the power button, silence reigning for a moment. There was scratching on the roof again, this time headed to the front. Something shiny and green hopped onto the hood, turning quickly on six multi-jointed limbs. Sharon caught a glimpse of hell as a mouth opened up beneath a wide, domed head—a mouth filled with a hundred sharp teeth.

"Monster, mommy!" Sydney called out from the back.

Sharon screamed, throwing the car in drive and mashing the pedal to the floor. The Equinox's inline-four roared to life, lurching forward as they sped away from the gas station. She watched the thing on her hood tumble up her windshield, skittering for purchase as it hit the roof. She listened closely as the scrabbling sound receded towards the back, eyes glued to the rearview mirror as she waited for it to fall to the road.

Nothing happened. Cold dread spread through her in waves as the mad scrabbling stopped, replaced with a defiant, resolute scratching sound that crawled slowly to the middle of the roof. And then there was silence.

Sharon sped down Santa Fe, thoughts racing to match her pounding heart.

Green.

Teeth.

A plaid-covered arm reaching for the roof.

Blood.

Is Sydney safe?

Sharon's eyes snapped up to the rearview mirror. Sydney sat calmly in her belted seat, bouncing the plush elephant in her lap. Sharon dropped her eyes back to the road. Ahead of her the light turned yellow, then to red.

She sped through anyways.

A rash of horns sounded behind her from drivers cut off mid-turn. Sharon forced herself to breathe.

In.

And out.

She eased her foot off the pedal, slowing the SUV from its breakneck speed.

Is it even still there?

Sharon pulled her foot from the gas, slowing down further. Immediately the scratching resumed, moving towards the vehicle's front. A sharp green forelimb drifted into view at the top of the windshield.

Yes!

Sharon mashed the pedal to the floor, the forelimb dipping back out of view as they accelerated. The scratching receded back to the center of the roof. Then silence again. Sharon swallowed hard, letting the speedometer drop to sixty miles per hour, just twenty miles over the speed limit.

Breathe in. And out.

She checked in on Sydney again.

She's fine, drive. Don't crash.

Sharon nodded to herself as she sucked in a deep breath, cheeks puffing out as she exhaled. She forced her hands to unclench from the steering wheel, color returning to her knuckles when she did.

Breathe in. And out.

She checked on Sydney again. Her daughter busied herself with whispering secrets to the plush elephant.

Where are we going?

It was a valid question, one that took three intersections to break through the frantic morass of her mind.

Home?

Home was still an option, the right-hand turn into their neighborhood was only a few blocks away. She could call Gregory, have him waiting when she got home.

Have him shoot it?

She banished the thought with a shake of her head. There were no guns in the house, the closest thing they had was the twenty-pound recurve bow she used to practice archery. And Gregory was anything but a sportsman.

Maybe he can distract it? Give us time to run inside?

A vision unfolded in her mind. The blue Equinox pulling into the driveway. Gregory running outside and waving his arms. Him getting too close to the car, not understanding the danger on the roof. A blur of green. Gregory reeling back with blood spraying from his throat. *Just like the man in plaid…*

Sharon winced, knuckles tightening on the wheel. Her turn was coming up. Sharon could see the wide mouth of the neighborhood drive, the *Crestview Hills* sign flanked by maple trees. She began to slow for the turn, heart beating faster as the sign drew nearer. The scratching resumed on the roof.

No! I can't bring this thing home.

She bit her lower lip, steeling herself as resolve crept through her, pushing aside her fear for the moment.

I won't let it get Gregory.

Sharon gasped, forcing out a breath she hadn't meant to hold. She sped past her turn, barreling away from her neighborhood.

Breathe in. And out.

Don't crash.

The road began to narrow, trimming down to two lanes as they moved away from town. She checked on Sydney again, now staring out the window as their neighborhood dwindled in the distance. Sharon nodded to herself, puffing out her cheeks with another deep breath.

I need more time to figure this out. And more road.

There was a sign up ahead for the highway on-ramp.

Perfect.

Sharon approached the northbound on-ramp with cautious optimism. Dusk had settled, the sun's last rays trailing from behind the western mountains. Well past rush hour, she prayed the traffic had cleared enough for her to merge without slowing.

She felt a flutter of relief as she turned on the empty ramp, merging with ease amid the smattering of cars on I-25. Keeping the speedometer at sixty-five, she sped up with traffic but only just above the speed limit. The last thing she needed now was a ticket.

Or do I?

The thought turned over in her mind. Cops have guns, and she knew from the evening news that they were more than willing to use them.

But what if they hit Sydney?

A shiver of worry passed through her. If she got pulled over, the thing might startle a cop before she got a chance to explain. Her mind's eye envisioned the Equinox, riddled with bullets and shattered glass.

No, she shook her head, *no cops. Not until I figure out a way to explain this.*

She checked on Sydney in the rear-view mirror, she'd been unusually quiet.

"Sweetie," Sharon called back, forcing calm into her voice. "You okay back there?"

"Hungry," Sydney said, watching the cars pass by the window.

Sharon looked at the clock on the dash, trying to shake the pang of guilt in her stomach. Any normal day and she would have been home an hour ago. *You've got bigger worries at the moment, Sharon.*

"We'll get dinner soon, sweetie," she replied, voice lilting up at the end. "McDonalds?"

"With a shake?"

"Chocolate shake," Sharon nodded. "For sure."

Cheers filled the cabin's silence as she dropped her attention back to the road. Her guilt temporarily assuaged, she returned to the thing on the roof, and the problem of what to do about it. Cops sprang again to mind. *Or the army*, she mused, *someone with guns. Assuming, of course, that it isn't bulletproof.*

That was something to consider. She didn't actually know what *it* was, let alone how to stop it. She churned over what little she did know, informed by the briefest of impressions she gained when it was on top of her hood. It was green, about the size of their neighbor's German Shepherd, and shiny, almost oily. She remembered a blur of legs, segmented and spiny, like a crab. There were more than four, but how many she couldn't quite recall. *And the teeth.* She shuddered at the thought, her mind filled with flashing rows of white, jagged teeth.

Beyond appearances, she knew it was dangerous. *And quick.* At the gas station it'd moved in a blur. She shivered again, deliberately blocking out the image of blood-soaked plaid. She focused instead on its connection to the car. Any speed above fifty miles-per-hour seemed to keep it in place. The scratching sound had settled in the middle of the roof, no doubt tucked between the railings of the rack. Sharon frowned, none of that gave her insight into what to do next, but it was all she had for now.

She changed lanes, passing a grey minivan with *PAW Patrol* playing on the drop-down screen. Sharon allowed herself a small moment of pride in not being one of *those* moms. You know, a *soccer-van* mom. She ran her hands lightly over the leather-wrapped wheel. The 2016 Equinox wasn't the sportiest SUV, but at least it had all-wheel drive. And, critical though she was of her own failings as a parent, at least *her* kid could get through a car-ride without watching tv.

A chirping sound came from the dashboard screen, pulling her from her thoughts as Gregory's name popped up. She answered the

Bluetooth call, a momentary silence before her husband's voice poured out of the speakers.

"Are you close? If you're not in the neighborhood yet I need you to swing by King Soopers on your way in. We're out of milk. And beer." His tone was rushed and slightly distant, no doubt on speakerphone while he 'made' dinner.

"No, dear, I'm—"

"No? Where are you guys? You didn't take Lincoln, did you?"

"Yes but—"

"Are you still in traffic? Of *course* you are. I told you not to take Lincoln, just cut through the neighborhoods."

"I know, but—"

"I *told* you last time, take Baxter to Alberta, then left on Portier and a right on Hillside. Gets you home in thirty minutes every time."

Sharon ground her teeth. Somehow, even today, this was going exactly as predicted. "You did, but Greg—"

"Forget the milk. But just so you know, I put dinner in right when I got home. No bitching if it's cold by the time you finally get here—"

"GREG! Shut *the fuck* up for *ONE! SECOND!*"

There was silence on the other line, accompanied by the sound of the faucet switching off.

"Bad word, mommy," came a whisper from the back.

"I know," Sharon sighed, shaking her head as she collected her thoughts. "Gregory, listen, something happened."

Confused worry replaced the frustration in his tone. "Sharon, are you okay? What's wrong?"

Sharon opened her mouth and shut it, trying to find the right words.

"Was it another accident? I know I got mad last time, but that was only 'cause his turn signal was on and I really thought you should've seen it."

Sharon threw her head back against the seat, a waterfall of exasperation pouring out of her.

"No, *Greg*, it wasn't another accident," she said through gritted teeth. Trust her husband to find yet another way to remind her of the fender-bender she had last year.

"Well, what is it? Whatever it is, you can tell me, Sharon."

I'm TRYING to, she fumed. Her windshield lit with flashing red as traffic flowed around an accident ahead. Sharon tapped the brakes, slowing down with the other cars. Organizing the events of the past hour in her mind, she tried to assemble them into a measure of sense.

"I pulled in to get gas," she explained, her words measured and slow.

"At the Sinclair on Santa Fe?"

"Yes, and the reader on the pump was broke—"

"The one on the far right? I think it was broken last week too."

"Yes, *Greg*." Sharon's knuckles tightened on the wheel, she could see the accident now, a small Nissan on the shoulder of the road. The cars around her slowed further, negotiating their way around the shattered glass and torn-off fender lying in the far-left lane. "But I need you not to interrupt me right now."

Sharon watched the speedometer dip below fifty, then to forty, then thirty-five. "The pump-reader was broken, and a man stopped me because he said he saw something on the roof."

"What roof? Of the gas station?"

Sharon shook her head. "No, my roof, on the rack by the RocketBox."

"What was it, Sharon? What was wrong with the roof?"

Traffic slowed to a crawl. Sharon felt her heart sinking as the speedometer dropped.

"Monster, mommy," Sydney replied quietly from the back.

Sharon nodded, acknowledging her. Keeping her eyes on the road, she reached behind to give her leg a reassuring squeeze. "That's right, sweetie, the monster was on the roof."

"The what?" Greg's voice was louder now, having taken the phone off speaker. "Sharon, sorry, I didn't hear you right."

Sharon steered around the wrecked Nissan. On the other side of the accident she could see traffic picking back up. "At the gas station, we were at pump and there was a thing on the roof."

"A thing? What kind of thing?" More confusion in his tone. She pictured him standing by the sink, eyebrows drawn together with his jaw slightly open.

"I don't know, Greg—some kind of animal."

"An animal? On the roof?"

"Monster, mommy," Sydney repeated, a little more urgently this time.

"I heard you, sweetie." Sharon nodded to her again, eyes still on the road. Clearing her throat, she spoke up louder. "Yes, an animal. On the roof. When we were at the gas station."

"No, mommy, monster *now!*"

Sharon froze, panic gripping her at the urgency in her daughter's voice. A tapping sound she hadn't recognized earlier filled the cabin, like nails clinking on a coffee mug.

OR GLASS! Sharon whipped around. She spotted the green domed head, craning down to peer at her daughter through the side window. Sydney looked up at her, pupils wide with terror as she death-gripped the plush elephant. Sharon watched in horror as a spikey forelimb drew back from the window, a chip of glass coming away with it. Sharon searched the road around her, but the lanes were packed with cars slowing to a stop. The spikey limb came down again, a small crack spiderwebbing from the point of impact. Sharon locked eyes with her daughter, trying to reassure her as she thought through a plan.

Greg's voice cut in over the speaker. "Sharon? Sharon? Are you still there?"

A van in front of them pulled away slightly, leaving them the briefest gap.

The forelimb drew back.

"HOLD ON!" Sharon shouted, mashing the gas pedal and roaring onto the highway's shoulder.

She watched in the rearview as the creature fought for balance, lurching back from the window. Sensing an opportunity, Sharon cranked the wheel hard to the right, scraping against the back corner of the white panel-van. Metal screeched on metal as the van's corner dug a trench through the SUV's bright blue paint. A horn blared behind her as she sped away, cabin vibrating in protest as she drove over the rumble strip marking the edge of the lane.

Sharon checked the rearview again, but the creature was nowhere in sight. A thin flicker of satisfaction pulled at the corners of her mouth. Straightening the SUV out as she drove around the stopped cars, she let out a small sigh of relief.

Until she heard the faintest sound of scratching from the roof.

Miles outside the city, Sharon eased the Equinox off the shoulder and back into the far-left lane. Sunset have given way to dusk, and she'd passed the last car over a half-mile ago. As the rumble of the lane-divider subsided, Sharon exhaled slowly through her nose, forcing herself to breathe. *In. And out. Just like yoga,* she thought absentmindedly, although she hadn't been to a class since giving birth. She'd been busy.

She checked in on her daughter. Sydney's eyes were shut, the stuffed elephant loose in her hands. *Hopefully asleep.*

The sky and the highway stretched before them, vast, open, and empty. A handful of stars sparkled in the east as they drove north along I-25. It was a quiet, clear night, and she hadn't heard scraping since they left the traffic behind, but Sharon knew better than to trust it. She felt that dread, deep within her bones, knowing the creature was still up there.

She changed to the right lane, more out of something to do than for any particular reason. The highway gave her a direction to follow, but no destination, and she dared not slow down enough to turn around. Setting cruise control once again, she ran a hand through her side-swept bob, mussing it a little as she reached for something, anything to do next.

Tragedy struck in the form of a small yellow light, blinking on the dash. Sharon read the fuel gauge with dismay, realization settling in that though the road ahead seemed infinite, their time on it was not.

Does that mean I have enough gas for fifty miles? Or only twenty-five? Sharon wracked her brain. She knew Gregory had told her once, she'd just never needed to remember it before. She always filled up when the gauge read a quarter-tank, just to be safe. Idly, she considered calling him to ask, but that last maneuver onto the highway shoulder had knocked her purse off the seat, slinging her phone into the crack of the passenger door. She'd tried to use the Bluetooth earlier, but couldn't get the screen to work right. She tapped the touch-screen in the dash again, rolling her finger back and forth on the menu before giving up in a frustrated huff, thwarted in her attempts to navigate to the previous calls list.

And so she drove, lost in thought, before being interrupted by a second set of flashing lights. Sharon cursed under her breath, her rearview mirror lit up with red and blue. She calmed herself down as the lights grew closer, reasoning with herself that this might be the break they needed. *Just as long as I can explain before he starts shooting…*

Sharon slowed the SUV, just in case the cop was trying to pass. The red and blue lights slowed as well but stayed behind her, and she resigned herself to pulling over. She held her breath as she guided the blue Equinox to a stop, listening the whole time for the tell-tale scratching. But the cabin was silent as she drifted to a stop on the shoulder of the road.

The lights stopped behind her as well. She considered rolling down the window to yell back at them, but they seemed too far away, and she was wary of doing anything that might be interpreted as 'threatening.' Sydney stirred in her seat, momentarily drawing her attention to the back. A rap at the window made her jump, but it was just the cop.

A young trooper in a wide-brimmed blue hat stood beside the car. "Colorado State Police. Ma'am, can you roll down your window."

Sharon held her breath, waiting for the sound of scratching from above.

The officer knocked again. "Ma'am, roll down the window."

Sharon nodded, reluctantly complying. Her face scrunched up

with worry as she watched the thin safety of the glass fade away into the door.

The officer stood back, resting his hands on his belt. "Ma'am, do you know why I pulled you over?"

The question caught her off guard. She hadn't considered *why* a cop had been following her. She paused for a moment before answering.

"Honestly? No. I wasn't speeding, was I?"

The young trooper shook his head. "No ma'am. I got a report of a hit-and-run from a vehicle matching this description."

Oh, right. Sharon nodded. "Yes. About that. Officer, I can explain—"

The officer cut her off with a wave of his hand. "License and registration, ma'am."

"Right, yes, but—"

His voice was coarser the second time. "License. And registration."

Sharon swallowed hard, eyes on the ceiling as she bent over to retrieve the documents. She handed them over, mouth opening to explain further. He ignored her and walked off, disappearing behind the glare of the flashing lights.

Seconds crawled by in silence, every fiber of her being stretched taut in fear. Out on the highway, a semitruck whipped by, rocking the SUV in its wake. There was a murmur in the back as Sydney stirred again. She reached around to quiet her, freezing in place as something sharp scraped against the roof.

Sharon whipped back, frantically pressing the button to raise the window. Looking up, she saw the shocked face of the officer as the glass slid shut between them. He reached forward, rapping the butt of his flashlight on the glass.

"The roof!" she hissed, "It's on the roof!"

The Officer tapped again, his voice muffled slightly by the glass. "Ma'am! Open the window!"

Up above, Sharon heard scraping on the move

"*THE ROOF!*" she shouted, tears in her eyes as she pointed upwards. The officer stepped back, confused. One hand hovered near the gun on his belt while the other panned the flashlight up. He swept his light over the roof-rack and RocketBox, taking another step back.

But not far enough.

Sharon watched in horror as the spikey forelimb struck out, a blur of motion almost too quick to see. The flashlight dropped from the officer's hand as he clutched at his torn throat. He reeled back, eyes wide in terror and disbelief. Blood sprayed against her window, obscuring her vision as he tumbled backwards into the road.

No scream escaped her this time as trembling hands threw the car in drive, speeding them off into the night.

Manicured nails dug into the wheel, supporting her as she suppressed a cold shiver. On the dash she watched the needle tick further down the 'E,' her stomach twisting and churning on itself. She had no idea how far they'd driven since the cop, and no idea how far they could go. Her mind was utterly consumed with two thoughts.

How do I get it off the roof? And how do I keep us safe after?

She glanced over to the passenger door; the edge of her cellphone just visible. She kicked herself for forgetting to grab it when they'd stopped, but she dared not slow down again. She pictured the spiderweb crack on the window in the back. The window right next to her daughter's car seat.

She glanced up at the rearview mirror. Sydney was curled up in her seat, knees tucked to her chest, and eyes shut a little too tight to actually be asleep. The stuffed elephant was on the floor, dropped in the panic of the traffic stop. Sharon gave a quick look to the road before reaching back and retrieving it. Tucking it back into her daughter's arms, a small whimper left Sydney's lips as her dainty fingers clutched the purple fur.

Sharon's heart broke as the turned back to the road. She longed to curl herself around her, shielding her from the terror outside with her own body.

That won't keep her safe, that will only slow it down.

The knot in her stomach tightened further. She cast her pale blue eyes to the heavens for inspiration.

Something, anything, please.

Her eyes settled on the row of switches on the ceiling. There, nestled among the buttons for the dome-light and the back release, was another button she'd never notice before. A small blue button, with two letters capped by a tiny star.

Blue's always been my lucky color…

Sharon snapped her eyes to the road, heart racing as an idea formed. The highway stretched before her, flanked by miles of pasture and rolling ranchlands. Verdant, empty plains dotted here and there by boulders. She looked back to Sydney, doublechecking the belts tightened around her chest. Glancing down at the dash, she saw the needle tick down, now fully below the 'E.' She prayed it would hold out just a little longer. For this to work, she needed speed.

Sharon picked her target two miles out, a lonely outcropping of limestone butting up against the highway shoulder. She'd slowed down briefly right before, the brief scratching above confirming the creature was still onboard.

No use risking this for nothing.

A mile-and-a-half out and she left the lane for the shoulder of the road, breaking the silence of the cabin with the ping of gravel kicked up underneath. She glanced in the rearview mirror. Sydney's eyes were open, wide and staring out the windshield. Sharon reached behind and squeezed her foot, pouring as much comfort and love into the gesture as she could.

Please, God, keep her safe.

Sharon turned to face the front, hammering the pedal down. She watched the needle on the speedometer slowly climb upwards, as sixty turned to seventy, then to eighty. A mile out and the outcropping loomed ahead, growing larger as they approached, bigger than expected.

Less chance of missing it then…

A half mile out and the Equinox's in-line four whined in protest as they hit ninety, coughing and shuddering as the fuel lines dried up.

Almost there…

A quarter-mile out, the needle passed ninety-five, the engine giving one last wheeze before dying. Sharon released the pedal, knuckles white as she steered. She only had one chance.

The outcropping rushed to meet them. She could see the cracks and crevices in the limestone face. She forced one hand off the wheel, reaching upwards and tapping the small blue button.

"OnStar services, what's your emergency?"

"I'm having an accident," she replied flatly, slamming her foot down on the brake.

The night was rent by the shrieking of worn pads biting into rotors. The wheel jerked in Sharon's hands as she fought to keep the SUV straight. She could feel the pedal fluttering beneath her feet as the anti-lock brakes fought to keep from seizing up. All around her, tires squealed, fighting against the momentum of 3,000 pounds of steel.

Grimly, Sharon clung to the steering wheel, keeping them straight through sheer force of will. The Equinox's nose dipped, front brakes bearing the greatest load.

C'mon, c'mon!

Her prayers were answered with series of dull thuds and frantic scrabbling. She watched as the creature tumbled off the roof, sailing uncontrollably through the air, borne forward by momentum. She didn't have time to cheer as she watched the creature smack against the wall of limestone.

Sharon glanced at her daughter one more time in the rearview mirror. Up ahead, the rocks were coming much too fast.

She said another prayer for Sydney.

And then her world went black.

Sharon came to slowly, like waves lapping against the shore. Her first sensation was of gloved hands, wrapping a brace around her neck. Then snippets of words floated to her ears.

"…Female, Caucasian, late-thirties…"

"…C-collar?"

"One-two-three lift!"

Sharon felt her body raise, then lower on a rigid bed. The word 'gurney' tumbled through her mind. Another sensation of lifting, and the distant sound of wheels locking into place.

She felt a bump, rocking gently against the Velcro restraints as they loaded her in. She cracked one eye, squinting hard against the glare of the light.

A lumpy shadow blocked her view as it bent over, poking and prodding as he affixed monitors and wires. She felt a tube enter her nose.

Her eyes snapped open.

"Sydney?" she coughed, struggling against the restraints. "Sydney!"

"Your daughter is fine," the EMT replied, leaning his weight on her to hold her down. "She was buckled in tight."

Sharon felt a prick in her elbow as the IV slid in, a sensation of numbness spreading out from her arm.

"Sydney? Sydney?" she whimpered, her eyes watering.

"She's fine, she's right here." The EMT sat back, revealing her daughter sitting safely in the jump-seat.

Tears of joy flowed down her cheek. As Sydney rushed forward from the seat, Sharon felt a dainty hand grasp her fingers tight as she shut her eyes.

She heard the EMT pound on the cab's metal divider as the numbness spread up her neck.

"Secured for transport, let's go."

Sharon felt the rumble as the ambulance drove off. She gripped Sydney's hand tight within her own, unwilling to ever let her go. The wind outside howled as the ambulance picked up speed. As her world faded to black, she could almost hear a faint scratching from the roof.

Chapter 2:

Tuesday

A stillness hung over the apartment of Charles Davner, a warm heaviness that blanketed the two-bedroom condo like a patchwork quilt. Amber street light filtered through tattered blinds, casting long shadows on the bed where he lay. Charles sprawled out in the two a.m. quiet, clinging to sleep with the hushed desperation that comes from going to bed far too late knowing you had to be up very, very early. Snuffled grunts broke out intermittently from the corner of the room as a fat French bulldog chased rabbits through her dreams.

A clatter arose from the bedside table, shattering the silence of the room as "Flight of the Bumblebee" blared from the cellphone's speaker. Bleary brown eyes snapped open, taking in the darkness of the room before shutting tight again. In that moment Charles Davner was aware of two things; Savannah had been messing with his phone again, and someone had died.

Blindly, he reached for the nightstand, fumbling his way to the vibrating phone. Unlocking it with a swipe of his thumb, he brought the phone to his ear, his eyes resolutely shut.

"Detective Davner."

"Hey, Chuck, it's Sam—"

"It's Todd's turn for on-call. I'm off tonight."

"I know, Todd didn't answer."

Fucker, Charles thought, scrunching his eyes further closed. "Perry's next up after him. Call him."

"Perry's phone's off," Sam replied, exasperation creeping in his tone. "And Allison's still out on maternity leave for three more weeks."

Should've turned my phone off—only way to get some damn sleep around here. Charles continued bitching to himself, letting silence stretch on the line.

"Chuck, you still there?"

Charles sighed, he knew ignoring Sam wasn't an option.

"Yeah," he grumbled, "I'm here. What's the deal?"

"Officer down. A CSP trooper on I-25."

Charles winced, bringing his other hand up to pinch the bridge of his nose. "What happened?"

"Hit by a truck," Sam answered slowly. "Few miles south of the Corvette Center."

Charles opened his eyes, brows knitting together in confusion. "And the State troopers aren't taking it? Why?"

There was a pause on the line.

Sam's voice took on a pitched, somber tone. "The driver said the trooper was lying in the road when he hit'em. CSP says he was on a traffic stop earlier and never called it complete. They think something happened with the stop."

Charles nodded to himself, details falling into place. Per an executive order from Governor Jarvis, any officer death that couldn't immediately be ruled as manslaughter had to run through another agency. If the Colorado State Police had the slightest inclination it wasn't an accident, it made sense they'd go to Colorado Springs as the nearest police department. Charles sighed again, the investigation made perfect sense, he just wished it wasn't him that had to run it.

"When?" he grunted, feeling for the lamp switch as he rolled over in the bed. He took a notepad and pen out of the nightstand, scattering empty Heineken bottles as he slammed the drawer shut.

"We got the call around one-thirty. CSP got the dispatch call from the truck driver around midnight. No details on the time of the traffic stop."

"Sure, sure," Charles mumbled, jotting notes down on the pad. "CSP still on scene?"

"Ummmmmm." There was another pause, Charles imagined the investigative technician leafing through his color-coded notes. "Yes, uh, I think so. I'll call them back to make sure. You heading in now?"

"Yeah, I'll stop by the scene first and talk to CSP there," Charles said, sitting up on the edge of the bed. "South of the Corvette Center?"

"Yes, I'll let the Sergeant know you're heading there first before you stop in."

Charles dropped the notepad on the bed, rubbing the last vestiges of sleep from his eyes. "Don't forget to call CSP and make sure they stick around."

"Copy," Sam replied, his usual chipper tone returning. "Thanks for taking this."

"No problem," Charles grunted, dragging a hand down his face. "Happy to help."

"One last thing, Chuck."

"Yeah?"

"Sarge says, 'Don't to be an asshole.'"

"No promises," grumbled Charles, hanging up the phone and dropping it on the bed. He dropped his head and rolled his shoulders, a chorus of pops and cricks echoing back as he stretched. Standing up from the bed, he hunted for his pants in the dim room. A snort came from the corner as Petunia rolled over, oblivious to the world around her.

"Good, keep sleeping," He said, pulling on a pair of jeans from the floor. "I know you had such a *long,* busy day."

Petunia ignored him, a contented sigh escaping as she found greater comfort on the pillow in the corner.

He stomped over to the bedside table, rifling through the drawer for his wallet, badge, and gun. The wallet and badge went into his back pockets, the phone and notepad into his front. He threaded his belt through the loops of his holster, securing the 9mm Smith & Wesson in its customary place on his right side. Bending over to retrieve his socks from beneath the bed, he felt the rough stippling of the pistol's backstrap rub up against his side. He frowned as he looked down on polymer butt scraping against a roll of pale skin. *That's new.* He looked from the roll on his side to the beginnings of a paunch in his front, connecting the two in his mind. He poked at his belly, watching it almost, but not quite, disappear as he stood up. *That's it, diet starts Monday,* Charles mused, pulling a wrinkled shirt off the back of a chair.

James had tried to get him to eat better the whole time they were together. *And workout more. And dress better,* he thought as he fastened the buttons on the plaid shirt. *And get a haircut more than once a month.* That last item was a particular sticking point for Charles as he checked himself in the mirror. He liked his messy swoop of tangled blond hair. He smoothed it out with a few quick strokes of his hand, forcing the top to run in a single direction. *There, nice and easy.* James had pushed him to shave the sides, feather the ends, use mousse—to do *something* with it. Charles' jaw clenched a little at the memory of their last fight, when he'd accused James of trying to mold him into the perfect social-media accessory instead of taking him as he was. Things hadn't gone well after that; he'd come home from work to find Petunia unfed, half the closet empty, and a post-it note on the door.

Charles shook his head, clearing away the memory and bridging his focus with the here and now. He ran a hand over the stubble on his cleft chin, the fine red hair just light enough to obscure the smattering of gray that'd cropped up after his thirtieth birthday. The thought of shaving occurred to him, but he dismissed it with a snort. *They called me in at two a.m., they get the two a.m. me.*

He stomped into the hallway to grab his boots, sitting down on the hardwood floor with a thud. The light flickered on in the office at the end of the hall. He looked up to see his little sister standing in the doorway, bright blue hair sticking in every direction as she rubbed her eyes.

"What's up?" Savannah asked, blinking her eyes into focus.

"Heading out," he grunted, tugging his boots on. "Got a call."

She covered a yawn with her hand. "Homicide?"

Savannah had been crashing with him for the last few weeks, ever since a guy from her class wouldn't take no for an answer and started waiting for her in the parking lot outside of Colorado College.

He nodded. "CSP trooper out on I-25."

Savannah blanched. "Yeesh."

"Yup," he answered, struggling with the stubborn laces. He straightened up, smoothing his pants over the top of the boots before fixing an eye on her. "Didn't I tell you not to fuck with my phone? You *know* I hate that song."

She grinned. "Didn't *I* tell you not to stay up late creeping on your ex's Instagram?"

Charles muttered something unintelligibly derisive in reply, fishing his keys off the hook in the center of the hallway.

"Don't give me that guff," snapped Savannah, hands finding their way to her hips in the same way their mother's did when they were kids. "Doesn't take a detective to figure out why half the beer's gone the same night James uploads his cliff-diving story from Cabo."

Charles ignored her as he trudged over to the door.

"I'll be gone all day," he grumbled. "Feed Petunia."

"I always do. You want some coffee first?" Savannah asked, folding her arms over her chest. "Take some stink off that shitty attitude?"

"Got a RedBull in the car, *mom*," he called back, slamming the door behind him. Muttering to himself, he added, "And there's nothing wrong with my *attitude*."

Charles grouched his way down two flights of cement stairs and all the way to the cracked asphalt lot. Plodding over to the number fifteen spot, he yanked open the door on the golden 1987 Oldsmobile Delta 88. Jamming the key in the ignition, the 3.8-liter V6 rumbled to life with a cough. He leaned across the wide bench seat, flicking the pleather latch on the passenger side. The glovebox dropped open, revealing a rat's nest of maps, a flashlight, window punches, expired coupons, and canned energy drinks. He grabbed a can and slammed the glovebox shut, scattering a few old receipts in the process. Leaning back against the tan fabric seat, he cracked open the can and drank it, grimacing a little as the taste of stale bubblegum and taurine rolled down his throat.

Charles belched, tossing the empty can in the passenger footwell as he rubbed his tired eyes. He put the car in gear amid two more burps and backed out of the lot, speeding off towards the highway.

The roads were empty in the early morning, just a smattering of shift-workers and semitrucks. Charles spun the dial on the dash radio, searching for a late-night station. Finding one, he watched the city slip away behind him as classic rock crackled out of the sedan's aging speakers.

About twenty-five miles outside the city the scene of the incident came into view. Three State Police Chargers and a mid-90s F-150, all clustered on the northbound shoulder. Charles pulled the Delta 88 to the side and parked, looking both ways as he crossed over the median. This late at night and this far outside the city, he had the benefit of seeing traffic approach from miles away.

Two of the patrol cars had their lights on, the flashing red and blue bracketing the scene from the north and south. The center Charger had its lights off—no doubt belonging to the deceased officer—while just ahead of it was the F-150, hazard lights flashing dimly in the waning moonlight. Charles spied a stout, swarthy trooper leaning against the door of the southmost Charger and made his way to him.

"Detective Davner," he said, flashing his badge as he approached. "Colorado Springs."

"Sergeant Gomez," the trooper answered from behind a thick mustache, standing up from the car.

Charles smiled and offered a hand. "Charles."

"Cesar," the trooper said gruffly, shaking once before turning to the scene. "Thank you for coming."

Charles dropped the smile and followed him. "Happy to help."

"The officer was Jimmy Temmen, a two-year trooper from Pueblo," Sergeant Gomez said, gesturing to the patrol car in the middle. The walked past it to the F-150. "The truck belongs to a Wayne Algado, a Larimer County resident driving up from Pueblo after fishing with his cousin."

Charles looked in on empty pickup. "Where's he now?"

"We took him to the patrol station in the Springs for a statement," Sergeant Gomez said, shining his flashlight over the truck. "He claims Trooper Temmen was lying on the road as he drove up. Says he tried to brake but didn't have enough time to swerve."

"Headlights are on, so he shouldn't have had visibility issues." Charles looked around the front of the truck. He found the usual scrapes and dings, but nothing major, nothing that couldn't be explained by time on the road. "Point of impact?"

Sergeant Gomez circled his light around the front left tire. "No dents in the bumper, no damage to the lights or mirror—Algado says he tried to steer around him but drove over Trooper Temmen with the left front wheel."

"Blood or tissue residue?" Chuck asked, pulling out his own flashlight and examining the worn tread of the tire.

"None that we could see, but we'll have techs out later to swab. We're not expecting much though, took him about a hundred feet to stop after hitting Trooper Temmen, so any material probably rubbed off."

"Maybe," Charles nodded, shining his light in the rusty wheel well. "Probably some back-scatter in the well though. Maybe even some damage to the shocks. Not that it matters much, he's not contesting that he hit'em." He shrugged, standing back up from the truck. "Was the deceased dragged? Can you show me where the body was hit?"

"Yes," Sergeant Gomez said flatly, pivoting on the spot and walking towards the road. He pointed with his flashlight, illuminating a dark stain on the road by the lane marker. "*Trooper Temmen* was found here, in the left lane, but we believe the point of impact was about ten feet down. There were two sets of tire marks, one on his abdomen and one across his ankles."

"Consistent with the truck swerving to miss him," Charles finished, walking over to the middle of the road. "You said you found him in the lane? Driver didn't try to help him or anything?"

Sergeant Gomez shook his head. "Algado says he was too freaked out. He called 9-1-1 but stayed in the truck the whole time."

"And left your guy smeared on the road. Fuckin' A." Charles let out a low whistle. He bent over the stain on the road, failing to notice the Sergeant's glare. "You breathalyze him?"

"Clear." Sergeant Gomez grunted.

"What about other substances? SFSTs?" Charles asked, walking over to suspected impact site.

"No," Sergeant Gomez answered, crossing his arms over his chest. "We skipped the roadsides, we'll do a DRE after we process him at the station. Then grab a warrant for blood."

"Interesting technique," Charles muttered to himself just loud enough to be heard. *He* was always taught to perform field sobriety testing on scene, that way even if the bloodwork came back clear you could establish proof that the driver was impaired when operating the vehicle. But different departments ran their own procedures, and bloodwork might be enough in this case anyway. He found a trail of shattered plastic, following it back to a few strips of torn blue fabric. He circled the trail with his flashlight and hollered to Sergeant Gomez, "From your man?"

Sergeant Gomez marched over, mustache twitching in irritation. "Yes," he said stiffly. "From his gear."

Charles nodded. "Fits with him being struck in the abdomen, and it lines up the driver's story too. There's not much scattering here with the debris, more like it crunched up when the truck rolled over him. And if he wasn't dragged far, it makes sense that he was already in the road when he was hit. Just a clean hit and decent length skid."

"Just as we thought," Sergeant Gomez replied through gritted teeth.

"Alright," Charles said, squatting down where the trail of debris stopped. He panned the flashlight from the lane marker to the shoulder. "So what was your guy doing in the road?"

"We think it had something to do with the traffic stop he called in earlier," Sergeant Gomez answered, walking over to the shoulder. "He called in a stop around 21:00 on a vehicle suspected of a hit-and-run outside of Pueblo. No call for completion."

Charles frowned, removing the notepad from his back pocket and checking his notes. "Nine p.m.? I thought the 9-1-1 call from Algado came in around midnight?"

"It did," Sergeant Gomez answered, pulling a patrol binder from the front seat of his car.

Charles' confusion deepened. He tapped the notebook on the side of his leg. "So Temmen makes a stop around nine, never calls it complete, and nobody thinks to check in on him before midnight?"

"It was a busy night, and Trooper Temmen was an experienced trooper," Sergeant Gomez said hotly. "We have lots of highway to cover and not a lot of officers. Sometimes things slip by."

Maybe in SOME departments, Charles thought, unable to stop himself from rolling his eyes. He looked up to see Sergeant Gomez staring daggers at him. *Shit.*

"Who was the stop for?" he asked quickly, ducking the Sergeant's gaze. "Did he get a chance to call in the vehicle?"

"Sharon Kruschek," came the taut reply. "Driving a blue 2016 Chevy Equinox registered to a Gregory Kruschek, both from Pueblo."

Charles nodded, busying himself with his notebook. "Any lead on her? BOLO? APB?"

Sergeant Gomez shook his head. "No need. EMS responded to a

single vehicle accident about fifteen miles north of here, an SUV impacting a rock face near the racetrack. Kruschek was the driver, operating the same vehicle."

"They transport her?"

"EMS took her and a child passenger to UC Health in the Springs. We took over the scene after EMS."

Charles nodded, making a note to stop at that scene on the way into town. He wandered over to the dead Trooper's car, jotting down the registration number. "Do we have footage of the stop?"

"Dash cam from the patrol car, we can pull that after the techs finish photographing the scene. Body cam is…tougher."

"Tougher?" Charles looked up sharply.

Sergeant Gomez frowned, the bristling ends of his mustache dragging lower. "His camera was damaged when he was hit. We're not sure yet if it's recoverable."

"Well, if your lab can't hack it, try sending it our way so my techs can take a look. In the meantime, though," Charles shrugged, "keep me in the loop with what you get."

"Of course," fumed Sergeant Gomez. "*Happy* to help."

Charles walked along the shoulder of the road, tracing the path of the fallen officer to where he imagined the traffic stop to be. He stopped by another dark stain on the road, pooled on the edge of the rumble strip. Yelling back to Sergeant Gomez, "Blood?"

"Yes, we think from Trooper Temmen," Sergeant Gomez called back. "There was a wound on his neck when we found him."

You couldn't mention that earlier? Charles bristled, crouching lower to examine the stain. He panned his flashlight in a line from the stain to the center of the road. Squinting hard, he could just make out the start of the debris trail from earlier. He took out his phone and snapped a few pictures of the scene. He'd get the shots from the crime techs but evidence transfers between departments always took more time. *Better to have a few shots to draw impressions from initially.* He looked back at Sergeant Gomez, mustache curled in fury as he texted someone from his phone. As the Sergeant looked up at him, Charles got the distinct impression that the flow of evidence from the CSP might be a little slower this time around.

Charles jotted some more notes as he walked the length of the scene back to the front of the pickup truck, pausing every few steps to take more pictures. In his head he was assembling a list of evidence to further examine, departments to call, and transcripts to request. He finished his examination and walked back to exchange information with Sergeant Gomez. A quick discussion ensued, confirming the location of the second scene and who was currently posted there. They exchanged cards and promises to share information as it came up. As he crossed the highway to the Delta 88, Charles tried not to take it personally when he saw the Sergeant toss his card in the back seat of the patrol car.

Charles sighed as he slid into the wide bench seat of the Delta 88. *That could have gone better*, he thought bitterly, setting the car in gear. Although upon reflection he was hard pressed to figure out exactly where. He chewed on it for another few moments, replaying their conversations before dismissing it with a shrug. Flipping a u-turn, he drove the wrong way on the southbound shoulder until he cleared the scene. Crossing over to the northbound lanes, he set a course for the scene of the accident.

Events at the next scene went *much* smoother. He spotted the wreckage of the ruined SUV from a few miles out, coasting to a stop behind a CSP Tahoe. After a brief exchange with the bored trooper securing the scene, Charles set out, stopping every few feet to take pictures with his phone.

The blue Equinox was ruined, an accordion of collapsed steel mashed against the limestone bluff. The entire front end had molded to the rocky face as it caved in on itself. Deflated airbags hung from the steering wheel beneath a shattered windshield, the driver's side door hanging open and loose on its hinges. Congealed blood coated the door window in streaks, fanning back in the direction of travel. *Curious*, Charles thought, peering at the bloody trail. He stepped around it, looking inside the front seat, careful not to disturb the mess of broken glass and twisted plastic. Taking a few more pictures, he jotted notes of things to ask the crime techs when they'd finished with the scene.

He walked around towards the back, passing his flashlight over a car seat in the back. *Child passenger*, he mused. Kids were tough in cases, most of the time they were too young to give an accurate statement, and their testimony was notoriously unreliable in court. *Still, an unreliable witness is better than no witness.*

He circled the rear of the car, a low whistle escaping him as he saw the damage on other side. A massive gouge stretched from the fender to the tailgate, the scrape in the paint fresh and clean. *That's a hell of a hit-and-run.* He made a note to check the toxicology report for the driver. *No way she was sober during that.*

The rear passenger door hung open like the front, no doubt left there by the EMTs as they removed the kid from the back seat. Charles shook his head as he photographed the interior, capturing the cut belts of the car seat swaying in the light breeze. There wasn't much to go on here, the interior was clean—far cleaner than his own car—and he wouldn't have a detailed look at any evidence inside until the crime techs had torn it apart.

He backed up further into the open field, trying, and failing, to piece together the events that had unfolded. As he did so, he noticed something on the window over the car seat, a small crack spiderwebbing from a chip near the top. At first, he dismissed it as more damage from the hit and run, but the longer he looked at it the less sense that made. There were no scratches in the glass, nothing to connect it in parallel to the damaged metal. He looked at it further; it also looked fresh, the center chip a little too round to be from a rock. The side windows were designed to shatter on impact anyway, so that ruled out an errant rock. Charles snapped a few pictures of the chip, shrugging as he walked back to his car.

He exchanged a few more words with the Trooper, offering his card before he left. As the sun rose, he drove to town—his list of questions and leads expanded with a subsection for Sharon Kruschek.

"Gawdamnit, Chuck! What did I tell you?!"

Charles winced as he heard Sergeant Briske's sonorous twang thundering down the hall. He froze in place, glancing around the bullpen for something to duck behind. He sized up a nearby ficus, hesitating just a little too long as his section chief rounded the corner. *Get this over quick, like a band-aid,* he thought, turning to face the furious stomping headed in his direction. Charles had nicknames for all of Sergeant Briske's moods—this is one he'd termed 'hopping mad.' Charles watched his section chief shift his weight from side to side, cracking his knuckles repeatedly in front of him.

Charles put up his hands to shield his face. "I know, Sarge, it wasn—"

"Sam!" Sergeant Briske hollered, turning to shout across the open bullpen. His bushy grey eyebrows animated to match his words, forehead wrinkles pitching up in steep waves that rolled back endlessly onto his bald, shiny head. "Sam! What did *I* tell *you* to tell *him?*"

Charles watched Sam Marken's spindly hornrims and bushy clipper-cut pop up from one of the cubicles.

"You said, 'Tell him not to be an asshole,'" Sam answered, pushing the hornrims further up the bridge of his straight, dark brown nose.

"And what did *you* tell *him?*"

"I told him, 'Sarge said, 'Don't be an asshole.'"

"So, you can confirm that you relayed to him my carefully crafted instructions?" Sergeant Briske demanded, voice echoing across the room.

Charles rolled his eyes behind the section chief. Sergeant Briske prided himself on his courtroom delivery—his son was a prosecutor in Denver's 2nd District—but outside of sworn statements he tended towards the theatrical.

"Yes, Sarge," Sam answered, offering a conciliatory nod in Charles' direction.

"And what was his reply to this set of artisanal-brewed, finely-tuned, expertly-detailed directionals?"

"No promises," replied Charles, taking the lead on the conversation. He ducked the swing of a particularly exaggerated hand-gesture as Sergeant Briske turned back to him. "Again, Sarge, it wasn't my fau—"

Sergeant Briske cut him off, a thick finger stabbing into his chest. "Of course not! It's never *your* fault! Seven billion people on this planet and everyone *you* meet—*apropos of nothing*—hates you on sight. For. No. *Reason.*"

He punctuated those last words with more jabs into Charles' sternum.

Charles took a step back, sputtering as he rubbed his chest. He wasn't sure which stung more, the finger or the fact that his section chief was using scrabble words against him. "It wasn't me, Sarge. It was that Sergeant Gomez guy—he's got anger problems or something."

"I've known Sergeant Gomez for five *years!*" Sergeant Briske bellowed, eyebrows wagging to match his tone. "He's the calmest cop I know. He teaches *yoga* at the rec center on Saturdays and his wife is a librarian. *You're* the only one I've ever heard of who pissed him off!"

Charles gave a sheepish shrug. "Sorry, Sarge, I got nothing."

Sergeant Briske raised his hands and his eyes towards the heavens, seeking the divine patience before he smote his errant detective.

Sensing an opportunity, Charles started inching his way down the hall. "Anyway, Sarge, it's been a long morning. And I've got a *lot* of evidence to request. So, if you need me, I'll be—"

Sergeant Briske lowered his hands, and his focus, to the mortal plane, cutting Charles off mid-step.

"I don't know what you did, or how you did it, but you're lucky your dear Sergeant was around to smooth things over and bail your ass out." The section chief dragged a weary hand down his face, gesturing with the other to the office at the end of the hall. "On my desk is a copy of the dashcam from last night. I got CSP to pull it before the techs were done with the scene and send it over."

Charles brightened, pivoting on his back foot to go grab the tape. "Thanks, Sarge, that's a huge load off my plate."

He stopped when he felt a heavy hand on his shoulder, rooting him in place.

"Chuck, this is an officer-related homicide. It requires *sensitivity*. And *tact*. And playing well with *others*." Sergeant Briske said, his voice a low whisper in Charles' ear. "So, I need you to hear these next few words clearly. Carry them close. Deep in your heart. Do you understand me?"

Charles nodded.

"Don't be an asshole."

Charles spent the next hour reviewing the dashcam footage, matching it to the time stamp on the dispatch transcript. He heard the call come in over Temmen's radio, a blue Chevy SUV, license plate XGI 752 with a scrape on the right side from a hit-and-run during major traffic, heading north on I-25 up from Pueblo. Charles fast-forwarded after Trooper Temmen replied in confirmation, speeding along until he saw an Equinox with a familiar set of plates pop up on the screen. The dashcam was newer, so he had a nice, color picture of the flashing red and blue as the Trooper switched on his overheads. He watched as the Equinox slowed, then pulled over for a stop. The tape was clear as Temmen called in the stop to the dispatch center in Pueblo, relaying that he had Id'd the vehicle from the previous BOLO. Charles watched the officer exited the vehicle, approaching the driver's side with caution. He saw an exchange between the driver and Trooper Temmen, and the passing of her driver's license and registration.

Trooper Temmen walked back to the patrol car with the easy-going confidence of a seasoned trooper, disappearing from the feed as he entered the vehicle. He called in the driver—Sharon Kruschek, of Pueblo, Colorado. There were a few minutes of silence while he checked her for outstanding warrants and wrote out the ticket. There was a cough as he exited the patrol car. Charles watched Temmen approach the blue Equinox, shining his flashlight in the driver's side. He saw the state trooper extend his arm—presumably to return Sharon Kruschek's license and hand her the ticket—then abruptly take a step back.

Charles' brow furrowed as he watched the trooper take another step backwards, one hand hovering near his gun belt. The footage from the dashcam was too angled to see what was going on inside the blue

SUV, and they were too far away to be picked up by the dashcam's microphone. There was a flash of something, Charles watched Trooper Temmen drop his flashlight and reach for his throat. Blood sprayed out from the Trooper's neck as he stumbled back further into the road. *So that explains the bloody door*, Charles thought, watching the patrolman take his final steps before collapsing in the middle of the highway. A few seconds of stillness passed, then the Equinox quickly pulled away.

Charles fast-forwarded through the rest of the tape. Several cars passed in the far-left lane, avoiding the dark lump in the edge of the right. He slowed it back down when a mid-90s F-150 appeared in view, watching its brakes light up as Mr. Algado swerved to miss Trooper Temmen. Charles winced a little as the wheels on the left side lifted up and down, knowing that was the point of impact. He fast-forwarded the tape again, watching as the truck pulled over to the side, followed closely by the arrival of the CSP officers securing the scene.

Charles stopped the video, rewinding back to the initial traffic stop to replay it, again and again. No matter how many times he saw it, he still couldn't get an exact picture of what happened. He just saw Temmen stepping back, a flash of movement, and then stumbling into the road as his life poured out of his ruined throat.

She slashed him, of that Charles was certain. It was the only thing that made sense. But how she'd managed to get the drop on an experienced trooper with his hand on his gun, and how she'd rolled the window up fast enough to catch the spray of blood afterwards, Charles didn't know.

He stood up from his cubicle desk, rubbing his bleary eyes as he grabbed his coat. Heading for the door, the puzzles of the case turned over in his mind as left the station. He knew one thing for sure, tomorrow he needed to talk to Sharon Kruschek.

Chapter 3

Wednesday

UC Health Memorial Hospital towered over the surrounding neighborhood, the undulating waves of glass that adorned its façade catching the early light of the morning. Charles Davner turned the corner on the winding sidewalk, leaving the lingering chill of the morning behind as he stepped up to the sliding glass doors. He flashed his badge to the lobby clerk, stopping for directions to room 318. He'd called ahead the night before, confirming her spot in the third-floor psychiatric ward. It was standard procedure for criminal cases following trauma care—the Velcro cuffs came on as soon as the surgeons stepped out. He turned down a bright-lit hallway, sidestepping doctors and gurneys as he walked to the stairs. Making his way up, he ran through his list of questions for the care staff.

Charles paused at the top of the third flight of stairs, catching his breath as he rubbed the bags under his eyes. He'd been up late last night trawling through social media—for work this time—as he followed her thread across different platforms. He'd learned a lot about Sharon Kruschek in last twenty-four hours, tracing her through profiles on LinkedIn, Facebook, and a Twitter account with twenty-seven followers. He knew she was a Colorado native, growing up in Longmont and working as a court reporter in Denver during the mid-2000s. Her maiden name was Thomas, but she changed it when she married Gregory Kruschek in 2010. Gregory was an engineering consultant working for a patent company in Pueblo, although he'd worked at Davis Manufacturing when they met. It was around that time that Sharon went back to school for a paralegal certificate from the Community College of Denver. After finishing that, she'd taken a job at Baxter & Sammon, a small defense firm. That was the last entry on her LinkedIn, but the story continued on her Facebook profile with the birth of her daughter, Sydney, on August 5th, 2016.

That part marked a transformation of sorts for Sharon, as pictures of mountain hikes and brewery tours faded away, replaced with a wave of pictures, posts, and shared stories documenting her daughter's life from day one. Scrolling through the hundreds of posts, Charles couldn't help but marvel at the type of person who felt it necessary to link to an article on the importance of creativity in raising a child, then post a fifteen-minute video of their daughter's first somersault, following that only minutes later with a shared meme of a Minion juggling bottles of wine. The internet was a godsend for cops, taking most of the legwork out of preliminary investigations. *Used to be you had to canvas the whole neighborhood, knocking on every door just to find out a suspect's job and close associates.* Charles shook his head, glad that those days were behind them—personal interviews were never his strong suit.

He followed the signs for the ward's front desk, staffed by a smiling young brunette wearing bright green eyeshadow. 'Cindy' read her nameplate, adorned in stick-on pink jewels.

"Hi there!" beamed Cindy, cocking her head to one side as she waved. "Can I help you?"

Charles attempted a smile in return, trying, and failing, to match her energy. "I'm here for Sharon Kruschek, I need to talk to her care staff first though."

"Okay!" Cindy bobbed her head, ponytail bouncing as she looked up the information on her screen. "Friend? Or family?"

"Homicide," Charles answered, laying his badge on the counter. Cindy's eyes narrowed when she saw the badge, the bouncing ponytail slowing down in somber realization.

"Okay," she said after a moment, tapping the screen with a neon green fingernail. "Her primary care is Dr. Kutlack, he's making his rounds now, but I'll have him escort you back as soon as he's done."

Charles nodded in reply, taking a second stab at a smile and arriving somewhere in the middle of 'jovial' and 'grimace.' He watched her smile falter in response to the pained expression on his face, and gave up entirely on his attempts at human interaction.

"Great, thanks," he muttered, stomping over to the waiting area. He sank down into the vinyl depths of the narrow chair, sighing as he pulled out his notepad to review the facts. Laying it down on his leg, he fished his phone and opened it up to pictures from the crime scene. As he swiped through them, he stopped again at the blood splattered on the driver's side window. There was something odd about it, some aspect he couldn't quite place that didn't jive with the rest of the scene. He zoomed in on the picture, lost in thought.

A polite cough brought him back to the present. A tall woman with narrow cheeks and close-cropped grey hair stood over him, a clipboard tucked neatly under one arm.

"Dr. Kutlack," she announced, extending a hand.

"Detective Davner, CSPD," he replied, taking the hand as rose from the chair. "I'm here about Sharon Kru—"

"Kruschek, yes," she interrupted, pivoting away on her heel. "Follow me."

Charles shrugged as he fell in behind her, walking briskly to match her long strides.

"As I already explained, you can't interview her," Dr. Kutlack said brusquely, turning the corner. Charles' brow furrowed, but he refrained from correcting her. *Must have been CSP*. Passing another nurses' desk, she tucked the clipboard in an empty tray without slowing her pace. "I know she's tied to a homicide of yours, but she's in no condition to give a statement. She suffered a lot of trauma in the wreck."

"Injuries?"

"Three broken ribs, minor abrasions and contusions on her forearms from the airbags deploying, and a severe TBI." She continued down the hallway, rattling off the list without looking back.

Charles' brow steeped further.

"Traumatic brain injury," she explained, cutting him off before he could ask. "She spent twelve hours in a coma—and required sedation when she woke up."

"Sedation? Why?" he asked, dodging around an empty IV stand in the hallway. *Would it kill her to slow down? Not everyone's built like a giraffe...*

"She seemed lucid when she woke up, but lost focus when a tree branch scratched against the window." Dr. Kutlack stopped for a moment, reading the chart outside a room before carrying on. "We normally don't sedate after a brain injury—we need the patient conscious for monitoring—but we couldn't get her to stop screaming. We put her under to avoid the risk of further injury."

"She say anything during the screaming?" Charles asked, catching up with her during the momentary pause. "Any words or statements might be helpful."

Dr. Kutlack shook her head. "Mostly unintelligible. She asked for her daughter when she first woke up. The rest was just a few words here or there—something about a roof—but that was it. Hard to tell in between all the screaming." Dr. Kutlack sighed, stopping in front of the door to room 318. "There was a *lot* of screaming"

Charles peered through the slit window in the door, catching a glimpse of a blond woman restrained to the corner bed. He watched her chest rise and fall slowly under the shadows cast the by tree outside. He jotted down a few notes before turning back to Dr. Kutlack. "Toxicology? Anything in her system when they brought her in?"

Dr. Kutlack thought for a moment, grabbing the chart out of the tray on the door. She flipped back and forth through a few pages before setting it back. "Nothing, no trace of alcohol, cannabis, or other substances."

"Any sign of previous or habitual use? Track marks? Scabs? Blisters on her lips?"

Dr. Kutlack shook her head.

Charles frowned, writing quickly in his notepad. He'd been hoping for something easy—soccer mom takes PCP and goes on a rampage while freaking out. It wouldn't have been the first time either, his third homicide was a stay-at-home mother of three who shot her husband in the face while going through withdrawals. One of the speakers at the Rocky Mountain Law Enforcement Conference last year had devoted an entire talk to the proliferation of methamphetamine in the suburbs. Drug use would have gone a long way towards explaining the events of the day before.

"There was a daughter transported with her at the time of the accident. Do you know what happened to her?"

"Daughter was fine," she said. "Minor bruising from the seatbelt straps. Sent home with the father before Mrs. Kruschek went in for x-rays."

Charles' frown deepened. "He didn't stay here? During the exams and procedures?"

The doctor thought for a moment, grabbing the chart out of the tray and flipping through it again. "Nope, we gave him a call when she woke up, but she hasn't had any visitors before you."

Charles flipped the notebook closed and pocketed it, mulling over this latest puzzle.

"I appreciate the help, I know you're busy," he said, offering his card to Dr. Kutlack. "Call me if she stabilizes enough to talk."

"Will do," she replied, tucking the card into the clipboard chart on the door. Then, turning abruptly on a heel, she left him behind, striding off to continue her rounds.

Alone in the hallway, Charles looked through the window of room 318, a hundred question turning in his mind.

He'd just reached his car when the phone rang, 'Flight of the Bumblebee' blaring loudly from his pocket. He grit his teeth as he pulled it out—*I've got to get her back for this*—swiping it open when he saw

Sam Marken's name on the screen.

"Chuck," he said, sliding into the tan bench seat. "What's up?"

"Coroner finished with Trooper Temmen, says you can catch him if you get there in the next hour."

Perfect, he thought, clicking his seatbelt into place. "Thanks Sam, I'll head over."

"No problem," said Sam, hanging up the line.

Charles tossed the phone on the empty seat. He'd just grabbed the column shifter when it rang again, grimacing as the sound of buzzing violin strings filled the cab.

"I'm going to get you for this," he growled, tapping the speaker button and setting the phone back down on the seat. "You should respect other people's stuff."

"Maybe other people should respect themselves enough to move on when they've been dumped," said Savannah, voice echoing tinnily from the small speaker.

"It was mutual," Charles snapped, backing the enormous gold sedan out of the parking space.

"*Mmm-hmm.* You gonna be home for dinner? What should I pull out?"

He threw the shifter back in drive, cranking the wide, tan wheel hard to the left to straighten out. "I dunno. Pizza? There's one in the freezer."

"We had pizza on Monday."

Charles sighed, looking both ways before gunning it onto the main road. "What do you want from me? A menu? You know what's in there, hell, you picked most of it out. Why'd you call?"

There was a pause.

"Petunia got into the blinds again."

Gawdamnit. Horns blared behind him as he cut off a Honda Civic, he answered them with a raised middle finger. "Was it the bird again?"

"Yep," Savannah replied. "The big gray one in the fountain."

Her sworn nemesis, he thought, leaning in as he steered the golden barge onto Hancock avenue. "I thought I told you to make sure the blinds were up. She can't break them if they're already up."

"I forgot, okay? It's been a busy morning."

You're telling me. He took another left, the H-body sedan rolling on its aging springs as he cut west on Fountain Boulevard. "What's up? Another paper? Or is it still that presentation?"

He heard the rustle of a bag of chips opening.

"Presentation," said Savannah, her words muffled around a

mouthful of food. "Bernie's being a real dick because I've been emailing him my updates instead of coming into the meetings."

"Fucker," Charles remarked, both about her classmate and the black GTR that swerved into his lane.

"Ed Zachary. It's like, why do you need me to sit there and explain what I already wrote in my email? Total fogey move."

He made a left at the recycling plant, driving past the sheriff's office and the county jail. "Uh-huh. Total fogey."

Coasting into the parking lot of the El Paso County Coroner, he killed the engine on the Delta 88. "I gotta go. Anything else?"

The line filled with the sounds of thoughtful crunching.

"No," She said at last, swallowing a mouthful of chips. "I saw a guy hanging out in the parking lot today after I grabbed Petunia."

Charles raised an eyebrow. "And?"

"Not him, too tall. But I wasn't sure at first."

Charles nodded, giving her some space to elaborate as he undid his belt. The cabin filled with the sound of more crunching.

"Anyway, I think that's it. Love you."

"Love you too," he replied, hanging up the phone.

The lobby of the El Paso County Coroner's office was cool and slightly damp, the air redolent with the smell of disinfectant. Charles signed in at the front counter, walking through a pair of dark wood doors to the cubicles in the back. He spotted movement in one near the middle, weaving in and around desks as he made his way over. The lone occupant typed away on an ancient Dell desktop, bopping his head to the punk music blasting from a pair of enormous headphones. They were black to match his hoodie, standing out in stark contrast to his curly red hair, and thick, gnarly beard. Charles tapped him on the shoulder, drawing his attention away from the report on screen.

"Detective Davner, CSPD," Charles said, showing his badge.

"Jeffrey," the man said, pulling off his headphones as he stood up from the desk. 'The Working Stiffs' stood out in bold white letters on the black hoodie, just above a cartoon of a body's chalk outline. As they shook hands, Charles noticed a half-dozen tattoos poking out from the cotton sleeves.

"I'm here about Jimmy Temmen," Charles said, gesturing around the empty office. "I heard you guys had finished up with him."

Jeffrey nodded. "Yeah, I'm almost done with the written report, but I can take you back and talk you through it first."

Charles was surprised. "That was fast, must've been slow around here."

"Nah, four bodies. Usual Wednesday," Jeffrey shrugged, stepping around Charles and heading to the autopsy room. "But when a cop shows up on your table you, uh, you tend to put him as the priority."

Jeffrey led him through a pair of steel doors. The autopsy room was lit from above with a dozen fluorescent lights, glinting off the scuffed government-white tiles and the stainless-steel tables. Jeffrey walked over to one of the tables, checking the tag on the body before he drew back the sheet.

"Jimmy Temmen, twenty-seven-year-old Caucasian male," he said, piling the sheet on a nearby counter.

Charles looked down on the deceased state trooper. His skin was pale, with purple bruising along his back where his fluids had settled. Aside from the Y-shaped stitching from his clavicle to his waist, his body was marred by a thick band of crushed tissue spreading horizontally across his chest. A second band crossed both legs just above the knee— the second tire mark from the F-150.

"He was crunched pretty bad, shattered ribs, a cracked sternum from the CPR they tried on-scene," Jeffrey explained, gesturing up and down to the twin marks. "But it's all post-mortem. They told me when they brought him that he'd been lying in the road for a while before the truck rolled over him."

Jeffrey pulled on a pair of gloves, offering a pair to Charles. Charles declined, watching the coroner shrug before raising the corpse's head from the table.

"He's got some abrasions and scraping on his head and back," said Jeffrey, twisting the dead trooper's neck to give Charles a better view. "Truck musta dragged him a little bit when it hit him—but nothing to indicate movement on his part at the time of impact."

Charles nodded as Jeffrey set the head back down. He pointed to the corpse's throat, a ragged gash running across it from ear to ear.

"Yup," Jeffrey nodded, poking a finger into the wound. "That's your cause of death. Deep lateral laceration running left to right. Severed the carotids, jugular—even nicked the vertebrae at C5."

Charles let out a low whistle. "That's deep. Takes a lot of force to get that deep."

"Lots of force," Jeffrey added. "You see that kind of damage when something mechanical's involved, like a truck whipping by with something hanging off the side. That would make sense here too, since he was found in the middle of a road. A truck driving by with something jagged hanging off the side that catches him in the throat."

Charles nodded, jotting down notes but saying nothing about

Sharon Kruschek and the traffic stop.

"Jagged?" he asked, looking up from his notes. "What about serrated? Like a kitchen knife?"

"*Pffffffft*," Jeffrey snorted, pointing to the ragged edges of the wound. "Kitchen knives are thin, even the serrated ones. Wound's too wide, too torn on the ends. Anything that did this was thick, sharp, and again, jagged."

"What about an axe?" Charles asked, pointing to the wound with his pen. "Or a machete?"

Jeffrey considered it for a moment, stripping off a glove to stroke a hand through his thick beard.

"Maybe an axe," he said after a moment. "Machete's probably too thin—it'd still need to be jagged though, and I've never seen an axe like that."

The coroner looked down at the officer on the table, frowning behind his beard. "And it'd take a helluva lot of power to get an axe that deep as it swiped him."

He looked up as Charles tucked the notebook away in his pocket, raising a single eyebrow in the detective's direction. "We got a mad ax-man on the loose?"

"Worse," replied Charles, staring at the body lying on the table. "Soccer mom."

Stacks of papers waited on Charles' desk as he arrived at the station, a post-it note on top marking them as 'courtesy of Sam.' He settled into the swivel chair with a groan, propping his feet on the desk as he picked up the stack of papers.

The first was a transcript for the 9-1-1 call from Wayne Algado. He thumbed idly through the pages, skimming the lines. It was nothing he didn't already know or couldn't figure out. Just pages and pages of panicking chatter between Mr. Algado and the emergency operator. *And all while Temmen was lying in the road, fifty feet away*. It didn't matter to Charles that the trooper was already dead by that time—Mr. Algado hadn't known that. It completed his low estimation of his fellow man.

The last page had another sticky note from Sam affixed to the back. 'CSP called when this faxed over,' it read in Sam's usual, looping script, 'Algado requested a lawyer immediately. No statement from him.'

Charles sighed, this too was to be expected. Not that it made a difference either way, Mr. Algado twice admitted to hitting the officer in the 9-1-1 transcript and once again when Sergeant Gomez arrived on scene before he was arrested. *And again*, he reminded himself, *Temmen was dead long before he was hit.*

The next stack were the patrol statements from the CSP officers that arrived on scene. Each of the three statements described the same events as the first State Troopers arrived on-scene, approximately fifteen minutes after the initial call went out. The first of the troopers, Officer Jackson, attempted CPR on the deceased, while the second trooper, Officer Clintsky, detained and questioned the driver. An ambulance arrived, with EMTs calling Trooper Temmen dead thirty-five minutes after midnight. *And about three hours after he'd actually died*, Charles thought, reading through the statements. Sergeant Gomez was next on scene, arriving from the CSP station in Pueblo. After conferring with the EMTs, he made the call for the body to be loaded into the ambulance and delivered to the coroner's office. *Weird.* He usually had a coroner with him to examine the body on scene, ensuring a complete picture for the medical examiner. He shrugged, *par for the course in this fucking case.* Sergeant Gomez then conferred with Officer Clintsky, making the call to arrest Mr. Algado on suspicion of manslaughter and transport him to the Colorado State Trooper Station in the Springs. That marked the end of Officer Clintsky's statement, as well as Officer Jackson's when he was ordered to secure the north end of the crime scene. Sergeant Gomez's statement continued on for two more lines, where he described finding the bloodstain on the shoulder of the road and making the call to his lieutenant to bring in an outside agency.

In true cop fashion all of the statements were formulaic homologations of boilerplate 'official language' strung together in new ways to fit the night's events. Charles sighed again, pressing hard against his closed eyes. He knew the death of one of their own was a sensitive, heavily scrutinized subject, one that would leave any department on edge until the final report was published. But flipping through the three reports and spotting the same misspelling of the word 'could' in the second line, left him feeling that the sum was worth less than the total of their parts.

He took a break from the paperwork, calling around for an update on the processing for the two scenes. Significant progress had been made on the first, the one Charles had dubbed the 'Temmen scene.' Trooper Temmen's Charger had been towed in to the CSPD station for a full search, the trail of debris in the road had been bagged and entered into evidence, and DNA swabs had been taken from each of the bloodstains on the road. Algado's F-150 had likewise been impounded, awaiting search following the completion of the patrol car. Techs were still on scene, canvassing the shoulder of the road and part of the field in a hundred-foot radius around the scene.

"Tell them they're looking for an edged weapon," Charles said.

"Something with a thick blade, like an axe."

He thanked the scene supervisor and hung up, reaching out to the lead tech at the second scene.

Progress at the 'Kruschek scene' as he'd deemed it, was proceeding much slower. For one thing they only had two techs to work the area, the majority of effort spent at the 'Temmen scene.' For another, after finishing their initial photography, both techs were still engaged in trying to determine the least invasive way of disengaging the blue Equinox from the side of the rock face. Charles suppressed a sigh—he knew they were working as hard as they could—and repeated his request that they try and locate an edged weapon from the scene. Hanging up the phone, he looked over to the last two packets on the desk.

There were three pages in each, in total less than the stack of wasted ink and copy paper of the CSP statements. Charles picked up the first, a copy of the transcript of the 9-1-1 call for a hit-and-run on I-25, just outside Pueblo. The caller identified himself as Raymundo Sax, an electrician driving home from a job on the north end of town. He'd been stuck in traffic, Mr. Sax said, when a crazy lady had side-swiped his work van and sped off on the shoulder. It had taken Mr. Sax a few minutes to process what had happened, but he described in colorful language what he thought of the snooty white lady that had scraped up his livelihood just to save herself from waiting in traffic. Charles smiled as the operator reminded Mr. Sax numerous times that the call was recorded. *Give him credit though, he had a good eye for detail.* Mr. Sax had noted the make, model, color, and license plate of the offending vehicle—more than enough to generate the BOLO that Trooper Temmen used to pull Sharon Kruschek over.

The next packet was sparser in detail, but far more interesting. It was a transcript of the call from the OnStar emergency center to the 9-1-1 dispatchers in El-Paso county. The OnStar technician relayed a severe accident had occurred, transmitting the name of the driver and the GPS location for the damaged vehicle. The technician stated that the driver was unresponsive and requested immediate medical assistance. Charles nodded along as he read, freezing on the last page. It was a transcript of the call the OnStar center had received before dispatching help to the scene. The first line was standard, as the technician announced herself and inquired as to how to help. It was the next line that gave him pause— the only dialogue from Sharon Kruschek herself. Four words, comprising a single, declaratory statement. '*I'm having an accident,*' he read, the solitary finality of the sentence echoing in his mind. What followed was about a half-page of further clarifying questions from the technician—all to no response.

Charles dropped the packet down on the desk, setting it aside as he booted up the desktop. Navigating to Facebook, he pulled up the profile of a short-haired blonde in her late-thirties, beaming with pride at her daughter's tumbling class. Sharon Kruschek stared back at him from the glowing screen. He knew he couldn't talk to her, not under the steady drip of heavy sedation. *But she wasn't the only witness to the scene.* He looked past Sharon to the daughter, grinning ear to ear in the picture, sequins glinting from her pink leotard. *Tomorrow*, he decided, *I get some answers*.

Chapter 4

Thursday

Charles Davner rose with the dawn. He moved quickly and purposefully through his morning routine, neatly sidestepping Petunia as she snored in the middle of the room. Raising the tattered blinds and cracking open his bedroom window, he took a deep breath of the cool morning air. The sun was shining, his schedule was clear—he'd even gone to bed at a reasonable time. Everything was set for his drive down to Pueblo. Today he would talk to Sydney and Gregory Kruschek, and finally get some answers.

His phone buzzed in his pocket.

'Need to see you before you head to Pueblo,' read the text from Sergeant Briske.

Charles felt a frown coming on but shook it off. *It's fine. It's only 7:30, plenty of time for a quick stop by the station.* He ran a hand through his hair, smoothing it out in the mirror. *He probably just wants to make sure you're playing well with the Pueblo PD.* Charles nodded to the mirror, reassuring his reflection. He was working hard to toe the Sergeant's sensitive line on inter-agency relations. He'd left a message for the Pueblo cops that he'd be in their area conducting an interview for a homicide case, being especially polite on the phone when talking to the dispatcher about the transcripts—he'd even called CSP the day before to thank them for their mediocre statements.

"Petunia, breakfast!" Savannah called out from the other room.

At the sound of kibble pouring into a bowl, the French bulldog leapt up, snorting and chuffing as her short legs scrabbled across the hardwood floor. Charles shook his head as he belted on his gun and badge—nothing inspired that dog to move like food. He was down the hallway, hand on the front door when he heard Savannah call out again.

"Stop! You too! Get some breakfast first."

Charles grumbled as he looked down at his watch, the glowing green dial reading 7:50. *It's fine, still got plenty of time*, he told himself, releasing the brass doorknob. He made his way to the kitchen, studiously avoiding the look of maternal superiority Savannah beamed at him as he trudged over to the cabinet. Pushing past the PopTarts and family-size box of Cocoa Puffs, he felt around for the unopened box of organic quinoa bars all the way in the back—the only thing James left behind when he moved out. Charles pocketed two, stepping out the door at 7:53.

Only to storm back in at 8:07, fuming. As the engine turned over in the Delta 88, the tire pressure light had the audacity to make itself known, stubbornly refusing to turn off in spite of his repeated hammering on the dash. A huffing circle of the vehicle revealed a flat passenger tire, the shiny, crossed head of a screw poking out insidiously from between the treads. A frantic search of the trunk yielded a can of fix-a-flat and a missing air pump. Storming back inside the apartment only compounded his frustration, as he quickly discovered Savannah had borrowed it for a project and left it in her classroom at Colorado College ("I'm sorry! I needed it for airbrushing!" "*You should respect other people's stuff!*"). Stomping back out to the parking lot, he resigned himself to the task of mounting the spare.

It was a quarter past ten when Charles pulled into the station, a multi-car accident on Nevada Avenue having set him back another forty-five minutes. A foul mood cloaked him like a heavy coat as he stepped onto the second floor—the investigations division for the CSPD.

"Look what the cat dragged in," drawled Detective Daggert, beady blue eyes watching Charles over the mug clutched in his thick, hairy hands.

"Shut up, Todd," barked Charles, storming past the cubicle. "Your jokes are old enough to get a discount at Sizzler."

Todd smirked behind his mug, taking another sip of the cold, black coffee. "Boss was expecting you over an hour ago. What happened? Another late night cranking it to fuckboi Instagram models?"

Todd embellished his question with a few quick strokes of his free hand. He grinned as Charles shot daggers his way—some buttons were just too easy to push.

"Fat talk from the guy whose wife slipped a ball-gag in his lunchbox next to the turkey club," Charles snapped, poking his head in Sergeant Briske's office.

Todd shrugged. It was an open secret around the office that after twenty years of marriage the Daggert homelife had taken a dramatic turn for the better following Serena's enthusiastic completion of the 'Dom-In-Us' course at the Colorado Center for Alternative Lifestyles.

"It's called 'supporting your partner's interests,' you should try it sometime" said Todd, setting the mug down on his desk. "Boss is out, by the way. Some CSP sergeant stopped by while he was waiting for you, they took a walk."

"Some interests are easier to support than others," grumbled Charles, pulling back from the empty office. "And you're the *last* one who should be giving me shit. It was *your* turn for on-call when I caught this shitty case."

"I know, I know. I'm sorry," said Todd, dropping his head in apology. "Although if it's any consolation, I'm about to be up to my elbows in shit with this stabbing from Wednesday."

"Stabbing?" Charles cocked an eyebrow, walking over to Todd's desk.

"Yeah," Todd said, gesturing to the stack of printed pictures spread out on his desk. "Jogger on the Shooks trail, just south of Boulder Street. He caught it in the early morning around four a.m., found by a cyclist about an hour later and ID'd by the wife as Harold Whitlawn when she reported him missing around the same time."

Charles picked up a picture from the desk. It showed the victim, late forties or early fifties, lying on his back on the pavement beneath an elm tree. The victim's cyan jogging suit was marred by bright red stains as blood pooled from a number of vicious-looking stab wounds.

"What's your thinking?" he asked.

"Mugging? I guess?" Todd scratched the bald spot on the back of his head. "Guy's out in the dark, runs into the wrong guy who wants his money. No wallet at the scene, but the wife can't remember if he normally takes one with him."

Charles frowned, staring closer at the victim's picture, eyes narrowing as he counted the wounds. "What kind of mugger stabs a guy *eleven* times? Anything after the fifth stab seems kinda personal to me."

"I dunno," Todd shrugged. "Guy was a dentist, s'not like he had a bunch of enemies."

"Maybe he was the fifth dentist—the one who never recommends the toothpaste in the commercials." Charles cocked an eyebrow. "Have you called Johnson & Johnson? This could go all the way to the top."

"Might be," said Todd, picking up another picture from the spread on the desk. "Or maybe another jogger was pissed that he got cut off." Laughing as he looked down at the potbelly stretching the bottom of his yellow polo. "Either way, I'm marking it as another reason not to exercise."

Charles nodded, chuckling as he set the picture down. It was a curious truism of detective work that exercise and crime often intersected. Runners—out at all hours of the day or night—were always getting intro trouble, either stumbling across bodies or witnessing a crime in progress. Charles smiled to himself. *Score one for being a homebody, nobody ever got mugged sitting on their couch.*

"CHUCK!"

Charles winced and looked around, Sergeant Briske's baritone echoing off the walls.

"I know you're here, Chuck! I saw your piece-of-shit car in the parking lot!"

Charles looked from the Sergeant's office, to Todd, to the exit door.

Todd shook his head. "No chance. Better just get it over with."

Charles sighed, acknowledging the wisdom of his colleague. Head hanging low, he made his way through the cubicles and onwards to his certain doom.

Charles peered around the door frame of Sergeant Briske's office, determined to present the smallest target possible. "*Heyyy*, Sarge. You called?"

The section chief glared up at him from behind the wide, mahogany desk, bushy grey eyebrows bunching hard together.

"Yes, damnit, over two hours ago! Get in here!"

Charles entered Sergeant Briske's office with his hands raised and his eyes on his floor. "Sarge, I'm sorry, it's not my fault. There was a tire, and an accident—"

The Sergeant cut him off with a wave of his hand. "It's not about you being late, Chuck. It's about the words. The words, Chuck! Four little words. *Did you forget the four words, Chuck?*"

Charles cocked his head, puzzlement spreading across his face. "Four wor—"

"DON'T BE AN ASSHOLE!" roared the Sergeant, slapping a meaty hand on the dark wood, shockwaves rippling through the ornaments and papers on the desk. "Among the other words like *diplomacy, tact,* and *sensitivity!*"

"But, I didn't! I *wasn't!*" Charles blurted out, dropping his hands.

"You mean you *didn't* leave a snarky-ass voicemail with the CSP?" Sergeant Briske asked, staring down the wayward detective. "*Thanking* them for the *abundance* of investigative *detail* and *effort* they put into their patrol statements?!"

Charles was struck dumb for a few seconds. It had never occurred to him that his inner monologue might have colored that message's delivery. "Honestly, Sarge, I thought that one was pretty good…Tactful, I mean. You should of heard it the *first* time I recorded it."

Sergeant Briske tilted his tightly clenched jaw slowly to the left and right, the pops and cracks of his weary neck echoing in the office.

Seizing his moment, Charles spoke quickly to break the silence. "Anyway, Sarge, you should see those statements—*complete* horseshit—they've even got the same typo on all three pages. And I found out that they've been running around behind me, trying to talk to my lead suspect. How am I supposed to run a real investigation with that kind of bullshit interference from the CSP?"

Sergeant Briske sighed, dragging a heavy hand across his face. "There is a *long*, thoughtfully-worded, and punctilious explanation that I could give you regarding the history of this department and the inter-agency tensions that have pervaded its cooperation with the State Police. I could spend *hours* explaining to you—in full detail—the institutional ramifications and political ass-pain put upon a department that loses an officer in the line of duty. I could give you over a dozen different reasons why the patrol statements you were provided were worded as regimentally and mechanically as they were. But all of that would be a waste of time." Sergeant Briske looked up from his hands, locking eyes with Charles. "Because you. Don't. *Listen.*"

Charles opened and closed his mouth without speaking, a sheepish expression coloring his face. He shoved his hands in his pockets, dropping his eyes back to the floor.

"I…I'm sorry, Sarge," Charles said after a moment. "Is that what Sergeant Gomez was here for? To get me pulled from the case?"

"He was," said Sergeant Briske, continuing only after he spotted the requisite level of chagrin on the detective's face. "I managed to talk him out of it. I told him what a *smart*, and *talented* detective you are—with a clearance rate thirty percent higher than your closest peer…"

Nearly fifty percent, but sure, Charles mentally corrected. He suppressed a smile, continuing to stare at the floor.

"…And I told him that I would be keeping you under my extra-large thumb for the remainder of the investigation," Sergeant Briske finished slowly, eyes narrowing as he saw a glimmer of pride on the detective's face. "I said I would personally vet any of your work that leaves this office, and make sure you didn't further damage the fragile partnership between our departments. That was the *only* reason he didn't go straight to the Lieutenant for your head on a pike."

Charles nodded, on the whole, it was more freedom than he expected. "Was he here for anything else?"

"Yes," the section chief answered, rifling through a desk drawer and pulling out a thumb drive. "They were able to recover the bodycam footage from Trooper Temmen. I told him you were headed down to Pueblo to conduct some interviews, he insisted you watch the tape first."

He offered it to Charles, eyes intent on the detective as he handed it over.

"I need you to take this with the grace and delicacy with which it was delivered. By all accounts, Trooper Temmen was a good cop. Be thorough, but be mindful of the sensitivities that surround it. Try to remember that as you go poking around."

"I will, Sarge. I'll go through it before I head south," Charles said, turning the thumb drive over in his hands. "With consideration. And grace."

"Good, good." Sergeant Briske shooed him out the door with one hand. "Just remember that I can't bail you out if you fuck up again."

Charles nodded, pocketing the thumb drive as he headed for the door.

"Oh, Chuck, one last thing."

Charles stopped, one hand on the door.

"Probably a good idea to link up with PPD when you head down to Pueblo. Get a local cop to go with you when you—you know—*talk to people.*"

"Yes, Sarge," Charles sighed as he stepped out the door.

There were two stacks of photographs waiting on Charles' desk when he got to his cubicle, a note on top marking one as from the Temmen scene and the other from the Kruschek scene.

"Thanks, Sam," Charles called out, settling into the worn fabric of his swivel chair. There was a CD with all of the photos in a paper sleeve on top of the stack, but Sam knew that Charles and the other detectives preferred hard copies.

"No prob," said Sam, hornrims poking up from over his cubicle wall. "Techs said they got the Equinox un-mushed from the rock, they're loading it on a flatbed for processing now."

Perfect. Charles set aside the photos from the Kruschek scene, sorting the Temmen scene pictures on the floor of his cubicle. As best he could, he grouped them by geography, recreating a map of the area from south to north. After spreading them out, he overlaid the pictures of Trooper Temmen taken by Sergeant Gomez before they transported the body. He used the blood stain on the road to match the body's placement and the angle between the CSP photos and those of his techs.

Next, he picked up the photos of the evidence collected at the scene, matching the item descriptions and locations to the list on the bottom page. Most of it was the usual roadside junk—cigarette butts, fast food wrappers, bottles of piss. A few items were specifically implicated in the crime, of which Trooper Temmen's dropped flashlight was the most interesting, but all in all it was a sparse scene. Charles had a moment of excitement when he saw a detached lawnmower blade listed in the evidence, but the picture revealed it as a twisted pile of scrap— nowhere close to the right shape for the murder weapon. He set it down among the pictures of the field next to the highway. Grabbing a spare chair from the cubicle next to him, he stood on it to take the whole thing in.

"Pretty," Sam said as he walked behind him, gesturing to the pictures scattered across the floor. "Tell you anything new?"

"Unfortunately, no," replied Charles, frowning as he looked back over the evidence list. He took out his phone, snapping a few pictures of the gestalt image before stepping down and collecting it back into a single pile. He snatched the evidence listing from the bottom of the Kruschek photos, thumbing through the pages before he laid out the second scene.

Frowning, he called out to Sam from across the office. "They didn't find a weapon?"

"What you see is what you get. That's all the photos they had for me," Sam replied from inside his cubicle. Charles imagined the shrug that must have followed. "But they've still got to take the vehicle in for the detailed search."

"Yeah, I guess," muttered Charles, leafing through the stack of Kruschek photos. He'd seen the inside of the SUV on the first day of the investigation—it was pristine. Any weapon large enough to have killed Trooper Temmen would have stuck out during their first pass through. Charles sighed as he settled back into the worn swivel chair. *Everything in this case was one step forward, two steps back.*

He pressed the power button on the desktop, fishing the thumb drive with the bodycam footage out of his pocket and inserting into the computer. After dragging the video file onto his desktop for safe keeping, he pressed play. A box popped up on screen and the video began to play as he slipped on a pair of headphones.

Rising in popularity through the mid-2000s as digital camera technology proliferated and shrank, body-worn cameras were a staple of the modern police officer—a tool as ubiquitous and widely used as the TASER or pepper spray. One-part evidence custodian, one-part prying nannycam, there was an even split in the law enforcement community between the old guard that resented their intrusion, and the new recruits that had never known life without them. Charles had always been ambivalent towards the small, chest-mounted cameras. On one hand, he resented the Monday-morning quarterbacking associated with the release and reviewing of the footage, especially by commentators on the internet. On the other, they were an invaluable asset in any case involving a fatality and an officer in the line of duty.

Charles sped past the first few seconds of the Colorado State Police logo and rules for controlling the distribution of the video. He stopped on a black screen with text describing the time and date. Letting the video play out, the screen transitioned to a fish-eye view of the steering wheel and dash of Trooper Temmen's patrol car. Charles watched, from a slightly different perspective, the same sequence of events from the dashcam video. He saw the blue Equinox appear on screen, then pull over to the side ahead of Trooper Temmen. He heard Trooper Temmen call in the stop, and then watched the perspective shift as he exited the vehicle and approached the SUV.

Trooper Temmen walked to the vehicle with practiced caution. Traffic stops, no matter how routine, always carried an element of risk—especially on the open highway when you could never be too sure of who you were pulling over. Across the nation, dozens of cops were killed every year when an ordinary traffic stop became anything but. Charles watched him turn and face the driver's window, the camera getting a good shot of the occupant as the trooper leaned in and knocked on the glass. Sharon Kruschek was looking away from the camera, twisted around and talking to someone in the back—Sydney, he surmised—and she appeared startled by the officer's knock. Charles heard Trooper Temmen speak, the audio slightly distorted by the body.

"Colorado State Police. Ma'am, can you roll down your window."

Charles watched Sharon Kruschek ignore the trooper's instructions, her eyes wide and fearful as she stared up at the ceiling of the SUV cab.

Trooper Temmen leaned in and knocked again, a little more forcefully this time. "Ma'am, roll down the window."

Sharon Kruschek nodded and complied; a look of worry stretched across her face.

"Ma'am, do you know why I pulled you over?" Trooper Temmen asked.

Charles smiled to himself. It was the standard cop opening, perfectly designed to allow the guilty party to trip themselves up and admit to a wrongdoing the officer might not have been aware of. Charles watched Sharon Kruschek pause for a moment before answering.

"Honestly? No. I wasn't speeding, was I?"

"No ma'am," Trooper Temmen replied. "I got a report of a hit-and-run from a vehicle matching this description."

Charles watched recognition play over Sharon Kruschek's face. She nodded, acknowledging what he'd said.

"Yes. About that. Officer, I can explain—"

Trooper Temmen cut her off.

"License and registration, ma'am."

"Right, yes, but—"

"License. And registration."

Charles watched Sharon Kruschek gulp before bending over to retrieve the documents. She handed them over, opening her mouth to say something else but the camera turned sharply as the patrolman grabbed the papers and abruptly walked back to the patrol car. Charles rolled his eyes. *Typical trooper, so preoccupied with what he assumes the scene is that he doesn't stop to check if there's anything else going on*—it was a myopic mentality unfortunately common among cops on patrol.

Charles watched Trooper Temmen walk back to the patrol car and get in, the camera bobbling a bit with each step. The camera feed moved in and around the dash as the trooper leaned over, typing her name in the laptop mounted on the console. Charles sped the video as the officer searched for open warrants and wrote out the ticket. Out on the highway, a semitruck passed them by on the footage at hyper-speed. He pressed play again when the state trooper exited the patrol car, approaching the blue Equinox for the last time.

Trooper Temmen walked up to Sharon Kruschek's door, the ticket, license, and registration held out in his hand for her to take. Just like before, she was turned away from him, talking to someone in the back. Charles could imagine the frustration in the trooper as he opened his mouth to get her attention, only to be cut off as she whipped around and shut him out by raising the window.

Charles paused the video as the trooper took a surprised step back, lowering the hand holding the documents. Charles' brow furrowed, he'd expected her to roll the window up after she slashed him, not before. He jotted the video timestamp down in his notes, and pressed play again, the tingling suspicion that something wasn't right creeping up the back of his neck.

Charles watched as Trooper Temmen reached forward, tapping on the window with the back of his flashlight. Behind the glass, Sharon Kruschek was saying something, muffled by the window and the audio quality on the camera as the wind picked up out on the plains.

"Ma'am! Open the window!" He shouted, a concerned edge

seeping into his voice.

She ignored him, shaking her head and pointing wildly towards the SUV ceiling. Concentrating hard over the sound of rushing wind, Charles could barely discern her screaming the word 'roof' at the top of her lungs.

Charles saw the camera shift as Trooper Temmen took a step back from the car. The angle on the footage elevated slightly as he looked up but remained focused on the window and Sharon Kruschek through it. Charles watched her freeze in place, no more shouting, no more wild gestures, as Trooper Temmen took another step back. A strange expression crossed her face as fear was replaced with something odd and knowing—mixed with pity. Then the camera jerked violently, the strike on the officer coming from just off-screen. Charles watched as blood sprayed forward from the trooper's neck, coating the driver's side window. The camera backtracked some more in halting, stumbling steps, before pivoting upwards abruptly to the sky.

Charles paused the video and rubbed his eyes, unsure of what he just seen. *Or rather, didn't see.* He rewound the video, watching Sharon Kruschek roll up the window, Trooper Temmen knocking, her screaming, and then stopping as something sliced through the trooper's neck. Charles stopped the video again as her face became obscured behind the blood splattered glass. *So, she didn't slash him.* That much was certain, there was no way for her to cut the trooper's throat from behind a quarter inch of automotive glass. *Someone else did, someone just off-screen.* He knew the attack came from above, that must have been what Trooper Temmen was looking at when he stepped back. *Someone on the roof, with a machete or an axe.* Charles backed the video up for a third time, watching Sharon Kruschek crying and pointing from behind the glass. Realization crashed over Charles like a wave. *And she tried to warn him. That means that she knew someone was up there, someone dangerous.*

The sound of buzzing violin strings yanked Charles violently from his thoughts. He fumbled for the phone in his pocket, drawing it out and frowning when he saw a Colorado number he didn't recognize on the screen.

"Hello?" he asked. *If this is another damn robo-call…*

A woman's voice answered him. "Hello, yes? I'm looking for a Detective Davner."

"Speaking."

"Hi, I'm Detective Andrea Morales with the Pueblo Police Department," her voice was pleasant, but polite, with a touch of east coast accent. "My sergeant asked me to call you and offer some assistance in an investigation. Something about a favor for a Sergeant

Briske?"

Fucker. Charles imagined the smug look on the bald sergeant's face when he'd made the call down to Pueblo. He grit his teeth, determined not to let his annoyance show. "Yes, thank you. I'm working an investigation here in the Springs, but I was going to head down there for some interviews with a potential witness." He rolled his eyes, hard. "I was hoping someone from your office might assist me when I'm in the area, partner up as I knock on some doors."

"Sure thing, when were you planning to stop in?"

"Tomorrow, if possible," Charles replied, getting out a pen and paper to jot down her information at the end. "This case is kind of hot for me and I need to chase these leads quickly."

"I understand *completely*." There was a pause on the other end, along with the sound of someone flipping through a day planner. "Tomorrow works, I usually get in around seven. I'd prefer you to stop before eight so we can knock this out early, I've got my own caseload backed up as well."

Charles winced, getting in that early meant waking up at five a.m. *Fucking early risers*. "Sounds good. Is this a good number for you? I can call you when I get into town tomorrow to link up."

"Cool, do you have the witness names or addresses? That way I can get a run-down tomorrow before we meet."

"Uhhh, sure," Charles nodded, pulling out his notebook and flipping through the pages. "That'll be 3126 Tamerlane drive—we're interviewing Sydney and Gregory Kruschek. This is an initial interview though; they don't know we're coming."

There was a pause on the other line, long enough for Charles to check his phone to make sure the call hadn't dropped.

"He-hello?" he asked, readying himself to hang-up and redial.

"What type of investigation is this again?" the woman asked abruptly.

Charles' brow furrowed, confused. "Homicide. Why?"

There was another pause before the woman answered, her tone firmer, more pointed than before

"Because, Detective Davner, I'm *also* investigating a homicide— and the Kruscheks were my next lead."

Chapter 5

Friday

"So, she's an axe-murdering soccer mom?"

Andrea Morales cocked a perfectly threaded eyebrow as she leaned back in her chair. The Puerto Rican detective trusted only two things in this world—her grandmother and her gut—and one of them was telling her this story didn't add up.

"No, no, no," Charles said, taking another sip from the half-empty RedBull. "Based on the bodycam video she couldn't have done it; her window was up when the trooper was axed. I'm just saying she *knew* who the killer was—or at least that he was there."

"Right, right, because she pointed to the roof." Andrea ran her hands through her curly black hair, pulling it back with an elastic tie while she fit the pieces together in her mind. "So, you think she was trying to warn him. And that makes her what? A hostage?"

Charles nodded as he took another long sip, finishing the can and setting it down on the desk. "Or an accomplice. Watching that video put me back at square one with this case, I've got nothing but open-theories at this point."

Andrea sympathized. There were few things worse than watching your carefully crafted explanation for a case crumble away into dust when the evidence took a hard-left turn. She'd seen it plenty of times working with the gang unit in lower Manhattan, though not so much here in Pueblo. It was one of the perks of moving out to the mid-size mountain town after working New York's busy streets—the crimes seemed simpler, more straightforward.

Not that there was any less of it, as she'd learned moving out there when her grandmother retired from her florist business on the lower west side. Despite having a hundredth of the population, Pueblo boasted a crime rate nearly three times that of New York. Andrea had been pressed hard as soon as she'd sworn in with the Pueblo PD, hitting the ground running with a double homicide in a trailer park by Lake Minnequa. It'd taken nearly a year after moving for her to fully adjust, but she was finally reaching a happy equilibrium—finding time for work, checking in on her grandmother, and twice-a-day workouts. She hadn't competed since 2015's Olympia Physique Classic, but she trained hard, keeping her narrow frame compact, muscled, and lean. It would take serious focus to cut back down to her competition weight, but she had a hopeful eye on the Colorado Cup in the upcoming summer.

"If you think that video set you back, try working with this trash," Andrea said, leaning forward in the swivel chair. She faced the desktop screen towards Charles, double-clicking the MP4 file on the top left. It was Charles' turn to lean in on the desk, squinting hard as the screen filled with grainy footage of a short-haired blonde, standing half-inside the front seat of a blue SUV. "It's from one of the pump cameras at the Sinclair station on Santa Fe—I've seen better footage of the moon landing."

Charles agreed, he could almost count the pixels as the video played. He watched the blonde—Sharon Kruschek, he assumed—sway back and forth as she stood on the running board of the SUV. She was talking to someone just off-screen, but the pump camera's fish-eyed perspective was narrowly trained on the area immediately surrounding the card reader and the pump-handles. There was no audio either, the tiny camera only suitable for documenting minor gas theft and credit card fraud. Charles could only guess at what she was saying, but her shoulders and body language transmitted agitation clear enough. Something happened off-screen. Charles watched her tense up suddenly, then jump into the car and slam the door shut. Charles saw her fumble with the dash, then speed out of the camera's view.

"So that's when your guy bit it, huh?" Charles asked, meeting Andrea's brown eyes from across the desk. "Is that the only video from the scene?"

"Oh no," scoffed Andrea, double-clicking another video file. "I've also got *this* absolute beauty from inside the store."

Charles watched as the grainy footage was replaced by a slightly higher-quality video of a clerk scratching his ass behind the gas station's register.

"All class," Charles remarked, as the clerk transitioned to picking his nose.

"That's Pueblo for you." She circled the upper left corner of the video with her finger. "The action's up here."

Charles could make out the edge of the Equinox's back hatch, just visible through the glass of the station's front window. They both watched for a few seconds as the clerk idled behind the counter before a man in plaid stumbled into view, blood spurting from his neck onto the oil-stained pavement. The clerk screamed, throwing his hands into the air and ducking behind the counter as the man in plaid fell to the ground.

"Why's he screaming and ducking *inside* the store?" Charles asked, raising an incredulous eyebrow towards his fellow detective. "Did he see the killer and think he was next?"

"Nah, just panicked 'cause he never seen a body before." Andrea rolled her eyes. The bodega clerks were a little harder to rattle where she was from. They watched the Equinox peel away from the left corner as the clerk fumbled for his phone.

"He's calling the ambulance right there. EMS showed up on-scene about five minutes later," Andrea explained, stopping the video and turning her screen back. "I've got the 9-1-1 transcript and I rolled a field interview with him a few days ago, but it's nothing helpful. Clerk didn't see anything until the vic fell down."

"The clerk didn't leave the store? Didn't try to help?"

Andrea shook her head. "Nope, just a panicky 9-1-1 call."

Charles frowned. *Seems to be a trend around here.*

"I don't suppose there's any lead with the victim?" he asked, flipping through the pages of his notebook.

"Will Springsley, the thirty-nine-year-old HVAC-technician?" Andrea chuckled. "Nope. No known enemies, no criminal history, no long-standing debts—lived alone with five cats. I interviewed his family on Tuesday. Apart from them arguing over taking in the cats, his sister and her husband couldn't think of anything bad to say about him."

Charles nodded, jotting down in his notes before looking up. "So what's the connection with Sharon Kruschek then?"

"None, as far as I can tell." Andrea shrugged. "Just the gas station. She pulls in, takes pump #9, he pulls in behind her. The register footage shows her walk partway to the store before changing her mind and heading back, but then I've got nothing until she shows up on the pump camera. You can tell they're talking about something, and then you saw her reaction when someone cut him, but I can't fill in more between that."

Join the club, Charles thought bitterly. He'd hoped after talking with her on the phone that the Pueblo detective might just be the break he needed. Instead, she'd just added to his list of questions.

"What was the cause of death?" he asked after a moment. "Throat slashed?"

Andrea nodded, pulling up the coroner report on her desktop with a few quick clicks. "Throat lacerated from left to right, slight nick on the top of C6 indicating a deep, downward slice." She looked up sharply from the screen. "Yours have a wide blade too?"

"Yup, and jagged," Charles replied, his tongue tucked in his cheek as he filled in a few more notes. "Downward slash though, that's new. I don't know if my coroner caught that on ours." He absentmindedly reached for the can of RedBull on the desk, momentarily disappointed when he remembered it was empty. "How tall was your victim?"

"About five-eight," she said, scanning the screen. "Yours?"

"Six-two."

"A biggun," Andrea remarked offhand, tapping a finger on her pointy chin.

"I guess," shrugged Charles. *She probably thinks the same about most guys*, he thought, eyeing the diminutive detective. He couldn't see from across the desk, but somehow, he just knew her 5.11 boots were swinging right above the worn office carpet.

"Still, it explains the different angle on the cuts," she said after thinking another moment. "And it's a second link between your scene and mine. Both vics killed the same way, with the same weapon, only an hour apart—for sure the same killer. And they're both linked to Sharon Kruschek, my vic was talking to her at the gas station, your vic pulled her over." Andrea held her palms out, weighing the two victims in her open hands. "Both were targets of opportunity, catching it at the point they intersected with her."

"Maybe," Charles acknowledged, scratching the back of his head. "But that really only applies to Trooper Temmen. For all we know your victim's death might've been what set this in motion."

"So, what?" Andrea withdrew her hands, lips pursed as considered it. "Killer's just hanging out at the gas station while Kruschek is talking to my vic, decides to take an ax to him, then Kruschek is caught in between when he hijacks her for a getaway, then he didn't want to get caught so he axes a cop when they get pulled over?"

"That's one theory," Charles shrugged. "But that's what I was saying earlier, without talking to Sharon Kruschek and with so many gaps in the evidence, it's all just guesswork. Up until yesterday I had a cop killed on a traffic stop and her as my primary suspect, just working on the motive. Now?" He spread his empty hands out in front of him. "I've got less than that. I've got two bodies, a missing killer, no murder weapon, and still no motive."

"And you can't ask Kruschek what happened because she's still in a coma."

"Heavy sedation," he corrected. "But pretty much, yeah."

"You think the daughter can fill in those gaps?"

Charles sucked in a deep breath, truth be told, it was a question he feared answering. "She's my only conscious witness, and the only one else I know was in the car during both murders. I know she's young, and probably unreliable, but she's my best next step."

Andrea nodded, interlocking her fingers behind her head as she leaned back in the chair.

"Mine too."

They rode to the Kruschek house in Andrea's squad car. Charles would have objected under most circumstances—it wasn't that didn't trust others to drive, he just preferred to control his own vehicular destiny—but he'd pushed the Delta 88's aging spare tire enough in the drive down. He watched the shops and strip-malls of downtown Pueblo pass by outside the heavily tinted windows of the unmarked Charger, the twang of country guitars spilling out as the radio kicked on. He fished a quinoa bar out his pocket, more to give himself something to do rather than out of any real hunger.

"What kind?"

Charles looked over across the cab. "Huh?"

"The DexU bar, what flavor is it?" Andrea repeated, pointing to the bar in his hand.

"Uh…cherry-walnut," Charles answered, reading off the label.

"Lemon's better," she remarked nonchalantly, returning her attention to the traffic outside. "You cutting?"

Charles blinked at her in confusion, struggling through a bite of the dry, crumbly bar. "What?"

"Cutting weight," she replied, eyes still on the road ahead. "I used to go through boxes of 'em back when I competed. Not much taste, but they're a decent meal replacement." She looked over at Charles, eyeing him up and down. "I just figured, you know…"

Charles' brow furrowed. "Figured what?"

He followed her eyes down, catching sight of the slight swell of his gut.

"No!" Charles sputtered indignantly around a crumbling mouthful. "I just grabbed something quick this morning."

"Okay," she shrugged, turning back to the road. "Just figured you were making some lifestyle changes."

"Lifestyle changes?" Charles' eyes narrowed. *What the fuck does that mean?* He sucked his stomach in a little when he was sure she wasn't looking.

"Yeah, you know," Andrea added, changing lanes around a stopped city bus. "Lotta cops do stuff like that after a few years in a desk job. Although, if you were, I'd advise you to skip the bars and just change up your routine. You'd see changes a lot faster with sprints or HIIT training."

"Nope, no changes here," Charles replied, forcing a neutral tone. He turned back towards the window.

Andrea bobbed her head. "Gotcha."

"Besides," Charles said, coughing a little as he choked down another dry bite, "I happen to *like* the taste."

Traffic slowed up ahead, the pursuit-sedan's cab filling up with the drawling of a cowboy ode to growing corn coming from the speakers. Charles felt his pocket vibrate, buzzing violin strings momentarily blocking out the country radio. He stuffed the rest of the bar in one pocket, digging his phone out of another. Savannah's name lit up on the screen.

"What?" he asked, bringing the phone up to his ear.

"Mom said you didn't call yesterday."

Charles sighed, he could picture her standing with her hands on her hips. "They've been divorced for two years, why do I still have to call her on their anniversary?"

"You know she gets lonely; she doesn't have as many friends after the move. And you don't visit anymore."

Charles rolled his eyes. "Well, maybe she should have considered that before she picked up and moved to *Arkansas*."

Charles had never been to Arkansas, but he was sure it was a terrible place. Charles based most of his assumptions about the south on the movie *Deliverance*, and they'd yet to let him down.

Quiet stretched on the line, he could feel her disapproval emanating through the phone.

Charles sighed again, pinching the bridge of his nose with his fingers. "Fine, I'll call her tonight. Then she can tell me all about how stupid her neighbor is for planting snow-peas too early, or something."

"Thank you!" Savannah replied, her voice back to its usual cheer as she hung up on him.

Charles slid the phone back in his pocket, shaking his head.

"Good ringtone."

Charles started upright. For a moment, he'd forgotten Detective Morales was still in the car. "What?"

"Your ringtone," she replied. "I love that song. Always reminds me of *Looney Tunes*. You remember that one? With the vulture? And the bee?"

"No," Charles grunted, turning back to look out the window. He was spared further conversation as they pulled into the cul-de-sac of Tamerlane drive.

"Thank god," he heard Andrea whisper to herself. "We're here."

The shutters were drawn on the Kruschek house, a slate-grey split-level nearly identical to the row of tan-bricked homes that surrounded it. A tricycle was upended on the overgrown lawn, pink handle-streamers fluttering in the breeze. Charles and Andrea walked to the front door, sidestepping a chalk flower on the sidewalk along the way. Charles tucked in the front of his shirt, ensuring the badge on his belt was visible while Andrea rang the scuffed bell on the side of the door. The heard the chime echo inside, followed moments by muffled cursing as the deadbolt was pulled back.

"I already bought cookies," Gregory Kruschek snapped as he opened the door. "I told you guys we don't need anymo—"

He froze in place, the last syllable trailing off as he caught sight of the guns, the badges, and the detectives attached to them.

"Good afternoon, Mr. Kruschek," Andrea announced calmly, hooking her thumbs in her belt. "I'm Detective Morales of the Pueblo PD, this is—"

"Detective Davner," Charles interjected, raising his hand. "Colorado Springs PD."

"—And we're here because of an investigation involving your wife," Andrea finished. "We'd like to speak to you and your daughter. Do you have a minute?"

Gregory's eyes narrowed as he looked them both over.

"I fucking knew it," he muttered, shaking his head as he turned back inside. "Yeah, come on in."

The inside of the home was pure anarchy. A mob of stuffed animals greeted them at the door, half-dressed barbies littered the landing, laundry adorned the stairs in piles leading up, while the television downstairs showcased the latest exploits of *Peppa Pig*. Papers of important-looking graphs and notes marked up with crayon were scattered around a desk in the living room corner, and in the kitchen, steam rose from two pots bubbling on the stove. Gregory let out a stream of curses as his bare foot caught the sharp edge of a block, motioning for them to sit as he hopped on one foot. Charles and Andrea took a seat on a worn leather couch, first moving aside a rather large plastic Tyrannosaurus.

"So, was it PCP?" Gregory asked, settling onto a square stool opposite them.

Andrea's brow furrowed. "I'm sorry, was what PCP?"

"The drugs she was taking on Monday. Was it PCP?" Gregory leaned back against the wall, letting out a sigh as he closed his eyes.

Andrea shot a quizzical look at Charles, mouthing 'drugs?' Charles shrugged and shook his head.

"We're…not aware of any drug use at this time," Andrea replied slowly. "Why? Did Mrs. Kruschek have a history of drug use?"

"No. At least not when I married her," Gregory said flatly, his eyes still closed. "But on Monday she calls me, freaking out, and can't explain why or what's going on. Then she hangs up on me, and the next call I get is from the emergency center telling me she drove headfirst into a cliff—the only one for miles around—with my daughter in the backseat. So, I go, pick up my kid, and in the hospital they tell me that once she comes out of the ER she's going to the psych ward—something about police observation. The next day I get a call from some electrician's insurance company demanding payment for a hit-and-run. That same day the hospital calls me, telling me they have to keep her under heavy sedation because she's psychotic and won't stop screaming. And now, three days after that, police from two different cities are knocking on my door." Gregory paused, sucking in a long breath before continuing. "So what was it? PCP? LSD? Meth?"

Charles cleared his throat, nodding to Andrea as he waded into the conversation. "Mr. Kruschek, as of now there's no indication of drug involvement. Now as my partner was say—"

"Well, it had to be something!" Gregory snapped, keeping his eyes tightly shut. "I don't know why she felt the need to do this. I don't know if it was something I'd done, or something at work, or if she was just frustrated at being stuck at home with Sydney for spring break. Whatever it was, it was enough that she felt she needed an escape, and so she took something. Something that caused…this." Gregory waved a hand around the room, summing a week's worth of chaos in one weary motion. He sighed again. "Sharon was a lot of things, but she wasn't all this. She was always…dependable."

Charles shut his open mouth, utterly unsure of where to go next. He raised an eyebrow at Andrea, imploring her to jump in and help. A timer went off inside the kitchen. Gregory sat still, nostrils flaring softly as he breathed in and out.

"Mr. Kruschek," Andrea began, treading cautiously back into the conversation. "We feel that something else was going on—*not drugs*—and so we need to talk about Sharon."

"And any associates she might have," Charles interjected.

"Associates?" Gregory cracked one eye open. "You mean like

she was having an affair?”

Andrea winced. “We think that someone else was involved in the incidents on Monday.”

“Right,” said Charles, jumping in. “Someone who may have coerced Sharon into driving them and is the real party responsible for the deaths.”

“Incidents? Deaths?” Gregory opened both eyes, shock rising on his face. “Just what the hell happened on Monday?”

Andrea shot Charles a dirty look. Interviews were a delicate business—one that required a sense of nuance and a deft touch.

“On Monday, around seven p.m., someone killed a man named Will Springsley at the Sinclair station on Santa Fe. We have video showing Sharon’s vehicle pulling into that station just before he was murdered,” she said slowly, choosing her words carefully. “And, approximately thirty minutes later Sharon’s vehicle was involved in a hit-and-run incident on I-25.”

“That’s around when she called me,” said Gregory. “She didn’t mention any dead guy though, she was just hysterical on the phone.”

Charles had to stop himself from rolling his eyes. *You don’t think those two are related?* He tipped a glance over to Andrea but she ignored him, so he busied himself in his notes instead.

“Roughly a half-hour after that,” Andrea continued, keeping her tone level and calm. “Sharon was pulled over by a Colorado State Trooper. Something happened during their interaction, and the officer was killed—in the same manner as the victim from the gas station. Now, we know Sharon was driving, and we know she wasn’t the one that killed him—either of them—but what we don’t know is who was in the car with her and what their connection might be.”

Gregory nodded, processing what she’d said.

“So what do you want from me?” he asked after a moment. “I can tell you a little more about the phone call, but like I said, she was real sharp, and frantic, and then she hung up on me.”

“We know,” Andrea said, gesturing to Charles as well. “And that information is very helpful to us in this investigation.”

Charles opened his mouth to correct her, but changed his mind, nodding and fiddling with his notes instead.

“But there was someone else in the car with Sharon that day, the real reason we’re here today,” said Andrea, watching her words sink in. “We need to speak to your daughter.”

Sydney Kruschek knelt at the glass coffee table, oblivious to the adults whirling around her as she colored. Charles sat on an ottoman across the table, admiring her concentration, the way she stuck her tongue out as she set one marker down and deliberated over the next color to pick up. Charles had always liked kids, they were straightforward and honest—letting loose with whatever thought popped into their little heads. Charles appreciated that about them, he found their bluntness refreshing.

"Okay, sweetie," Gregory said, kneeling down beside her. "Now I need you to talk to the nice policemen. They have some important questions for you."

"That's right," Andrea replied, drawing her words out as she sat down on the couch next to her. "We need to ask you *all about* last *Monday*. When you took a *drive* with *Mommy*."

Charles rolled his eyes. He'd never understood why some adults felt the need to speak slowly and over-enunciate when they were addressing children. *Like they're trying to calm down a scared horse.*

Sydney, for her part, ignored the detectives as she selected the yellow marker, looking up only as her father sat down on the square stool by the wall.

"Sweetie, please," he prodded her, hands clasped anxiously in front. "Tell them what happened."

Sydney returned her attention to the picture. "When?"

"Monday," Andrea repeated, voice lilting up on the end of the word.

"After tumbling class," Gregory hastily added.

Sydney thought for a moment.

"I saw Ms. Wiggles."

"Her teacher's dog," Gregory interjected, raising an apologetic hand. He turned back to his daughter, an urgent falsetto creeping into his voice. "Now, sweetie, tell them what happened *after* class."

"Yes," Andrea nodded, a reassuring smile stretched across her face. "What happened after your class? In the car with mommy?"

"Umm…" she thought for another moment, tapping the marker cap on her chin.

Andrea leaned in, radiating encouragement. "Did you stop somewhere? Like a *gas* station?"

"Ummm…"

"Did someone get in the *car* with *you* and *mommy*?"

"Ummmmm…"

"Did something *happen*? Like an *accident*?"

"Ummmmmmmm…"

"Was there anything *weird*? Did you see something *strange* that day?"

"Yes!" Sydney answered, raising the marker triumphantly in the air. "I also saw two birds!"

Andrea's face fell. Charles snorted. The smoke alarm went off in the kitchen as one of the pots started boiling over.

Gregory cursed, storming up the stairs to rescue his spaghetti.

"Bad word, daddy," said Sydney, finishing up her yellow shading.

Andrea leaned back, sighing as she dragged a hand across her face. Charles flipped his notebook closed and stood up from the ottoman.

"I'll tap in," he said quietly, stepping past Andrea. He took up a spot on the floor by Sydney, ignoring the popping of his knees as he sat cross-legged.

"Whatcha drawing?" He asked, looking over the table.

"A monster," she replied, switching over to the blue marker.

"She's been drawing them for weeks," Gregory called out from the kitchen, voice rising over the clattering of pans.

Charles nodded. "What kind of monster?"

"A *shiny* monster."

"Oh," he replied solemnly. "And what made you draw a shiny monster?"

"It's the one I saw on mommy's car."

"Sweetie, we talked about this" Gregory yelled out from the kitchen. There was crash as a potlid hit the floor. "There's no such thing as monsters!"

"Yes there is, daddy," Sydney replied matter-of-factly. She continued her drawing, sharp blue lines filling in a set of teeth on the monster.

Charles nodded again, flipping his notebook to an empty page. "And when did you see the monster on mommy's car?"

"After tum'ling class," she announced, filling in another line of teeth.

Andrea sat upright on the couch, dropping her hand and locking eyes with Charles from across the table. She opened her mouth to speak, but stopped when he waved her off.

"Oh," said Charles, his voice calm and purposefully aloof. "And was the monster in the car with you?"

"Nooooo." Sydney shook her head, brown curls bouncing around. "He was on the roof."

"The roof…" Charles repeated slowly, the phrase sticking out in his mind for some reason. He flipped back through his previous notes, but nothing jumped out at him. "And was anyone in the car with you?"

"Just mommy. And Harry."

"Harry?" Andrea asked earnestly, leaning back into the conversation.

"Harry," Sydney confirmed, pulling the plush, purple elephant out from under the table and holding it up.

"Harry," repeated Charles, chuckling to himself. He looked up at Andrea. "I think we've got all we're gonna get here."

"I think you're right," Andrea sighed, standing up from the couch. "Thank you for talking to us Sydney."

"*You're welcome,*" sang Sydney, still busy with her drawing.

"I'm sorry, I'm so sorry," Gregory apologized, sauce-splattered face appearing at the top of the stairs. "She watched that movie over a month ago and can't stop drawing that stupid alien."

"It's okay," Andrea said, making her way up the stairs. "What movie?"

"Uh, the new one," Gregory replied, wiping marinara off his chin with the back of his hand. "*Alien: Covenant.*"

"Terrible," Andrea scoffed, shaking her head. "Shoulda gone with the first one. Or *Aliens* at least."

Gregory shrugged. "*I* didn't pick it."

Andrea stopped on the landing, calling down to Charles. "You coming?"

"Yeah, one sec," he replied, getting up from the floor. Turning back to Sydney. "It was good talking to you."

He was just about to head to the stairs when he felt a tug on the back of his pantleg.

"Wait, here," she said, offering him the picture of the hideous monster. "S'case it comes back."

"Thanks," he said, the flicker of a smile on his face as he took the drawing. "We'll be on the lookout."

Back in the squad car, Charles set the picture down on the dash, rolling to one side as he buckled in.

"Well, that was a waste of fuckin' time," griped Andrea, slamming the door shut.

"Story of this fucking case," Charles said. "No answers, just more questions."

Andrea sighed, rolling her head around as she stretched. "I guess it went as well as it could've."

Charles dug his phone out, firing off a quick text to his sister asking about dinner. "Yup."

"And just think, now we've got a suspect," Andrea laughed, pointing towards the drawing on the dash.

"Yup," Charles chuckled. "Green and yellow with sharp teeth. I'll put out a BOLO as soon as we get back."

Andrea exhaled slowly, nodding to herself as she fired up the engine.

"You know, it's weird," she remarked, as they pulled out of the driveway.

Charles slipped the phone back into his pocket. "What is?"

"The alien," she said, pointing to the dash. "He said she saw it in a movie."

Charles shrugged. "So?"

"In the movie it was black."

Chapter 6

Saturday

Charles strode quickly though the parking lot, turning up the corduroy collar of his Carhartt jacket against the frigid, mid-morning gusts. The square red brick of the Colorado Springs Police Department loomed over him as he made his way to the vehicle bay door. The steel door handles were freezing in his hands as he pulled against the stuck door, cursing under his breath as the wind whipped his coat open.

He should be in bed. Any other Saturday and he'd be just waking up, forcing himself upright to tend to the urgent snorts and scratching as Petunia demanded to be let out. *But noooo, damn techs had to go and finish early.* He'd gotten the email from the scene supervisor last night letting him know processing on the Equinox had wrapped up ahead of schedule. He'd been fully prepared to let it ride over the weekend and tackle their findings on Monday, but something caught his eye as he clicked through the evidence collection list and the attached pictures. And so here he was, fighting with a door on a cold, spring morning. *All because of a grainy shot of a fucked-up roof...* Grunting with effort, he gave it one last heave, the door popping free in his hands and swinging open. Grumbling under his breath, Charles stepped inside onto the dingy concrete of the garage bay.

Flipping the switch by the door, Charles watched the fluorescent lights flicker to life across the garage. There, in the back, he spotted a glint of blue, the black swell of the RocketBox just visible on the other side of a Tahoe with an empty engine bay. Walking past the rows of lifts, he wove around a Charger with the front axle dropped and past a Ford Taurus with the interior molding stripped out. The last bay stood out from the others, its concrete a polished white square in stark contrast to the surrounding oil-stains and grime. No forgotten tools or greasy parts littered the floor of the last bay, this was the processing area for the CSPD crime techs and for that purpose it had to be immaculate. Charles spotted the logbook hanging by a screw on a nearby column. He signed in, pulling on a pair of nitrile gloves and taking his first step over the line of yellow-and-black striped tape on the floor.

Sharon Kruschek's blue Chevy Equinox sat suspended on the yellow lift, its smashed headlights peering forlornly at the floor from the crumpled front end. The doors were open, the driver's side hanging loose on its hinges. The wheel wells were empty, the drooping rotors adding to the melancholy of the crushed SUV. The rims and tires were leaned in a row against the wall with marker numbers in front of each, while a shelving unit beside them displayed the pieces and particulates removed from the totaled vehicle.

Charles walked the length of the shelf, comparing the numbered items to the list on his phone. It was the usual mixed detritus of a personal car—a momentary window into the suburban life of the woman who drove it. Three tubes of lip gloss lay next to a half-empty bottle of Purell and an empty bag of cheddar whales. A pair of cracked sunglasses rested next to a stack of McDonald's napkins and a dented LaCroix can. The usual mix of charging cords and USB outlet plugs were coiled near a combination seatbelt cutter and window punch. Looking back to the SUV, Charles made a note to compare the punch to the chip on the rear passenger window. A knock-off Versace purse sagged open, its contents of old receipts, concealer, and a mostly empty checkbook arranged with care and precision beside a two-year-old cellphone with a smashed screen. Charles looked it over to make sure it wasn't an iPhone—he wasn't sure he'd need it unlocked but it was good to have the option just in case, and Apple was notoriously reluctant to assist law enforcement.

Charles scrolled through the list as he looked over the lower shelves, a motley collection of rubber floor mats, a roadside emergency kit, and Sydney's car seat. He sighed to himself as he came to the end of the shelves. He knew from the list that the techs hadn't recovered any machetes or axes from the scene—the most dangerous item they'd found was a tire iron—and even that had been tucked away with the jack in the unopened trunk panel. Four days, three vehicles, two scenes, and three-hundred man-hours later, and Charles was still no closer to understanding who'd killed Trooper Temmen, or how they did it. Charles shook his head, pocketing his phone as he turned back to the Equinox. He'd known the recovered evidence was a bust from the email, it was the pictures of the SUV itself that had kept him up late last night, and drew him out early on a Saturday morning.

He took a slow lap around the smashed SUV. The blood splattered on the driver's side window was gone, chipped away and packaged for DNA testing—along with dozens of other samples of hair and bits found in the car. The CSPD was lucky to have its own crime lab on site that it shared with the rest of El Paso county—most departments had to ship theirs off to a regional lab.

Charles poked his head inside the cab, the shattered glass and broken plastic present at the scene was cleaned up and filed in Ziploc bags on the shelves along the wall. He looked around, mentally comparing the stripped and empty cab with his recollection of the scene on the first day of the investigation. Then, as now, the interior was remarkably clean, although he spotted a few holofoil unicorn stickers on the C-pillar where the car seat used to sit.

Charles stepped back from the cab, continuing with his survey of the exterior. The rear bumper and the trunk hatch were clean, absent the usual array of honor-student stickers and stick-figure family decals he saw on most cars. *I guess that's one basic-mom stereotype I can cross off,* he thought, noting with some amusement that her registration expired at the end of the month. *Hope she didn't pay the renewal fee yet…*

Charles circled around to the passenger side, greeted once again by the long gash trailing from the front fender to the tailgate. He scratched the back of his head, puzzling over the gashed metal. He knew it happened after the killing at the gas station, when Sharon Kruschek had driven out onto the highway, but he still couldn't place it in the context of the two murders. *Was she a terrified hostage, trying to get someone's attention? Was it to throw him off during a struggle in the car? Or was it just an accident in a moment of distraction as she and the killer fled the scene?* Charles shook his head, setting aside that last theory. He knew he needed to be at least open to the consideration that she was working with the killer, but the longer the case went on, the less that theory fit. He'd re-watched the bodycam footage on his laptop last night, the terror on Sharon's face behind the car window fresh in his mind. He couldn't shake the earnestness and desperation in her eyes. *'Roof! Roof!'* she'd been screaming as she tried to warn Trooper Temmen—hardly the act of a murderous accomplice.

Which brought him to the real reason he'd left the comfort of his warm bed behind to drive in to work on his day off. Charles hopped up on the lift-joist suspending the car in the air, careful not to step inside the tan cab interior. Holding on to the lift's pillar for support, he craned his neck, looking past the roof rails to the top of the SUV.

The photos had utterly failed to do it justice. Between the crossbars of the rack, the glossy blue sheet metal was shredded—marred by long scratches running in every direction. Charles tested the depth of the nearest one with his pen, the tip disappearing up to the rubber grip. He let out a low whistle, snapping pictures with his phone of the devastation wrought in the thin sheet metal. He hopped down from the joist to grab a ruler off the shelves behind him, returning to get a better measurement for the gouges' width and depth. Three-quarters of an inch wide and almost a half-inch deep, Charles jotted the numbers down in his notebook. He'd have to call to make sure, but he had a hunch it'd be a match for the wide slash across Trooper Temmen's throat.

He snapped a few more pictures, stepping down from the yellow joist and stepping away from the ruined vehicle. He signed out of the log, stripping off his rubber gloves and heading to the door. The damage to the roof was bizarre—almost like someone was trying to cut their way into the vehicle from the top. Charles shook his head, *even the most deranged killer would try a window first.*

He froze mid-step, struck by a sudden realization as he went back to the evidence shelves. Pulling on another glove, he snatched up the window punch and measured its tip against the chip in the rear passenger window. *Too small,* he thought, setting it back down on the shelf. *Not that it made sense since the chip is on the outside.* He picked up the ruler again, holding it underneath the chip for reference and snapping another few pictures. Without the exact weapon for scale he couldn't be one hundred percent sure, but the width of the scratches matched the chip well enough. Heading toward the second floor, he chewed over this latest development. *I guess he started with the window after all…*

Charles passed through the glass doors at the end of the second floor, walking past rows of empty cubicles to his desk. He hung his coat on the back of the chair, setting his notebook down on the desk and booting up the computer as he sank into the worn fabric of the swivel chair. The office silent save for the soft whir of the desktop booting up. Looking over at the stack of crime scene photos and the pile of paperwork, the weight of questions unanswered pressed down on his shoulders. *One step forward, two steps back,* he mused bitterly, *that's the story of this whole fucking case.* There was a soft ding as the monitor came to life, the cubicle lighting up in the blue glow. Charles sighed, clasping his hands behind his head as he leaned back in the swivel chair. He'd had difficult cases before. He'd had cases that were unsolvable—no suspects, no motivations, just a corpse with an unnatural cause of death. And no cop had a perfect clearance rate—especially not in homicide. But as the stack of photos and paperwork glared at him from the corner of the desk, he knew this was one that couldn't make its way down to the cold case section. *Not with a dead cop as the primary victim…*

By the time the start-up loading bar had made its journey across the screen, Charles had planned out his next few steps. *Email the coroner, double-checking the weapon dimensions. Revisit the scenes for another pass at the murder weapon. Put in a call at the Colorado Bureau of Investigation, see if they've had anything similar. Put together an update email for the Sergeant.* He briefly considered calling up Andrea to talk though his findings on the roof, but thought better of it. Even seeing for himself under the cold fluorescent lights, they added nothing but more questions. *Probably not worth bothering her on a day off.*

His pocket buzzed. Pulling out his phone, he opened up a text message from Savannah.

'Back home soon?'

'Maybe.' he typed back. *'Afternoon at most.'*

'Ok' came the reply. *'Grab poptarts on your way home. We're out.'*

Charles felt his jaw clench.

'You opened that box YESTERDAY!' he typed. *'Stop eating all my FOOD!'*

'Not fair. Not just me. Petunia likes them too.'

Charles hissed through his teeth.

'Stop giving her poptarts! She's on a diet!'

Three dots appeared at the bottom of the screen, waving at him from her side of the conversation. They disappeared and reappeared a few times before resolving themselves into a message.

'She's beautiful at any size. You're just mean.'

Charles shook his head, tossing the phone aside on his desk. He knew better than to argue with her, he'd just find himself drawn deeper into a debate until he somehow wound up arguing about the systematic pressures of institutional body shaming or some other topic from her deep well of collegiate outrage. Besides, his frustration stemmed less from the French bulldog's weight so much as his dread for the gaseous horrors that would spill out of her as she processed through the frosted pastries.

He was broken out of his thoughts by the slamming into the glass doors at the end of the office. Charles popped his head up over the cubicle, catching sight of Perry Raines, rubbing his elbow and cursing as he pushed his way through the doors. Charles' brow furrowed. It wasn't like Perry to come in on an off day. Ex-military, the broad, musclebound detective was fanatical about his time off, zealously guarding every precious second he could spent with his wife and eight-year-old daughter.

"Hey, Perry." Charles offered a wave to the irate detective. "What are you here for?"

Perry grumbled his way over to his deck, tossing his empty coffee cup in the trash. He threw his coat down roughly, knocking his chair over in the process. More cursing followed, the length and breadth of which never failed to amaze Charles.

"Double-homicide," Perry grunted out. "Two *shit-fuckin'* bums decided to have a fuckin' *knife-fight* in *gawdamn* Acacia park!"

Charles nodded to himself, his curiosity momentarily satisfied. With so many businesses and restaurants nearby, CSPD would definitely want the investigation handled immediately to assuage any public fears.

"Coroner on scene?" he called out over the cubicle.

"Should be," Perry called back, briefly interrupted by tinkling piano keys as his phone began to ring. "Hold on Chuck, this is them."

Charles sat back down at his desk, starting in on his email to the assistant coroner.

"Gawdamnit!" echoed across the empty office.

"You're shittin' me!" came a few seconds later.

"*Aaaaaaauuurgh!*" followed just behind that, accompanied by the sound of a phone bouncing off a cubicle wall. Charles tapped away at his keyboard, listening to the strained creaking of Perry's chair as it protested holding up his massive size.

"Chuck, you're not going to fuckin' believe this."

Oh, I probably will. Charles continued to type, adding a few lines before his signature at the bottom. "What's up, Perry?"

"Coroner's not on scene. Apparently he's got himself tied up with some fuck-stick hiker that fell off a cliff at the Garden of the Gods. Won't be back for hours."

"Ah," said Charles, pressing send on the email.

Silence filled the office. Charles could feel a forbidding sense of what was about to come.

"*Chuuuck?*"

Charles grit his teeth. He knew what followed when someone stretched his name out like that.

"Yes?"

"Do you mind checkin' out the scene with me? With two eyes on this I might be able to wrap it up without waitin' around for the fuckin' coroner."

Charles closed his eyes, pinching the bridge of his nose between two fingers. Saw it coming, and yet powerless to avoid it.

"Yeah, Perry, I'll come with."

Charles ignored the grateful whoop of his coworker, standing up from his chair and pocketing his notebook and phone. He logged off from the computer and threw on his coat, rolling his shoulders back in resignation.

Perry met him at the edge of the cubicles, his XXL black coat draped over a thick forearm.

"Thanks again, Chuck," he said, pushing through the glass doors.

"I'll owe you one."

"Yeah, yeah," Charles muttered, and followed him out the door.

The sky was overcast and gray over Acacia Park, the bitter chill of the morning not yet evaporated in the weak light of the day. Two CSPD cruisers were parked on scene, flanking the coffee shop at the edge of the park. Charles pulled the Delta 88 in behind the nearest cruiser. He'd overridden Perry's objections about riding in the golden Oldsmobile—if he was stuck going out of his way to do a favor, he was damn well going to drive himself there. *Besides, Perry has nothing to complain about.* The tan bench seat boasted plenty of space for the big detective.

They exited the vehicle, walking over to the nearest patrolman and checking in before entering the scene.

"So where they at? And whatcha got?" asked Perry, towering over the young officer.

"Two Caucasian males, late forties, deceased behind the coffee stand," the patrolman answered, leading them back behind the shop. "We found a wallet on one—Robin Oberbauer—no ID on the other. They both look homeless though."

Charles smiled a little, with all the aging hippies and urban granola types of the Springs, it was often hard to tell. Charles and Perry stopped short as they turned the corner, taking in the scene before them. Two men sat facing each other on the concrete path, leaned up against the back wall of the Story Coffee Company. Judging from the greyed beards, they were both mid-forties. Judging from threadbare hoodies and the built-up dirt around their eyes, homeless too. They were both, most assuredly, dead. The one on the left sat with his eyes closed, his mouth hung open after drawing his last breath, while the grey eyes of the one on the right stared sightlessly out into the distance. The chests of both men were crisscrossed with deep slashes and stabs, Robin Oberbauer—the one on the right—had his throat slashed as well, a wide gash opening up under his chin from ear to ear. There was dried blood on his left hand, leftover from when he tried to stem the tide spilling out from his torn throat.

The sidewalk around them was streaked with blood, cast off in lines radiating out from where the two men sat. Charles and Perry walked out from the scene, following the splattering trail to where it disappeared on the edge of the sidewalk underneath a wide maple tree.

"Start point?" Charles asked, pointing at the ground beneath the tree.

Perry nodded, tracing the meandering blood trails back to the scene with his finger. "And, end point."

They walked back to the two dead men, pulling on nitrile gloves to examine them further. Charles snapped a few pictures before crouching down beside the late Mr. Oberbauer—until the crime techs finished, they'd want to make sure to disturb the scene as little as possible. Charles spotted the wallet on the ground beside the corpse, picking it up and thumbing through its contents. He saw the other body move out of the corner of his eye as Perry leaned it away from the wall to search it.

"Got a knife!" the detective called out, leaning the corpse further as he felt underneath it. Charles looked up from the wallet as Perry picked it up, holding the knife up for him to see. "Some kinda mall-ninja, Rambo-type bullshit."

Charles set the wallet down and walked over to Perry, careful to step around the blood-streaked concrete. The knife had a long, single-edged stainless-steel blade tapering into a clipped point. Aggressive saw-teeth sprouted from the back of the blade's spine, ending in a shiny stainless-steel guard and cylindrical handle. Dried blood marked the surface in patches on the handle, with very few drops on the blade itself.

"Yup, Rambo bullshit," said Perry. "They used to sell this shit to the POGs hanging out in the command tent all day. Watch this."

He unscrewed the pommel of the blade, revealing a hollow core in the center of the handle. Tipping it up, he shook it out, the contents dumping into one gloved palm.

"Look Chuck," Perry laughed, thumbing through to reveal some fishhooks, line, matches, and a small packet of meth. "It's a bum survival kit!"

Charles snorted, walking back to the other body while Perry slid the contents back into the knife. Leaning the body forward, he patted it down, searching for another weapon.

Charles frowned, looking over to Perry. "I got nothing over here. You find a second knife on yours?"

"Uhhh, lemme check," Perry answered, setting the knife on the sidewalk and patting down his body. "Nope. Try yours again?"

"Already on it," said Charles, finishing up with his second search. He'd found two glass pipes, a half-eaten granola bar, a flip phone with the buttons worn off, a brass fountain pen, a fifty-dollar bill tucked into each sock, two ounces of meth in a Ziploc bag, a folded-up poncho, three lighters, and a half-empty bottle of Purell. He spread all of these out on the sidewalk, stepping back when he was done. "No knife. No weapons at all."

"Huh."

Perry joined him on the edge of the sidewalk, eyes narrowing as he considered the scene. A few moments of silence passed as he thought it over, ending in a shrug.

"Alright, so it's a one-knife, knife-fight."

"A one-knife, knife-fight?" Charles frowned up at the big detective. "So what? They just took turns stabbing each other and passing it back and forth?"

Perry shrugged again. "I got two stabbed bums, a ten-foot blood trail that starts under a tree and ends at a wall with nothing else around it, and one knife. Makes sense to me."

Charles shook his head, walking back to the two dead men. He crouched down beside Robin Oberbauer, circling his many wounds with his finger. "That makes *zero* sense."

"Suuure it does," Perry said, groaning as he settled into a crouch beside Charles. He pointed to Robin's corpse. "Bum One is hangin' out here in the park last night, smokin' some meth, shootin' the shit—life is good, this is *his* park. Then along comes Bum Two." He pointed over to the second body. "Bum Two is angry, it should be *his* park, and he's got the big-ass, dumb-as-shit, Hollywood-horror knife to prove it…"

Charles rolled his eyes. Perry had strong opinions on everything connected to the military, and most things that weren't.

"…And so these two go at it under the maple tree. They struggle, knife changes hands a few times as they're fightin' back and forth, and then ol' boy Robin here catches it in the throat." Perry pointed back at the Oberbauer. "At this point, he's done, he stumbles against the wall, fuckin' dead to the world. Bum Two, he *thinks* he's won, but he's cut up bad too. Takes a few steps, decides to rest up against the wall, then bleeds out himself." Perry laughed. "It's almost poetic."

Charles frown deepened, it was a dumb theory, but he'd seen dumber ones get proven right. He looked back at his corpse. There was something off about it, something strangely familiar he couldn't quite shake. He resisted the urge to scratch the back of his head with his gloved hand. Standing up, he ignored the look on Perry's facing imploring him to agree.

Charles walked over to the knife, picking it up off the sidewalk.

He looked at the knife.

He looked at Robin Oberbauer.

He looked at the knife.

He looked at the other body, nine red stains pooling the chest.

He looked at the knife, sunlight reflecting off the shiny blade.

He looked at Robin Oberbauer, counting five stab wounds, and the slashed throat.

He looked back at the knife. Aside from a few drops near the guard, the blade was utterly clean.

He looked at Perry.

"No dice."

"*Gawdamnit, Chuck!*" Perry groaned, head hanging down between his broad shoulders. "Why the fuck not?"

"Blade's too clean," Charles explained, holding it out for him to see.

Perry rolled his eyes, walking over to stand next to the smaller detective. "I found it underneath him. Maybe it rubbed off."

Charles shook his head, pointing to the spine of the knife. "The saw-teeth are clean too. No way they stabbed each other with this and left nothing in the teeth."

Perry looked at the knife and sighed. "Look, Chuck, I've seen this kind of stuff before, *overseas.*" He locked eyes with Charles. "Knife-fights are confusing. They're a mess. Not everything lines up neatly when they're done."

Charles' eyes narrowed. He sincerely doubted Perry had military experience related to investigating murder scenes—he'd been an Army mechanic after all—but he was in no position to argue with the man. "But..."

Perry reached out a hand, patting Charles on the shoulder. "I respect the hell out you, Chuck, you know that. But this is my scene. I'm calling it."

Charles nodded. Backed into a corner like this, he had no choice but to concede. This was Perry's case, and it was Perry that had to answer for it in the end. Perry watched the shift on Charles' face, happy for the moment with what he saw. He turned away from the scene, hunting for the young patrolman from earlier.

Charles' eyes dropped to the knife, watching the thin edge shine as he turned it over in his hands.

Like a razor.

He flicked a thumb over it, it was damn sharp.

Thin...

His brow furrowed. That feeling was back, that something was off about the scene.

Thin edge...

Charles looked over to Perry, satisfied that the big detective's back was turned as he spoke to the patrolman by one of the police cruisers. Charles stormed back over to the two bodies. He crouched beside Robin Oberbauer, measuring the edge of the knife against the wide slash across his throat.

Too thin, he thought, setting the knife down on the concrete. *It'd take a stout blade to make a wound that wide. Like a machete…or an axe!*

Charles bolted upright, eyes wide. His twitching hands struggled to peel off the nitrile gloves. He whipped his phone out, swiping across the screen and thumbing over to the dialer. Typing out 'A-n,' he pushed the icon next to her name as soon as it came up. Charles tapped a nervous hand against his thigh as the call rang through.

It picked up on the third ring.

"Hey," Detective Morales panted. She was out of breath, like she'd just come back from a run. "What's up?"

"You said to call if I found something weird or I caught a break on our killer."

Quiet filled the other line. Charles could almost hear the gears turning in her head over the sound of her heavy breathing.

"And? Which is it?"

"Both."

Chapter 7

Monday

Andrea Morales pinched her finger on the screen, eyes narrowing as the dead man came closer in focus. One eyebrow raised as she took in the details—older white man wearing a tattered green hoodie under a dirty jacket, greasy salt-and-pepper hair matching a grey, scraggly beard, and, below the beard, a bloody gash stretching from ear to ear. She swiped her finger, moving on to a close-up of the wound. It was at least a half-inch wide with ragged edges, and even with the poor lighting of the phone's camera, she could tell it ran deep. Andrea fished her phone out of her purse, unlocking it and pulling up pictures from the autopsy of Will Springsley. She compared the pictures of the two dead men, eyes darting from each screen as she lined up the pictures of their torn throats. She shook her head, setting the two phones down on the desk.

"Well, when you're right, you're right," she said to Charles, a grim smile on her face. "Looks like our boy is alive and kicking in the Springs."

"Wounds match?" he asked, leaning over to look at the phones.

"Almost identical. Width, placement, all of it." She tapped a manicured nail on the screen, highlighting the slash across the victim's neck. "I can't tell from these shots, but I'm willing to bet the wound path matches too."

Charles jerked a thumb to the coroner report for Trooper Temmen displayed on his desktop screen. "Left to right on the trooper, same for Oberbauer in the park. Yours?"

"Same." Andrea nodded. She drew both hands together, swinging an imaginary bat from left to right. "So, our boy is left-handed."

Charles scratched the back of his head. "Only if he's using something with a long handle—like an axe. Now that we've got other victims, I'm not so sure."

Andrea raised an eyebrow. "Alright, walk me through it."

Charles tapped his phone, swiping to the wider shots of the scene. "An axe fit for our first two scenes; both of those victims only had their throats slashed. But the guys in the park, they had stab wounds too." He zoomed in on the marks crisscrossing Robin Oberbauer's chest. "Pretty hard to stab a guy with an axe."

Andrea nodded. "So, a machete then."

"See, that's where I get tripped up." Charles frowned, turning back to the desktop screen. He pulled up a search tab displaying pictures of machetes. "I checked some out at Home Depot yesterday, since I had time—"

Andrea winced. "I know, sorry, I had plans. My *abuela*—"

Charles waved her off. "It's fine, we couldn't have gotten much done on a Sunday anyway. But, like I was saying, I checked some out and they're all thin—too thin." He scrolled down the page, rolling through the pictures of long blades. "Even online, I couldn't find anything with a thick enough blade. And then there's the problem with reach, whatever we're looking for has to have enough reach that the killer can swing it while staying out of frame on every camera."

"So, a thick-edged machete mounted on an axe handle?" Andrea's eyes narrowed. "What? Like one of those medieval spears?"

Charles shrugged. "I guess? But the handle can't be too long. Pretty sure both our victims would've seen someone coming with a spear."

Andrea ran her hands through her curly hair, pulling it back in a loose bun as she thought it over. She broke it down into the base attributes they already knew—thick blade, pointed, and a medium-to-long handle—trying to assemble them into something that made sense. She felt a twinge of guilt watching Charles scroll through the pictures on the screen. She would have been there Sunday, but the weather was supposed to turn nice the following weekend, and her grandmother had needed help getting her gardening tools down from the rafters in the garage. They sat in silence for a few minutes before it hit her.

"What about a brush hook?"

Charles looked up from the screen. "A what?"

"A brush hook," Andrea repeated, leaning forward in her chair. "My *abuela* has one she uses for the tricky branches."

She pushed his hands out of the way, typing it into the search bar. The screen flashed, the machetes replaced with dozens of curved, sickle-bladed tools, each mounted at the end of a long handle. Charles watched the screen as the tools rolled by, most of them ended in a tip-less, sharply curved hook. Andrea stopped abruptly, double clicking one near the bottom. The image enlarged, showing one with a pointed blade and a subtle curve, mounted at the end of a two-foot handle.

"There, like that one," she said proudly, pointing to the screen with her finger. "It says it's used for bananas, but it fits everything we said so far."

Charles squinted at the oddly shaped tool, scratching the back of his head. It was a good fit, ticking all of the parameters for their mysterious murder weapon. *All but one...*

He looked over to Andrea, shaking his head. "No serrations."

Andrea frowned, her lips pursed tight as she considered the tool on the screen. "It doesn't have to be serrated though, just jagged. That still fits with a working tool, my abuela's is old—lots of chips and rolls in the edge over the years. I bet if you cut with it, it'd look like it was serrated too."

Charles nodded, mulling it over for himself. He wasn't ready to call it just yet, but he had to admit the weapon fit. He shrugged; it was a better theory than some kind of medieval polearm. "These brush hooks, are they pretty common?"

It was Andrea's turn to shrug. "'Bout as common as machetes. I think they're in the next aisle over at the garden store."

Charles saved the picture to his desktop as a reference for later. He turned back to Andrea, offering her a half-smile. "Alright, one mystery down. Ready for round two?"

She returned the smile. "Lay it on me."

He picked up his phone again, swiping through pictures to the ones he took in the vehicle bay. He pulled one up showing the Equinox's shredded roof, holding it out for her to see. "Thoughts?"

Andrea sucked a breath in through her teeth, taking the phone in her hands. Her eyes darted back and forth as she took in the details of the ragged metal. "I think it's a lotta work, but that'd probably buff out."

Charles rolled his eyes as he leaned back in the chair. "And?"

Andrea set the phone down on the desk. "And it means the kid was right.

Charles' brow furrowed. "What do you mean?"

"She said she saw a monster," Andrea said, looking over to the picture tacked up on the cubicle wall. "That looks like something I'd draw after someone murdered a guy in front of me, then hung on my roof and tried clawing his way in."

Charles followed her gaze to Sydney Kruschek's artistic work. The monster glared back at him in technicolor hues of Crayola markers. A jagged wave of blue teeth jutted out from the curved green head, while its yellow belly was flanked by pairs of spindly green legs, each ending in a sharp point. Charles had never considered it might be an impression of their killer—he'd just written it off as flight of fancy from an imaginative child.

He looked back at Andrea, a newfound respect creeping into his voice. "That's…smart work. I owe you a beer for that one."

"Thanks, I have my moments." Andrea smirked, biceps stretching the sleeves of her white blouse as she laced her fingers behind her head. "You got anything else? Beer's nice, but I prefer scotch."

"Sure," Charles laughed. "And if you get this one I'll pay your whole fucking bar tab."

Andrea's eyes glittered. She liked scotch. She liked winning even more. "Try me."

"Alright," Charles said, shaking his head. "You want to explain how our killer rode twenty miles on the roof of a speeding car, survived a thirty miles-per-hour, head-on collision with a cliff, and then walked twenty miles just to kill two homeless guys in a park?"

The parking lot was bathed in the warm light of the mountain sun as they stepped through the heavy steel doors. The air was crisp, with the smell of cut grass wafting in on a light breeze from the south. Charles took a deep breath in, closing his eyes and taking in the warmth. Sometimes it was nice to be reminded of the world outside of the plain red brick of the CSPD station.

"So, you gonna tell your boss there's a serial killer on the loose?" Andrea asked, speaking up as the steel door slammed shut behind them.

Charles sighed, forcing his eyes back open. *Back to fucking reality*, he thought, a frown settling onto his face.

"No, not until we've got a sharper lead on his ID or location," he said quickly, fishing for his keys in his pocket. He knew Sergeant Briske well enough to know not to go to him until they had something the section chief would consider 'actionable.' "And, I thought we agreed to call him a 'spree killer.' Serial killers usually take their time and space their victims out."

Andrea shrugged, stepping off the curb and onto the asphalt. "Whatever. A killer's a killer when you stack the bodies together."

Charles rolled his eyes. *She should try floating that by Sergeant Briske.* The sergeant was a notorious stickler for precise language.

Charles clicked the fob in his pocket, signaling the Delta 88's location at the far end with a quick beep of its horn. They walked past the rows of black and white squad cars, Andrea's lips pursing as the long, straight lines of the faded gold Oldsmobile drifted into view.

"Undercover, huh?" she asked, taking in the miles of aging sedan stretched before them. "Make sense. A heap like this won't stick out in the cheaper 'hoods."

"Nope," he snapped, yanking the door open and sliding onto the tan bench seat. "It's mine."

He jammed the key into the ignition, firing up the burbling V6 as Andrea got in on the other side. Choosing the route of diplomatic silence, she said nothing as she buckled in and shut the door with a gentle click. Charles scowled as he reversed out of the spot, narrowly avoiding scraping the side of a white Subaru with the audacity to park and leave him less than two feet of room on the side. Throwing the car in drive, he sped off onto Rio Grande street, heading west towards the Risen Hearts Homeless Shelter.

They drove without speaking, the only sounds in the cabin were a rattling of something loose within the passenger wheel-well, and the soft clinking of empty cans in the cupholders. Andrea looked over to Charles, opened her mouth to speak, but reconsidered after noticing the veins sticking out on the back of his hands as he gripped the steering wheel. She turned to look out the window.

"What?"

She turned back towards Charles. "Huh?"

"I thought you said something."

"Oh, no."

"Okay."

Quiet filled the cabin again. Briefly, she considered turning on the radio to cover the rattling. She looked back over at Charles, noticing the clench in his jaw as his narrowed eyes focused on the road, and reconsidered that too. She sighed under her breath, turning back to the window.

"What?"

She continued to look out the window. "Huh?"

"I thought you said something again."

She gave half a thought to a sarcastic reply, but amended it in favor of something with a bit more tact. They were in this investigation for the long haul she reckoned, and bruising his ego wouldn't help.

"I said, 'I'm sorry.'"

"About what?"

"What I said earlier, about the car. That was rude of me. Inconsiderate."

He looked over at her, surprised once again. Apologies were a rarity among cops.

"Uh…thanks," Charles said, a sheepish flush rising in his cheeks. He instantly regretted his earlier response. Ball-busting was a way of life among police, and he knew better than to be so sensitive—especially about his car. It wasn't much to look at, he was well aware of that, the faded paint on the long hood marred with rock chips and dents. And it wasn't much to drive either, with a spongy suspension that reverberated over every pothole and a turn radius only a hair tighter than an aircraft carrier's. But it was big, one time fitting everything he owned as he moved south to Colorado Springs, and comfy, the beige bench seats worn soft in their age. Most importantly, it was the first and only car he'd ever owned. He'd bought it just after graduating from Colorado State, and, with some minimal attention and maintenance, it had borne him unfailingly over the past nine years.

Charles opened his mouth to offer his own apology but was spared further awkwardness as "Flight of the Bumblebee" blared from his pocket. He pulled it out, answering the phone and tossing it on the seat.

"What's up?" he called out. "You're on speaker."

Savannah's cheery voice filled the cabin. "Hi, Todd! How's Serena?"

"Todd's off today," Charles corrected, stopping for a red light. "Say 'hi' to Detective Morales."

Andrea waved at the phone. "Hey!"

"Hi! Are you a new detective?"

"What's up?" Charles interrupted, prodding the conversation back on course. The last thing he needed was Savannah making another friend in his office. She was already swapping daily SnapChats with Detective Jimenez while she was out on maternity leave.

"Nothing much, just got done talking to my zoology professor about the TPO."

Charles nodded. The Temporary Protection Order was Savannah's next step towards dealing with that creep from class. Charles felt a flicker of pride for his little sister, navigating hearings and filing a JDF-402 form weren't easy, and she'd handled the paperwork almost entirely on her own. "Good, so he's going to move you sections?"

"Yep, three p.m. afternoon section instead of mornings now."

Charles frowned. "Three? Won't you miss the bus?"

Charles could almost hear her shrug on the other line. "Nah, I'll hitch a ride with La'shea. She works at the ColdStone by our place anyway."

Charles liked La'shea, she usually gave him an extra scoop for free when he walked by with Petunia. "Alright, so you're set then? Classes and paperwork squared away?"

"Not quite." Savannah paused, some of the bubbliness evaporating from her voice. "I still need to serve him with the TPO. The judge said I could either hire a process server or ask a sheriff. I figured it shouldn't be you, since then he'd know what your car looks like, but I was wondering if you knew anyone."

"No worries," Charles said, pulling into the shelter's parking lot. He cranked the shifter up into 'park,' picking the phone up off the seat. "There's a big guy who owes me a favor…"

The Risen Hearts Homeless Shelter sat on the corner of Bijou and Cascade Avenues, sharing a parking lot with the church next door. Charles and Andrea left the Oldsmobile and headed to the front, passing a family sharing McDonalds on the grass in front. They walked up to the double-doors, robin egg blue with a painting of a yellow sun radiating across them. Stepping through, they were greeted by a pleasant old lady sitting behind a plexiglass window.

"Volunteers?" she asked, sliding a clipboard through a slot in the window. "Sign in. I'll let Cynthia know you're here."

She turned away from them, tottering off through the door behind her desk in search of the shelter's assistant manager.

"No, wait," Charles called after her, but she was already gone. He looked back at Andrea, who shrugged. They took a seat on a patch-worn green couch in the lobby, a pile of ESPN magazines from years past spread out on the coffee table in front of them. He picked up the June edition, thumbing through the article announcing the great expectations for Derrick Rose following his MVP season with the Chicago Bulls. Andrea tapped him on the arm, drawing his attention to the woman approaching them from the hall.

Cynthia Baysere was short and heavyset, with wavy black hair streaked through with grey, and a wide smile that stretched across her round face.

"Cynthia," she announced, waving excitedly with both hands. "Wasn't expecting you guys, but I'm glad you're here. Follow me, and I'll get you set up in the kitchen."

And with that she turned away, disappearing back up the hallway.

"No, wait," Charles called after her. He looked back to Andrea for support.

Andrea shrugged again. "You heard her. *Follow*."

They caught up with her around the corner, interrupting Cynthia mid-sentence as she explained the shelter's rotating menu policy.

"Detective Davner, CSPD," Charles said, throwing his introduction in before Cynthia could start in on the shelter's glove and hairnet policy.

"Detective Morales, Pueblo PD," added Andrea, sticking out her hand.

"Oh!" Cynthia's eyes widened, she shook her hand firmly. "I'm so glad you guys came! You usually ignore my calls!"

Andrea's brows pinched together, she looked at Charles. "Calls?"

Charles shook his head. "No calls, ma'am. We're here for an investigation—"

"Right, the missing residents," Cynthia interrupted, kind blue eyes darting between the two detectives. "The ones I called about on Sunday."

Charles frowned, taking his notebook out of his pocket. "I don't know about a call, was it for Robin Oberbauer by chance?"

Cynthia nodded, wavy hair shaking around her head. "Robin was one, along with three others: Nicholas, Marcus, and Celeste. They're some of our more permanent residents, they show up every Sunday for service, brunch, and laundry."

Charles nodded, jotting down the names.

"We found Robin Oberbauer," Andrea said slowly, taking the initiative while Charles busied himself with his notes. "Could you describe the other three? Was one a white man, mid-forties, brown eyes and a grey beard?"

"That's Nicholas," said Cynthia, closing her eyes. "And since he didn't tell you himself, I'm guessing he's dead."

Andrea reached out a hand, resting it on the woman's trembling shoulder. "Yes ma'am, it seems we may have found Robin and Nicholas in Acacia Park. We were hoping you might give us some answers about them?"

Cynthia swallowed hard, nodding. She'd tended to the good folks of the Risen Heart Shelter for twelve years; this wasn't the first time her path crossed with the homicide investigators of the CSPD. "Nicholas Chambers and Robin Oberbauer were good friends, both of them served in the National Guard and they loved to swap stories from those days. They've come here every Sunday, Tuesday, and Friday, and most of the cold nights for the last four years. On Sundays they show up early to wash up before service, and they'd both leave after communion to help me set up the tables for the brunch. Most of the other residents clear out as soon as the food is done, but Nick and Robin always stayed behind to help me take down the tables and do the dishes. Then they'd set up a game of spades in the laundry room while they washed their clothes." She chuckled a little at the memory, eyes welling up a little in the corners. "About once a month I'd have to go in there and yell at them, 'cause they'd be smoking in their underwear, passing cigarettes to whoever was playing with them." Cynthia shook her head. "They were good folks. Fell on some hard times, but they had each other."

Andrea nodded, looking over Charles' shoulder as he wrote it all down. She looked back at the shelter manager. "And the others? Marcus and…"

"Celeste," Cynthia answered, dabbing her eyes with a finger. "I don't know their last names. Nick and Robin used theirs whenever they talked about their time in the army." She dropped her voice in a grumbling impersonation. "It was always stuff like, 'Private Chambers here, ma'am!' or 'Sergeant Oberbauer, reporting in, ma'am.'" She laughed again, a small, sad sound. "They were characters."

"What about Celeste and Marcus?" asked Charles, looking up from his notes.

"They're a couple," said Cynthia, looking up at the stained ceiling tiles as she drew from her memory. "They've only been here a year, but they stay most evenings of the week. Celeste is tall, late-twenties, pale, with long hair, usually dyed purple. She's got tattoos up and down her arm of tropical fish. Marcus is short, real short, dark-skinned, and skinny—I don't know how old, maybe in his thirties. He's quiet—got a bad stutter, so Celeste usually speaks for him. She's…a handful, always on the hustle. I've had to tell her off so many times for trying to sell knock-off CBD oil to the other residents, *among other things*."

Andrea nodded. She had an idea what those other things might be. "And you said you think they're missing too? Why? Did they normally show up early for Sunday too?"

Cynthia snorted. "Celeste doesn't believe in time before noon, she likes her rest. But, like I said, they were staying here regularly for the last year—and they never missed brunch—none of the regulars do."

Andrea pursed her lips, considering what the woman had said. "Most homeless people aren't permanent; you don't think they just left on their own? Went somewhere else?"

Cynthia shook her head. "They'd already stayed here every night for almost a full year. Celeste had talked about them leaving and heading out to Seattle, I guess Marcus had some family out there, but they were planning that for mid-summer, when they were sure the mountains would be free of snow. Celeste wanted to see the forests on the western slope one last time before they went."

"So that explains why you reported them missing," said Charles, finishing the sentence in his notes and looking up. "I don't suppose you've got any ideas where we might look for them?"

Cynthia thought for a moment, running a hand under her dainty chin. "You should try the parks around Monument Creek. A lot of our residents like to walk the trail along it—Celeste and Marcus included. And I know they got into trouble once for loitering in the industrial section on the west side of the creek."

"Thank you, that's very helpful. We'll try to find your friends," Andrea said, patting the woman on shoulder again. She nudged Charles with her elbow. "Won't we?"

"Uh, yeah, sure," Charles sputtered, stowing his notebook away in his pocket. "Of course."

"Before we do, we have one last thing to ask you." Andrea locked eyes with Cynthia, radiating sympathy to the caring woman. "It's two men in Acacia park. It's going to be hard, but I need you to look at some pictures. We think it's Nick and Robin, but we need you to confirm for us. Can you do that? Please?"

Cynthia took a deep breath, centering herself before nodding. Charles retrieved his phone, pulling up a picture of the two dead men. He passed it over to Andrea, who held the phone out for Cynthia to see.

"Is this them?" Andrea asked, her voice soft and low. "Is this Nick and Robin?"

Cynthia looked at the camera, blue eyes widening with tears as she took in the details of the bloody bodies. She closed her eyes, shedding a tear down her full cheek as she nodded.

"Yes, that's them."

Charles and Andrea stepped out through the bright blue doors, shaking off a chill as they stood under the beaming mountain sun. Andrea checked her watch; it was a quarter past four. They'd need to head back now if she was going to beat traffic on her way back to Pueblo.

She looked over to Charles. "Wanna call it for today? Check out the creek and park tomorrow?"

Charles nodded, momentarily distracted by violins buzzing from his pocket. He fished a phone out, frowning at the screen.

Andrea watched him fiddle with it for a moment before answering. She shrugged, walking over to the Oldsmobile. She figured she'd eavesdropped enough on his personal life for one day. Folding her arms as she leaned up against the sedan's golden door, her mind turned away from the revelations of the day, examining the more pressing concern of what to do about dinner. The easy answer was grilled chicken, rice, and broccoli—her go-to meal for most nights. But her grandmother was coming over, and she always caused such a fit when she saw her granddaughter's modest cooking. Andrea sighed, if they hurried she might be able to pick up some ground beef to make *empanadillas* when she got home. She heard Charles talking as he approached, not paying attention until he tapped her on the arm.

"What's up?" she asked, looking up as he hung up the phone. He had a strange look on his face.

"That was UC Health Memorial," he said, sounding oddly distant. "Sharon Kruschek is awake. She'd like to speak to us."

Chapter 8

Tuesday

Charles pushed through the glass double-doors, swallowing the last dregs of a Redbull on his way to his desk. Passing through the rows of grey cubicles, he caught sight of Detective Daggert, hunched over and pecking away at his keyboard with two index fingers.

"You're here early," said Charles, tossing the empty can in the trash as he passed.

"That's 'cause I haven't left," grumbled Todd, eyes narrowed in concentration as he hunted for the right letters. "Caught a body last night."

"They hit you with another one?" Charles stopped, brow furrowing in confusion. With the Temmen case heating up he was loathe to call attention to it, but he was fairly certain it should have been him that was next in the rotation.

"Yeah, Sam said you worked the bums' scene with Perry on Saturday, so he gave you a bye on this one," said Todd, scowling as he highlighted and deleted a section of text.

Charles considered his fortune for a moment before shrugging it off. *Sometimes it's better to be lucky than good.* "So, who's the stiff?"

"Another fucking jogger," Todd sighed as he tapped out another sentence, keyboard bouncing on the desk with each poke of a meaty finger. "Stabbed over by Monument Creek."

"Monument Creek?" Charles frowned. He'd planned on checking out the creek with Detective Morales after their interview today with Sharon Kruschek. "Where at? Up by the industrial section?"

Todd shook his head, eyes still on the screen as he typed out another line. "Nah, just off the greenway, south of the fountain and that Judo place. Guy walking his dog found him lying in the creek, dragged him out and was about to start CPR before he realized the guy was dead." Todd paused to read the text on the screen, lips moving silently as he scanned each line for clarity. Satisfied, he nodded to himself before continuing. "Real mess too. Coroner and I had to break out the waders while we processed the scene. And *of course* we had a cold snap last night, so the water was fucking freezing the whole time. I mean, how come nobody ever dies when it's nice out?"

Charles was silent, staring off as he tried to picture the scene in his mind. He realized he'd drifted off for a few moments when he looked back to see Todd staring at him.

Charles raised an eyebrow. "What?"

Todd rolled his baggy eyes. "I'm *so* sorry. Was I *boring* you with details of my *murder* scene? I was just saying that on top of being waterlogged, the fucking coyotes got to the body before we did."

"Yeesh," Charles grimaced. It seemed like every year they got a little bolder, foraging for scraps further into the city. Like most Coloradans, he bore no love for the feral scavengers—there'd been plenty of times he'd needed to scoop Petunia up for her protection when he caught sight of one during an evening walk.

"'Yeesh' is fucking right," said Todd, leaning back in his swivel chair. He reached over, picking up his phone from the desk and passing them to Charles. "Take a look at this mess. They took his damn *arm*."

Charles swiped through the photos on the phone, eyes darting as he took in the details of the scene. The dead man was young, mid-twenties at most, with the lean build of a marathon runner. He was dressed in black, thermal-spandex running tights and a matching shirt, the reflective stitching along the seams glowing bright silver in the camera's flash. Splattered with mud from his time in the river, his long blond hair was a knotted mess matted with pond scum. Pale, greying skin peaked out along the edges of the seven deep stab wounds in his chest. True to Todd's word, the man's left arm was missing, torn off at the shoulder. Charles zoomed in, the frayed edges of the spandex sleeve forming a ring as it shrank around the ripped flesh. He zoomed out, reexamining the lacerations across the chest. They were wide, easily over a quarter inch, and looked deep. Charles' nose wrinkled, they were an eerie match for the wounds on Nicholas Chambers.

"Face pic?" Todd asked, catching sight of the look on Charles' face.

"What? No, not yet." Charles' brow furrowed as he swiped through the pictures, stopping when he got to a series of close-ups of the corpse's head. In all the previous shots it looked to the right, but the last shot showed the coroner's gloved hands, lifting and rotating the head over. Charles' eyes went wide. "Oh, *fuck*."

"Yep," said Todd, turning back to the desktop screen.

The right side of the face was shredded, the soft tissue torn away to the bone. His eye was missing, the cracked white bone of the orbital socket poking through the edges where it had been ripped away. Charles could see the outlines of teeth through a hole in the corpse's cheek. He let out a low whistle, passing the phone back to Todd. "Messy scene."

"Mmhmm." Todd tossed the phone in the corner of the desk. "Nothing like being dragged out of my warm bed at one a.m. for a muddy, half-eaten stiff." He sighed, rubbing his tired eyes with both hands. "They could've finished him off at least, then it'd be Animal Control's problem."

"Sorry, Todd, that sucks." Charles gave him a sympathetic look, momentarily grateful he hadn't dealt with scavengers at any of *his* scenes. "Got any leads?"

"Course not, just another average, white-bread guy." Todd snorted, scratching the bald spot on the back of his head. "One of these days I need to catch a cut-and-dry scene like those bums in the park."

"Yeah, cut-and-dry," murmured Charles as he looked across the office to Detective Raines' cubicle. He compared the two scenes in his mind, ever more certain they were connected. Catching himself drifting, he turned back towards Todd before the other detective noticed. "Anyway, tough break on the soggy jogger. You should get out of here though, get some sleep."

"I will," said Todd, turning his attention back to his screen. "Need to finish typing out these preliminary findings first. Now that we've got a spike in the workload, Sarge is asking for updates on all open cases twice a week."

Charles nodded, he'd gotten the section chief's email earlier that morning. He debated with himself as he walked to his desk, ultimately settling on drafting his findings after they'd finished the interview with Sharon Kruschek. *No use sending him something half-baked.* He looked down on the piles of photos and paperwork littering the desk, deliberating over what to bring with him. Witness interviews could be tough, especially considering this particular witness had spent most of the past week in a state of semi-consciousness. Charles had been shocked when he'd gotten the call from Dr. Kutlack telling him Sharon was awake, and further stunned to hear she'd specifically requested to speak to the police. After dropping off Andrea at her car, he'd spent most of the evening looking through his notes and drafting a list of questions for the interview. Flipping through the stacks of pictures, he pulled out a few to use as reference during the interview—two of the scrapes along the passenger side of her car, one of the gouges on the roof, and a close-up of the chipped rear window. He tucked them into a binder, along with a picture of Trooper Temmen in his dress uniform, a photo of Will Springsley taken from the DMV database, and a printout collage of banana-knives and brush hooks. He ruled out any shots of the corpses or bloody scenes, figuring that someone traumatized to the point of sedation needed no further reminding of the violence that had occurred. Closing the binder, he bumped the desk as he turned to head out, knocking Sydney Kruschek's drawing askew on its pin. Charles turned back to straighten it, his efforts rewarded with the thumbtack holding it up falling and disappearing behind the desk. Charles sighed, readying himself to hunt for it when he stopped. He looked at the drawing in one hand, and the binder in his other.

"Screw it," he said, and tossed it in the binder as well.

Charles met Andrea in the waiting area on the third floor of UC Health Memorial Hospital. She was leaning on the counter of the ward's front desk, eagerly chatting with a bubbly brunette nurse wearing bright green eyeshadow.

"So, you're saying there's footnotes on top of the endnotes? Like an encyclopedia?" Andrea asked incredulously, black curls bouncing as she shook her head. "And this is supposed to be *fun* reading?"

The young nurse laughed. Charles couldn't quite make out her nameplate, but he recognized the outline of pink stick-on jewels.

"Hey Charles," Andrea said, looking up as he approached. "Cindy here is telling me all about *Infinite Jest*."

"It's *so* good," the nurse gushed, the pink lipstick around her mouth accentuating the drawn out 'o'. "I mean, it's long. Kinda dense. But, like, really deep."

"So I hear," said Andrea, shaking her head again. "And *how* long have you been reading it?"

"Four years," she answered. Seeing the shocked look on Charles face, she blurted out, "But it's worth it! I promise!"

Andrea snickered. "I'll check it out when I get a few years' spare time. Maybe after this case is done." She turned to Charles. "You good? They said she's awake and ready to talk."

Charles nodded, following along behind her as she set off down the hall.

"Cindy told me she switched rooms from the last time you were here," said Andrea, deftly weaving a gurney as she turned the corner. "Something about a tree branch outside kept setting her off, so they moved her."

"Makes sense," replied Charles, ducking as a nurse popped out of a room with a dirty lunch tray.

"Apparently she was pretty lucid yesterday. Woke up in the

afternoon, asked how her daughter was and then demanded to speak to a cop." Andrea crossed over behind a nurses' station, turning left down another hall.

"Uh-huh," said Charles, stepping over a mop bucket in the middle of the floor. "Anyone else talk to her first?"

Andrea shook her head, stepping past a nurse balancing a stack of charts. "The husband and kid are supposed to stop by sometime this evening. I figured we'd get our interview in before he had a chance to muddle with her details."

"Gotcha," muttered Charles, following her around another corner. His brow furrowed. "Do you even know where you're going?"

"Sure," Andrea said, stopping suddenly. She pointed to the sign on the next door over. "Room 357."

Charles read the sign, confusion stretched across his face. He mouthed the question, "How?"

"Right, then left, left at the nurses' station, then two more rights. Room 357," Andrea recited, adjusting the purse slung over her shoulder.

He blinked at her.

"City skills. I have an *excellent* sense of direction," she said, tapping two fingers to her temple. She circled the air around him with her fingers. "You good? Need a minute?"

"Yes, I mean no. I'm good." Charles shook his head, flipping open his binder and clearing his thoughts. He looked up at her and nodded. "Let's do this."

Sharon Kruschek dozed in the hospital bed, CNN playing softly on the TV in the corner. Andrea knocked twice, easing the door open slowly. She saw Sharon's eyes flutter open as they entered, her brow drawn in momentary confusion when she realized they weren't wearing scrubs.

"Mrs. Kruschek," she said, offering a friendly wave. "Hi, I'm Detective Morales of the Pueblo PD, this is—"

"Detective Davner," Charles interjected, raising his hand. "Colorado Springs PD."

Sharon blinked twice before recognition set in. "Oh! Yes, sorry."

She started to sit upright, the Velcro cuffs abruptly stopping her short. Sharon tossed her head back and sighed, fishing around for the remote embedded in the bed rail. Locating the right button, the whir of motors momentarily replaced the drone of the television as the bed raised her up to a sitting position. She looked back at Charles and Andrea. "I'm sorry. I'm all out of sorts today." She flashed them a weak smile. "It's been a rough week."

"You're telling me," muttered Charles, pulling two chairs over from the table in the corner. He pushed one over to Andrea.

She thanked him and sat down across from Sharon, favoring her with a sympathetic smile. "Mrs. Kruschek, how are you feeling?"

"Oh, you know," Sharon said, voice trailing off airily. She looked down, jerking her arm against the cuff encircling her wrist. "*Living the dream.*"

Andrea nodded, beginning again. "Mrs. Kruschek—"

"Sharon, please," she corrected. "It sounds better under the circumstances."

Andrea's sympathetic smile strained at the edges. "Okay, Sharon, do you know why we're here?"

"*Yes.*" Sharon's eyes narrowed, thin lips pursing as she looked from Andrea to Charles. "*I* called *you.*"

Charles took up a seat next to Andrea, chuckling in spite of himself. He had no frame of reference for what this woman had been through, but he liked to think that if he had, he'd keep his sense of humor too.

He tapped Andrea's foot, letting her know he was ready to wade into the conversation. "Ma'am—"

"*Sharon.*"

"I'm sorry," Charles nodded, clearing his throat and correcting himself. "*Sharon*, we'd like to talk to you about what happened last Monday."

"And are you going to listen to me?"

Charles stopped, thrown off guard by the question. "What?"

"Are you going to listen?" Sharon repeated, pale blue eyes staring them down.

Charles exchanged a confused look with Andrea.

"Yes…" Andrea said, nodding slowly as she drew out her answer. "That's why we're here. To listen to your story."

"Good. The last cop didn't listen," said Sharon, closing her eyes as she leaned back against the stack of pillows. "That's why he died."

Andrea and Charles worked quickly to set up. As Charles flipped through the questions in his notes, Andrea set about positioning her phone on a stand in the corner. Bending the articulated legs for the best angle, she tapped the record icon and sat back down next to Charles.

"Okay, Sharon," Andrea said, pointing to the phone. "This interview is being recorded. I need you to speak up so we get everything on tape.”

“Not my first deposition,” Sharon said, settling herself into a comfortable spot on the bed. “Go ahead with the preliminary stuff.”

Charles kept his smile to himself as he looked down on his notes.

“Alright,” she said, clearing her throat. Her voice was a hair louder than it needed to be when she spoke again. “This is Detective Andrea Morales of the Pueblo Police Department, joined by Detective Charles Davner of the Colorado Springs Police Department on Tuesday, March 19th for an interview with Sharon Kruschek regarding the murders of Will Springsley and Officer Jimmy Temmen, of the Colorado State Police.”

Among others, thought Charles, flipping through his list of questions.

“Mrs. Kruschek, would you spell your name for us please?”

“Sharon Kruschek. S-H-A-R-O-N K-R-U-S-C-H-E-K.”

“Thank you,” said Andrea. “Address?”

“3126 Tamerlane drive, Pueblo, Colorado. Resided there for five years.”

“Thank you. Occupation?”

“Paralegal for Baxter & Sammon. Also five years.”

“Thank you.”

Charles nodded along as Andrea worked through the remaining preliminary questions, looking up when she asked Sharon about previous Monday.

“What can you tell me about the events at the Sinclair Station on Santa Fe last Monday?”

“I was driving home from Sydney’s tumbling class. I pulled in to get gas.”

“And did you get gas?” Charles interrupted. He knew the answer—they’d pulled all the credit transactions for the time period of the murder—but he wanted a double check on her memory.

Sharon shook her head. “No, I didn’t get the chance.”

“Thank you.” Charles pretended to jot the answer in his notes. He waved her on.

“I pulled into the gas station. I was in my car—a blue Chevy Equinox—with my daughter Sydney in the backseat. I pulled by pump…number…” Sharon looked up to ceiling, working to piece together a coherent narrative. She thought for a moment before giving up with a shake of her head. “I can’t remember the number, but it had a broken card reader.”

“We’ll verify the number later,” said Andrea. “What happened when you pulled in by the pump?”

"I was walking into the gas station to prepay for the pump when a man stopped me."

"Did you know him? Have you seen him before?" asked Andrea.

Sharon shook her head. "No, he just pulled up to the pump behind me in a truck. I've never seen him before."

"Is this him?" Charles held up the photo of Will Springsley.

Sharon squinted at the picture, face scrunched in concentration. "I think so. I can't be sure though. I wasn't paying too much attention to him."

Andrea nodded. "And why did he stop you?"

"He was trying to get my attention. Trying to tell me there was something on the roof of my car." Sharon closed her eyes, her voice echoing flatly. "I thought he was being weird, so I went back. He was trying to tell me though, about *it*."

Charles looked up sharply. "It?"

"The creature, the thing on my roof," Sharon said slowly. A shudder passed over her. "He was trying to warn me about it. He got too close. Then it killed him."

Andrea and Charles shared a look. He shrugged.

Andrea cleared her throat and began again. "When you say a creature killed him, you mean…"

"A creature!" Sharon snapped, fighting to sit up further in the bed. "A monster. A *thing*. It was on the roof of my car. It killed him. It killed the cop. *And it tried to kill Sydney!*" Sharon paused, chest heaving. Her eyes darted back and forth between the two detectives before she leaned back with a sigh. "I know how it sounds. I get it. But if you search the rocks where I crashed you'll find it. Then everything will make sense."

"Sharon, we processed the crash scene already," Charles said gently, "We didn't find anything out of the ordinary."

"Then it's still out there!" yelled Sharon, eyes widening as she stuggled against her Velcro restraints. "You have to find it! *You have to kill it!*"

"Okay, okay," said Andrea, putting up her hands to reestablish the calm of the room. "We'll look for it. That's what we're trying to do now. Find out what happened and find who—or what's—responsible."

Sharon glowered at her; thin lips pursed tight. "You don't believe me."

"We believe you," replied Andrea, keeping her face neutral and motioning for Charles to nod along.

"No, you *don't*," hissed Sharon. She let out a long sigh, settling back down against the pile of pillows. "It doesn't matter though. You'll figure it out. If it's out there, you'll find it eventually—when the bodies stack up."

Charles felt a cold trickle down the back of his spine. "What makes you think there'd be more bodies?"

Sharon fixed her pale blue eyes on him, propping herself up on her elbows. "Because I watched that *thing* kill two men right in front of me—*one of them a cop*—in the blink of an eye. It cut their throats out like it was nothing—*just because they got too close*. And then it tried to get *us*. So if it's still out there, whatever it is, wherever it is, it's going to kill again."

Andrea took a deep breath. "Okay. We'll take what you say as true—"

Sharon snorted.

"We'll take what you say as true," Charles repeated, nodding along to back Andrea up. "You said the creature killed Will Springsley."

"And the cop," Sharon stressed.

"And Trooper Temmen," Charles added, turning to a fresh page in his notes. "How?"

Sharon thought for a moment, another shudder passing over her. "It slashed their throats. It had these…*claws*. It had a bunch of legs and they were sharp, pointed, like a crab or some kind of giant praying mantis. And it moved *quick*…so, so quick. Like a blur." She shivered again. "I think that's how it managed to hold onto my roof while I was driving. Those claws. That's why I had to keep driving, every time I slowed down it would scratch at my roof—like it was trying to claw its way in."

Charles' brow furrowed. He considered showing her the picture of the gouges on the roof but thought better of it, the last thing he needed was to feed the delusion with further justification.

Cutting him a break, Andrea took over. "Okay, so the creature on your roof killed Mr. Springsley and Trooper Temmen. *Fine*. What was it doing on your roof?"

Sharon looked over at the detective, puzzlement crossing her face. "I…don't know. It wasn't on there when I left Sydney's tumbling class. Maybe it was when I stopped at the gas station." She closed her eyes, racking her memory. Suddenly, she bolted upright. "No! *The truck!* When I was stopped for the red light, I thought it was just snow, but that must have been it. It jumped off the truck onto my car."

Andrea crossed her arms over her chest, leaning back in her chair. "It jumped off the truck onto your car. What kind of truck?"

"A semi-truck. It had a trailer," Sharon said. "And it was covered in snow, like it'd just come in from the mountains."

Charles figured he might as well humor her. *There's always a little truth in the craziest stories.* "Any special markings on the trailer?"

Sharon thought for a moment. "It had an American flag across it, and a big red-and-blue 'X.' Does that help?"

"Sure does," said Charles, making a note to look up trailer logos later.

Andrea saw her opening and jumped back into the conversation. "So you're driving home with your daughter from class and you're stopped at a light. A semi-truck is next to you and this thing jumps onto your roof. You pull into a gas station and a guy tries to warn you about it, but it kills him. Then what?"

"I panicked," said Sharon, conviction ringing out in her voice. "I didn't know what to do, so I drove off. I could hear it move every time I slowed down, so I just kept driving. I headed for the highway and everything was going fine until I hit traffic."

Charles thought for a moment, tapping the pen against his notepad. "Was that when the hit-and-run happened?"

"*Yes!*" Sharon looked at him sharply, a flicker of gratitude flashing behind her blue eyes. "When I slowed down it was trying to get inside, it kept chipping away at the window to get to Sydney. I had to do something, so I tried to scrape it off."

"On a work van," mused Charles, flipping back through the pages of his notes.

"Exactly," said Sharon, readjusting herself on the bed. "I was doing better when I got out of traffic, further out from the city. But then my gas light came on, and the cop pulled me over."

"Trooper Temmen," Andrea added, rolling her shoulders back as she sat. "You said the thing killed him too?"

"It did." Sharon winced, closing her eyes but suppressing another shiver. "I tried to warn him. I really did. He didn't listen to me. He got too close, and it killed him too."

"How?" asked Andrea, her voice flat as she looked up at the ceiling.

Sharon brow wrinkled as she tilted her head. "Cut his throat— same as the guy at the gas station. Didn't you listen?"

Charles dove in, diverting her attention with another question. "What happened after it killed Trooper Temmen?"

It worked; Sharon looked back at him. "I drove off again—only thing I could do. But I was running out of gas, so I needed a plan. I got the idea to hit some rocks. I figured if I crashed into them hard enough, we'd be safe because of the airbags but it would die. I picked out some boulders by the highway and sped into them."

"And used OnStar to call 9-1-1?" probed Charles.

"Maybe?" Sharon's face scrunched as she searched her memory. "I don't know. The last thing I remember was picking out the rocks and speeding up." She shrugged. "Then I woke up yesterday."

"Well, okay then," said Andrea, voice straining as she leaned forward in her chair. "That was *very* helpful for us. We'll be sure to look into this further. Let you know what we find."

"That's it?" asked Sharon.

"Yep, all we need," said Andrea. "We'll call you again if we need any more info."

She got up, moving towards the camera to shut it off.

"Wait, I've got one more thing" Charles said, motioning for Andrea to join him as he flipped through his binder. "This creature, can you describe it?"

"Yes," Sharon said, trembling slightly.

"Go on, please," Charles said gently. He pulled out the picture Sydney had drawn, hiding it so only he and Andrea could see it.

"It was green, and shiny, with a pale underside. It had a six legs, sharp and jagged—like a crab's," she said, a shudder passing through her again. "It was about the size of dog—like a German Shepherd—and it had a round, long head, with teeth. *Lots* and *lots* of *teeth*."

Charles looked at Andrea, circling each of the traits she'd named on the technicolor drawing. Charles looked up at Sharon over the edge of the binder.

"Thank you, Sharon, that should be all."

Charles met Andrea out in the hallway, cracking her knuckles as she paced back and forth.

"So?" he asked, catching her attention as he shut the door behind him.

"So?" she repeated, cocking an eyebrow at him.

"Got what you needed?"

She snorted. "That a monster killed our vics, and now it's on the loose? The fuck do *you* think?"

"I know, just figured I'd ask." Charles scratched the back of his head. "Weird that the drawing matched her description."

"Coincidence? Projection? Both watchin' too many movies?" Andrea shrugged. "I've seen weirder. You?"

"Sure," said Charles, scuffing the tile with his shoe heel. "Check out Monument Creek tomorrow?"

Andrea tapped her chin. "By the industrial park? Like the shelter lady said?"

"No, another spot. There was a stabbing further south, I want to check out the scene."

Andrea thought for a moment before shrugging again. "Sure."

Chapter 9

Wednesday

He heard it before he saw it, the low, warbling drone announcing that terror approached on glittering wings. Charles froze, the gentle flow of the creek lapping around his rubber boots. Up on the embankment Andrea stopped as well, black ballcap tucked low against the glare of the morning light.

"You find something?" she called down, squinting at the water around Charles' feet.

His body tense and perfectly still, Charles shook only his head. The drone was louder now, undulating in waves ahead of the erratic flight path. He searched the air around him from the corners of his eyes.

Andrea pulled off the cap and ran a hand through her curly hair, tightening her ponytail as she threaded it through the back of the hat. "How far do you want to go down? Another hundred feet or so?"

"Uh-huh," Charles replied through gritted teeth. His eyes continued darting all around him. *There!* He spotted it, the telltale flash of yellow and black meandering about on the edges of his vision. He watched it barrel through the air, unable to suppress the shudder that passed through his rigid body. It stopped just ahead of him, transparent wings folding against the bloated, fuzzy body as it alighted on a purple flower. Apologists like his sister and James had chastised him for years, cajoling and proselytizing against his hatred. *'They're essential pollinators. They're good for the environment. You like honey, don't you?'* Charles' eyes narrowed as he watched it crawl through the yellow center, rude globs of pollen sticking to its hairy back as it shoved aside the petals. He'd heard all their quisling arguments before, running together with the pinnacle of their useless advice. *'Don't bother them and they won't bother you.'* Its floral pillaging complete, it took off, lumbering forth in a lazy, chaotic spiral. Charles felt his heart rate slow as the drone faded away, replaced with the gentle whistling of the breeze and the burbling water around his boots. He shook the stiff fear from his body, forcing his mind back to the task at hand. No matter what anyone told him, he knew the truth. He felt it deep, an instinct that pre-dated memory or words. *They fly, they sting you, and they should all be destroyed.*

Charles and Andrea continued their search slowly and deliberately, following the path of Monument Creek up from the bend where the dead jogger had been found the previous day. It was probably a wasted effort; the techs had already gone through the scene the day before. Charles had no expectations for what they'd find, but he and Andrea agreed it was best to give the scene a personal look. *Especially since no one else knows about the spree killer*, he thought as he tramped through the marshy edges of the creek, tendrils of algae trailing from his boots. Andrea bent over the dewy grass ahead of him, midway up the hill between the creek and the concrete jogging trail.

"Find something?" he yelled up to her, fighting to free a boot from the mud as he took another step.

She shook her head. "Just a dead snake."

There was a mighty squelch as the mud released its grip on his foot, throwing him off balance and threatening to pitch him forward into the water. Charles sighed as he righted himself, pushing his way further against the creek. He looked ahead, looking for a landmark to use as a backstop to their search. He spotted a culvert ahead, concrete flaring up from the side of the hill as it drained into the creek.

"Stop at the culvert?" he asked.

Andrea stood up and looked back, mentally measuring the distance from their starting point. "Yeah, that's about two hundred feet. Then we can regroup and try downstream."

"Sounds good," grunted Charles, using both hands to pry a boot up from the mud.

They trudged on, eyes scanning the ground as they crept forward step by step. As they reached the culvert, Charles sat down on the concrete wall.

Up the hill, Andrea leaned over the flared edge, looking down the five-foot drop at the silt lines draining into the creek. "This it?"

"Think so," said Charles, knocking the pond scum off his boots on the lip of the drain. "The current's not that strong. I doubt it could have pulled the body even this far."

Andrea nodded, peering around the edge to the iron grate at the inlet of the drain. It was due for a replacement, the majority of it having rusted and fallen away years ago. Only a few cross bars remained, jagged edges sticking up from the concrete like trailing fingers. She squinted against the shadow as something caught her eye.

"Hey Charles, what was the vic wearing again?"

Charles stood up, finished with scraping the bottom of his boots. "Black athletic wear, with silver reflective stripes.

Andrea pointed at a tear of fabric, caught on one of the bottom crossbars. "Like that?"

Charles held a hand up to block the sun, following the direction of her finger. He spotted the shred of black spandex, a few silver threads trailing from the edges. Stepping forward towards the grate, he crouched by the iron bar, pulling out his phone to snap a few pictures.

"Got a bag?" he asked, looking up at Andrea.

She nodded, fishing a Ziploc and a pair of nitrile gloves out of her purse. She passed them to Charles, watching him delicately lift the torn fabric off the grate.

"Guess we should rethink our backstop," Charles said, sealing the scrap of shirt away in the plastic bag.

"S'pose so," Andrea said, bracing herself with one hand as she jumped down from the concrete lip. She joined him at the grate, peering into the gloom of the drain. She eyeballed the three-foot gap between the rusty edges before looking back at Charles. "I don't suppose this is one of those drains that cuts off a few feet in?"

"Nope," answered Charles, slipping the bag in a cargo pocket. He pulled a flashlight out of another, clicking it on and shining it into the storm drain. It widened past the gate, swelling to a concrete pipe roughly six feet in diameter. Charles drew a circle with the light, tracing the edges from floor to ceiling. He looked back at Andrea, cocking an eyebrow. "In?"

Andrea looked past him into the drain. About twenty feet in and the light disappeared, swallowed up by the gloom as the pipe jogged east towards the city. She took a deep breath and nodded, digging in her purse for her pocket maglight. Andrea sighed as she pulled it out, her light joining his in illuminating the damp darkness.

"Gawdamnit," she muttered under her breath. "I hate sewers."

"Man, I fucking *hate* sewers."

Charles grit his teeth, rubber boots splashing in a puddle of water at the bottom the drain. "So you've said."

"Well, it bears repeating," quipped Andrea, flashlight bouncing as she stepped to the side of the puddle. "Not all of us are wearing waders. I didn't know this was gonna be a fuckin' fishing trip."

What's she got to complain about? Charles thought as he ducked his head further to narrowly avoid something dark and sticky hanging from the low ceiling. *At least she can stand up straight.* Peering in the gloom as he stomped ahead, he muttered to himself. "It's not even a sewer."

"What?"

"It's not a sewer," Charles repeated, voice echoing a little off the concrete walls. "It's just a storm drain. It feeds runoff from the city to the creeks."

"We're in an underground pipe." Andrea rolled her eyes behind him. "It's dark, and it fuckin' stinks. It's a fuckin' sewer."

Hard to beat that logic, Charles mused, following the bobbing sway of his flashlight beam. He kicked a rock out from underfoot, watching it skip off the floor and disappear into the dark. He looked back to Andrea. "How much further do you want to go?"

"Me?" she scoffed, shining the flashlight on him in an accusatory point. "This is *your* fuckin' idea. *You* tell *me*."

Charles shifted his light further forward, squinting to make out details of the tunnel ahead. "It looks like the pipe splits. If we don't find anything by the intersection, we can call it then." He looked back at Andrea. "Sound good to you?"

She thought for a moment, arms folding over her chest before grumbling out a terse "Fine."

This isn't my idea of a fucking picnic, either. He was about to turn back when he heard a louder, rumbling grumble come from her stomach.

"Hungry?" he asked.

She nodded. Waking up early for the drive up to the Springs, she'd already missed two of her usual six meals. "Starving."

Charles tucked the flashlight under one arm, searching around in his cargo pockets. Letting out a grunt of success, he pulled out something small and square, holding it up for her to see. Andrea's eyes widened as she recognized the wrapper on the quinoa bar in his hand.

"Cherry-walnut," he apologized he offered it to her. "But it might be a little squished."

"Don't care," she blurted, snatching the bar out his hand and unwrapping it. She was halfway through the dry, crumbly granola before she remembered her manners. Wiping crumbs off with the back of her hand, she mumbled out, "Thanks."

"Don't mention it," said Charles, smirking a little as he turned back to head on. Taking another step, he felt his boot catch on the lip of a pipe junction. He caught himself on the sidewall as he tripped forward, cursing to himself as he scraped his hand on the rough concrete. There was a 'tink' as his flashlight bounced off the pipe and skittered into the muck ahead.

"You okay?" Andrea rushed forward, helping him up by the shoulder.

"Fine," said Charles, wiping his palms on the side of his pants. "Thanks."

"Don't mention it," she replied, searching around for his flashlight. She found it half-buried in the mud, black aluminum handle bearing a few new scuffs. As Andrea reached for it, she caught sight of something jagged and white poking out from the corner of the tunnel's intersection. She passed Charles his flashlight, motioning for him to join her as she walked down the tunnel. Reaching the intersection, she panned the light around the corner.

"Is that a fuckin' arm?" she blurted, illuminating a length of white bone laying in the mud.

Charles bent over the broken bone, tracing the twin outlines of the radius and ulna back to a hand half-stripped of flesh as it lay on the dirty floor. "Sure is."

"*Fuck!*" Andrea barked, the curse echoing down the tunnel walls. She locked eyes with Charles. "What're the odds it's not our guy?"

Charles shrugged. "Does it matter?"

Andreas shoulders slumped as she swept her flashlight left then right, watching the beam disappear down the length of tunnel in either direction. "*Fuuuuuuuuck.* I guess we should do some poking around before we call in a full scene team, see if there's any other vics." She turned back to Charles, sighing heavily. "Left, or right?"

"I'll take right," Charles said, following the direction of the severed arm with his flashlight. He pulled out his phone, checking the time on the screen. "It's 10:40 now, want to follow each side and meet back here?"

"No," Andrea muttered, glaring down the left tunnel. She caught his disapproving look and rolled her eyes. "*Fine.* No more than twenty minutes down each way before we meet back up. Any longer and my cop-curiosity gets buried under the heebie-jeebies." She looked at him sharply. "You gonna be able to find your way back?"

Charles watched the flashlight beam fade away at the end of the tunnel. "The lines follow the city roads. How hard could it be?"

It was around ten minutes in that doubt began to creep into Charles' mind. The tunnel split up ahead in another intersection, the third one he'd passed since they'd left. He deliberated over which way to turn, dragging his rubber heel on the concrete as he weighed his options. Charles flashed the light behind him, the crushing darkness swallowing up the narrow beam. Pulling out his phone, he checked the time—10:49. *Might as well make one last turn before heading back*, he thought, stowing the phone back in his pocket. He turned the flashlight down the right tunnel, settling on his chosen direction. He'd gotten this far making only right turns to ensure he had a reasonable idea of how to get back. *And if it ain't broke…*

He got another hundred feet down before reaching another split. Panning his flashlight to the right, he saw it glinting off a dead end. Charles pulled out his phone—10:51. *So much for the perfect system*, he sighed as he tucked it away. *Guess I'm heading left.* Turning down the tunnel, he saw it went about twenty feet before jogging sharply to the left. Doubt nibbled at the corners of his mind. He hadn't found anything yet to justify going forward, but he couldn't shake the nagging feeling that if he gave up now, he'd be missing out on some big break just around the next corner. *Nice hunch, but how's it work if you get lost?* Charles sighed again, he'd never half-assed a case before, and he wasn't about to start with this one. Resolving to keep going for a few more minutes, he fished around in his pockets, pulling out two quarters and a metallic green ballpoint pen. He stuck the pen straight into the silt in the middle of the floor and laid a quarter flat on either side of the intersection. Passing his flashlight over it the three markers shone brightly against the dingy concrete. Charles snorted in approval, heading down the left tunnel.

He noticed a chill the further he went, the stale air growing damp and clammy underground. Charles rubbed his arms, feeling goosebumps rising, and pined for the jacket he'd left in the Delta 88. He'd just made up his mind to turn back—big break or not—when the tunnel opened up in front of him. Finally able to strand up straight, he rolled his shoulders back, stretching out the kinks in his neck.

Charles took a deep breath, surveying the underground atrium he'd stumbled into. Craning his head up, he saw daylight peeking around the edges of a manhole cover nearly twenty feet above him. As he panned his flashlight around, he saw more tunnels peeling off in all directions. *Must be some kind of cistern.* He stepped further into the center of the chamber, flicking the light up and down on the curved, dingy concrete walls. In addition to the tunnels, the walls were pockmarked with smaller inlets of varying sizes. Charles could hear the steady drip of water falling from cracks in the ceiling.

He took another deep breath, reveling in the space of the room after nearly an hour of cramped tunnels. He let it out slow, stopping when he caught a whiff of something odd. Amid the usual smells of rotting algae and damp earth he'd enjoyed for the last hour was something decidedly different, something bitter and pungent, mixed with a coppery tang—like new pennies. Charles dropped the flashlight beam low—he'd seen enough crime scenes to pick out the smell of blood—and to smell it in a room this big there had to be a lot of it. As he trained the circle of light on the floor he spotted a dark stain near the center. The coppery smell grew stronger, confirming his suspicions as he drew closer. A thick trail led away from the pool, fading into one of the smaller inlets in the wall. He followed it over, crouching down and shining his flashlight against the gloom of the hole. There was a mound of something in the center, coming into focus as he tilted the flashlight around.

"*Fuck!*" snapped Charles, stumbling back from the wall.

Years spent working homicide hadn't prepared him for the sudden sight of a bare torso, stuffed in the side of a wall with its ribs cracked and splayed open. He stood back, muttering to himself as he walked out a quick circle to muster his nerve. He shook off his shock, steeling himself as he crouched back down. The pale beam of the flashlight illuminated the corpse's white skin. Properly guarded after the initial surprise, Charles noted that the torso was missing its head and most of its limbs—only the left arm remained. Passing the light over it, Charles saw the faded outline of tropical fish tattooed up and down its length. *Celeste*, he presumed, remembering the shelter manager's description of the missing woman. He let out a low whistle as he looked over the rest of the body. In addition to the missing limbs, most of the soft tissue was gone from the pelvis and abdomen, just a hollow bowl flanked by ragged edges of bone. The chest was likewise empty, the bottom four ribs cracked open, jutting up and out after something had forced its way under them.

Charles suppressed a shudder as he reached into his pocket for his phone, determined to maintain his composure in the face of the grisly scene. Holding the flashlight up in one hand to illuminate the body and offset the glare of the shutter, he maneuvered himself into the best angle for the shot, ever mindful not to step in the trail of blood. Focusing on the pictures, he barely noticed that the bitter, pungent smell had returned, stronger than before. Charles turned away from the inlet, thumbing through the pictures on his phone as he deleted the ones the flash washed out or were out of focus. He was just about to step away when he realized he hadn't gotten a good shot of the arm—he'd need it to show to Cynthia at the shelter. Turning back to the hole he panned the flashlight, lighting up the two mounds within.

Charles stopped. There was something wrong about that, something about the scene his brain hadn't quite processed.

Charles glanced at the phone in his hand, the screen lit up with the last picture of the inlet. It took him a fraction of a second to compare the one mound from the photo to the two mounds in front of him.

And then the second mound moved.

Charles jumped back. Base instinct assumed control, yanking him to his feet. Blood pounded in his ears, he could just make out the sound of something sharp scraping on concrete. He took another step back, slipping on the puddle of blood in the center of the chamber. Heels went up as he fell down, the wind leaving his chest as he hit the concrete with a dull thud. Charles fought for breath, as up ahead, something emerged from the shadows of the inlet.

A domed, shield-shaped head came first, shining with an oily green glint in the thin circle of Charles' flashlight. Six spiky limbs followed, fanning out around the edges of the inlet. Charles watched the multi-jointed legs pull, unfurling the rest of the narrow body out of the hole like the blooming of a monstrous flower.

Charles' regained his breath as the domed head shook from side to side.

Rising up nearly five-foot tall on the segmented limbs, Charles' first thought was that Sharon was wrong, this was *way* bigger than any dog.

As it took a single step forward on a jagged forelimb, Charles' second thought was that the phone in his hand had been replaced with his gun, and he couldn't remember doing that.

As Charles watched a mouth open up under the wide, domed head—a mouth filled with hundreds of sharp, needle-like teeth—he didn't have space for a third thought.

Charles pulled the trigger, the M&P's muzzle erupting in his hands.

The dark chamber lit up with the flash of the pistol's barrel as 9mm rounds roared out, pitting the concrete wall around the creature. Muscle memory took over as Charles rose to his feet and backed up, hands tightening on the grips to steady his shots.

The creature's head snapped back as a few of his hollow-point rounds found their place. Charles stopped firing, his finger on the trigger as he watched the legs sway unsteadily. He waited, watching the shaking stop, the domed head twisting back to face him. Four red eyes blinked beneath the edge of the flared skull. The sharp-toothed mouth opened up again, and the chamber filled with the creature's unholy screech.

Charles yelled back, pulling the trigger again and peppering the domed head with jacketed hollow-points. He watched the creature shudder under the impact but take another step forward. His slide locked back as his gun went dry, the last of his firing echoing off the concrete walls like thunder. Ears ringing, he felt around on his belt for his spare magazine. His fingers connecting with empty space as he realized it had fallen out. Ahead of him the creature shook its head, the oily surface unmarked as it glinted the light of the dropped flashlight.

Charles took a step back as the red eyes looked once more in his direction. The back of his rubber boot connected with the flared lip of one of the larger drainpipes. He spared a glance into the tunnel behind him. He could only hope it was the right one. The creature took another step forward, knocking the flashlight spinning.

Fuck it, thought Charles, and ran.

Charles sprinted down the narrow tunnel, pedaling his arms as he tucked his head down. His breath came out in gasps as his rubber soles thudded on the concrete, the roar of blood in his ears just drowning out the ringing from before. Just above that, he could hear the faint scratching of claws digging into concrete behind him.

There was a sharp turn ahead. He cut right, clipping the wall with his shoulder as the momentum carried him forward. He stumbled forward but kept moving, heart pounding in his chest. Unable to see clearly in the dark tunnel, he dragged his fingers on the wall, praying for an opening as he darted ahead.

He passed an opening on the right, gripping the corner of the wall to spin him around the intersection turn.

RIGHT! THEN RIGHT! THEN LEFT! THEN LEFT! THEN LEFT!

He repeated the directions over and over again in his mind, just praying he'd backed his way into the right tunnel. Rocks kicked up beneath his rubber wading boots, skittering off the concrete behind him.

RIGHT! THEN RIGHT! THEN LEFT! THEN LEFT! THEN LEFT!

There was scraping on the concrete behind him. He pushed on, fingers scraping against the rough concrete. If his prayers were answered, the first left turn was just ahead. Hope flickered to life in his chest as his fingers passed into empty air. He bared his teeth in a desperate grin, throwing himself left and down the next tunnel.

Unbidden, a song from *The Dirty Dozen Brass Band* sprang up and began playing in his mind. Charles had never liked jazz—but James had—playing it most mornings as he got ready for work.

'My feet don't fail me now! My feet don't fail me now!'

Rubber boots pounded on the muddy concrete. He heard the scraping growing louder behind him.

'My Feet Don't Fail Me Now! My Feet Don't Fail Me Now!'

He turned left again. A light flickered in the tunnel ahead.

'MY FEET DON'T FAIL ME NOW! MY FEET DON'T FAIL ME

NOW!'

Charles saw Andrea's face backlit by the flashlight in one hand, the other gripped tight around her pistol.

"Charles!" she called out, voice echoing down the tunnel.

Charles held a hand in front of his face, shielding against the glare as she shined the light in his eyes.

"Charles?" she asked, her question resolving itself into recognition as he came into focus in the flashlight beam. *"Charles!* What the fuck is going on?"

"That!" he gasped, jerking a thumb backwards as he caught up with her.

Andrea's brow furrowed as she squinted in the dark. She watched something glossy and green tumble into the edges of the light. Her eyes widened as realization flashed through her. Her finger left the guard of her pistol, finding its way to the trigger. She was beginning to pull when she felt his hand yank her shoulder, spinning her around.

"Won't work!" he gasped, dragging her behind him. *"Just run!"*

They ran, murky water splashing up around their ankles as feet hammered on the dingy concrete. Andrea began to pull ahead, superior conditioning winning out over longer legs.

"C'mon!" she shouted, voice hoarse as she sped past him.

Charles nodded but said nothing, eyes bulging as he wheezed in and out of his open mouth.

Rounding another turn, she could tell he was beginning to falter, his breath coming out in shorter gasps the longer they went. Andrea tried to listen for the creature, ears straining to hear over the echoes in the concrete drain. She gave up as Charles slipped a few lengths further back, his pace plodding as he fought for air. Worry creased her brow as she watched sweat pouring down his reddened face.

He looked back to the dark tunnel behind them, then ahead, locking eyes with her.

"Go on!" he panted, weary arms waving for her to leave him.

Andreas face scrunched up. She sucked in a deep breath and slowed down, determined not to leave him behind.

The tunnel lightened up ahead, the shadows giving way to daylight filtering from the culvert entrance. Relief soared in Andrea's chest. She looked back, reaching an arm behind her and grabbed him by the hand.

She pulled hard, and together they stumbled past the rusty grate and into the blazing sunshine.

Chapter 10

Wednesday

"What the fuck?!"

Andrea trained her gun on the tunnel entrance, panting as she looked past the narrow white dot of her front sight to the darkness beyond. Heart pounding, the barrel of her gun traced tight figure-eights as she tracked the flickering shadows within. She squinted against the glare of the midday sun, the rusty edges of the broken grate jutted out like gnarled fingers grasping for her. A bead of sweat rolling down her temple and into her eye, as she waited for the emergence of sharp teeth and shining claws.

"What the fuck?" she repeated under her breath, keeping her gun pointed with one hand while she wiped the sweat pooling in her eye.

"I …know…right?" gasped Charles, doubled over and leaning against the concrete wall for support.

"I just…it just…how's that…" Andrea's shoulders slumped as words failed her. She paused to collect herself, mustering up the only relevant question she could think to ask. "What the *FUCK?!*"

"So much…for…banana-knives," said Charles, sucking in a deep breath as he pushed himself upright from the wall.

"Fuck *you*, man!" Andrea's gun stayed straight while she tore her eyes away just long enough to glare at him. "How the fuck was I s'posed to know *monsters* exist?!"

Charles walked a tight circle on the concrete mouth of the culvert, hands on his hips as he tried to breath through the stitch in his side.

"We…should…talk…about that," he wheezed, rivers of sweat collecting in the collar of his shirt.

"What's there to talk about?" griped Andrea, gun still darting to cover the tunnel's entrance. "Our parents lied. Monsters are real. The X-Files are true. And I'm never sleeping again."

Charles gulped in air through his open mouth, red cheeks puffing out as he tried to slow down the thundering in his chest. "Guess…we owe…Sharon an…apology."

"Oh, you got fuckin' jokes, now huh?" She snapped, looking over her shoulder to glare at him again. "How's about you fuckin' join me?"

It was funny, he'd barely heard her accent when they'd first met. She was obviously east-coast, but he noticed she tended to tamp down on it during interviews or whenever they were around someone new. In the excitement of the moment though, the five-borough brogue was on full blast.

"Can't…I'm out." Charles pulled the gun from his holster, showing her the slide locked back on the empty magazine.

Andrea stared at him. "What? *How?*"

Charles blinked at her, nodding his head at the tunnel. "I *used* it."

"Oh! Right," said Andrea, ponytail bouncing as she shook her head clear. She unclipped the spare magazine from her belt, handing it out to him. "Nine-mil M&P?"

"Yeah, thanks," he said, taking it from her and swapping it for the empty one in his gun. He sent the pistol's slide forward, chambering a round before dropping it back in his holster. "But it won't help. I shot it at least five times, straight in the face—no dice. It just shrugged it off and kept coming."

Andrea dropped her gun, keeping one eye on the tunnel as she turned back to face him. "So what? We just leave it?"

"I dunno. I know as much about it as you do." Charles sucked in another deep breath, wincing as he massaged the knot in his side. "I just know that handguns didn't leave a scratch."

Andrea thought for a moment, then shrugged. "Alright, go get some long-guns. I'll stay here and cover the tunnel. When you get back, we'll head in and hunt it down."

Charles shook his head. "Those tunnels stretch for miles throughout the entire city. We have no idea what it is, where it is, how to find it, or if *any* gun will do the job. That thing already caught us off guard once and we barely got away, the next time we might not be so lucky." Charles dragged his heel across the concrete, marking lines in the silt. "Besides, I have to give a reason for checking larger weapons out of the armory, and I sure as hell can't say it's to hunt *monsters*."

Andrea sighed, holstering her weapon. "Well we have to do *something*. I can't go back to my precinct with a 'Sorry, Sarge, I was workin' that case real good but then a monster popped up and I got spooked. Anyway, case closed.'"

You're not the only one. He pictured the furious confusion contorting Sergeant Briske's face as he tried out a similar line. Charles snorted. "I have no idea how this will shake out in the report, but we need hard evidence. Something actionable."

Andrea nodded. "Too bad we didn't get a picture of it."

"Maybe?" Charles frowned, thinking it over before digging his phone out of his pocket. He swiped through his pictures, finding nothing but a few shots of Celeste's dismembered corpse. "Nope, nothing."

He tucked the phone away, looking back up at Andrea. "You know who we need to talk to about this?"

"Yeah, I do." Andrea sighed again, hopping the culvert wall and heading towards the car. "And she's going to be insufferable."

Sharon Kruschek was propped up in the hospital bed, a half-dozen white pillows surrounding her. The picked over remains of her lunch sat on a tray on the side, along with a few scattered snacks and a stuffed purple elephant. Sydney curled up by her feet, working her way through her second *Pretty, Pretty, Pretty Princesses* coloring book. Sharon dozed, a juice box in her hand as she watched the afternoon news. She looked over as the door opened, Charles and Andrea letting themselves in with a gentle knock.

"Hi, Mrs. Kruschek," Andrea said, offering a friendly wave as she stepped through the doorway. There was a forced casualness in her voice, just slightly out of step with the extra-wide smile on her face. "It's Detective Morales and Detective Davner again."

Charles looked around the hospital room, saying nothing until Andrea elbowed him in the ribs. "*Oof*. Uh, hey Sharon, Sydney."

Sydney ignored him, her tongue sticking out as she concentrated on appropriately shading the jewels on the princess' crown. Sharon looked over the two disheveled detectives, taking in the dark sweat stains under their arms, the numerous fly-away strands missed by Andrea's ponytail, and Charles' muddy-stained rubber boots. Pale blue eyes narrowed, piecing it together.

"You saw it, didn't you?"

Andrea's mouth opened and shut without a word. Charles started chuckling, stopping short when he caught another elbow to the ribs.

Sharon nodded, lips pursed in triumph. "I *knew* it. What did I say, if it wasn't at the crash it was still out there?"

Andrea spoke up. "Now Sharon, this isn't the time for 'I told you so—"

"Sure, it is," Sharon sniped, cutting her off. She pointed at the two detectives, taking a hard pull of her juice box. "Because I absolutely did. I *fucking* told you so."

"Bad word, mommy."

"I'm sorry, sweetie," Sharon said, setting the juice box down to stroke Sydney's hair. She looked up at the two detectives. "Where was it?"

Andrea spoke again, "In the sewer—"

"Storm drain," corrected Charles. He put up his hand, catching her elbow as she glared at him.

Sharon nodded. "And you didn't kill it, did you?"

Andrea looked at Charles, unsure of how much to disclose.

Charles shrugged. "No. We lost it when we ran."

"Which is why you're here." Sharon took another sip from the juice box, shaking her head. "I warned you. I tried to tell you it was dangerous. You didn't listen."

"Well, let's talk about that actually," snapped Charles, wagging an accusing finger. "Because you said it was the size of a dog, and let *me* tell *you*, that's the biggest fucking *DOG* I've ever *SEEN!*"

"Bad word, p'liceman," said Sydney, switching over to a fat-tipped purple marker.

"Sorry, Sydney," muttered Charles. He frowned at Sharon. "Well?"

"It *was*," Sharon said, shimmying her way up straighter in the bed. Her eyes searched between the two detectives before giving up with a shrug. "Maybe it got bigger?"

"*Hmmph.*" Charles' face crumpled as he folded his arms over his chest.

Andrea stepped in, raising her hands diplomatically. "The point is we saw it. We're here now. We believe you, and we need to know what you know." She turned to her partner, beckoning him with her eyes. "Right, *Charles?*"

"Right," Charles grumbled as he pulled up a chair.

Andrea sighed, summoning all of the tact and patience left in her body. She turned back to Sharon. "Mrs. Kruschek—Sharon—*please*. We need to know what you know."

Sharon took in a deep breath. "It's not much. Not more than I told you already, anyway. It's green and vicious, with sharp claws and teeth—but if you saw it then you already know that. It killed everyone that approached the car. And it's tough—tough enough to hang onto the roof on the highway, and tough enough to survive a car crash too."

Not to mention some hollow-points to the face, mused Charles.

"Where did it come from?" asked Andrea, pulling up her own chair and sitting down. "Where were you when you came across it."

"Pueblo," said Sharon. "I was driving along when it landed on my roof."

"From the truck?" asked Charles, pulling out his notebook.

Sharon nodded. "A semi-truck. With a red-and-blue 'X' on the side and an American flag. It fell off that truck with a pile of snow and onto my car."

"What kind of brand is that?" Charles asked, looking to Andrea for help. Andrea shook her head.

"Did you get a plate on the truck?" Andrea asked Sharon. "Any idea where the truck was heading or where it came from?"

Sharon thought on it, worried crease in her forehead deepening as she searched her memory. She gave up after a moment. "I'm sorry, no. But it was covered in snow, so it had to have come from the mountains."

Andrea nodded. "And you've never seen it before it landed on your car? No prior connections at all?"

Charles and Sharon turned to stare at her, bewilderment stretching the silence between them.

"Alright, okay!" Andrea threw up her hands. "Screw me for asking, but this is my first case of monster-induced homicide. I'm making this shit up as I go!"

"Bad word, p'licelady," said Sydney, slapping the cap onto her purple marker.

Andrea dragged a hand across her face, cursing in Spanish under her breath. She looked over at Charles. "Well, do *you* have any all-star questions?"

Charles mulled it over, flipping back and forth through the pages of his notes. "Red-and-blue 'X' on the side?"

"Yes," Sharon said, the cardboard sides caving in as she sipped on the juice box.

Charles flipped the notebook closed, mumbling a 'thanks' as he stood up from the chair. He cocked an eyebrow at Sharon. "Need anything from us?"

"Cuffs already came off, so at least I can scratch my nose without calling for the nurse," Sharon said dryly, setting the empty juice box down on the tray. "I don't suppose you could let the hospital staff know I'm not a dangerous murder suspect? So they let me go home?"

"Deal," replied Charles. He exchanged a goodbye wave with Sydney before turning back to Andrea, pointing towards the door. "You ready?"

Andrea's brow furrowed. "For what?"

"To go find that truck."

It was late evening when they arrived at the Colorado Springs Police Department. The sun had already sunk behind the mountains, its last golden rays glowing around the edges of the squat brick building. Charles pulled the Delta 88 deftly into an open space, letting it glide to stop on the heavy brakes. Throwing the column shifter up, he turned to the detective dozing against the beige bench seat.

"Ready?" he asked, rousing her with a poke in the arm.

Andrea yawned and stretched, forcing her eyes open and focusing them on the dash clock. "Fuck me, it's only eight?"

Charles nodded, suppressing his own yawn as he rubbed his bleary eyes. "Time flies when you spend the morning running for your life."

Andrea shut her eyes, leaning back against the worn headrest. Charles considered doing the same, but didn't trust himself not to fall asleep. Another yawn came on, and this time he was powerless to stop it.

"Charles," Andrea said at last, her eyes snapping open as she pushed herself up from the warm comfort of the worn seat. "You know I'm all in on this case, but I'm crashing hard now. If I don't leave now, I'm not gonna make it on the drive back."

Charles nodded. "It's been a long day."

"Understatement of the fuckin' year," Andrea laughed, unbuckling her belt and rolling out the passenger door. "What about you, man? Gonna call it a night?"

In that moment, Charles wanted nothing more than to do just that, but he had questions he knew would nag at him the whole night. He shook his head. "I'm going to dig up what I can on the truck, then I'll head out."

Andrea studied him for a moment before shrugging. "Suit yourself. I'll see you first thing in the morning." She stood up from the low car, arching her back and stretching her toned arms. She looked back, flashing him a smile. "Right now, I'm gonna head home, take a warm shower, and pass-the-fuck-out."

Charles returned a lopsided smile. "Thought you were never sleeping again."

"Life, uh, finds a way," quipped Andrea, fly-away hair catching the sun's dying light. "And if it doesn't, there's a full bottle of *Laphroaig* waiting back home to nudge it along."

Charles strode through the empty parking lot, barely remembering to lock the car behind him as he walked up to the squat brick building. Climbing the narrow stairs to the second floor, he found the office quiet and still. As he pushed through the glass doors at the end of the hall, Charles flipped on the lights as he passed, the bullpen illuminating under the long fluorescents.

"Thanks, bud," Detective Daggert called out from among the cubicles.

"No problem, Todd," Charles said as he wound his past the rows of empty desks. "You're here late."

"Same t'you." Todd's balding head popped up from his desk, his hairy forearms following shortly as he leaned on the cubicle wall. "*I'm waiting on a call from the coroner for the second jogger, what's got you here?*" The detective's eyes narrowed as he took in his bedraggled compatriot, sizing up the mud-splattered pants, sweat-stained shirt, and rat's nest of tangled blond hair. "Damn, Chuck, is this where you say, 'You should've seen the other guy?'"

"Shut up, Todd," Charles griped. "Your jokes are…"

He trailed off, too tired to muster up any of his usual snappy retorts. Shaking his head, he found his desk and dropped wearily into the old swivel chair. A post-it note by the monitor let him know the blood splattered on the Equinox's window was confirmed as Trooper Temmen's.

Todd spoke up again from his desk. "Sam told me the lab finished blood analysis from the vehicle, and to remind you to send in your preliminary findings to Sergeant Briske."

"Thanks," replied Charles. Punching the power button on the desktop, he leaned back against the chair's flexed backing. His eyes drifted closed as he listened to the soft whirr of the computer booting up.

They jolted back open as the sound of a whip-crack echoed across the office. It repeated three more times before he heard Todd pick up the phone.

"No, honey, still at the office."

Charles shut his eyes again, waiting for the triple beep announcing his computer was finished.

"I know, I'm sorry." He heard Todd say, his voice a hair higher than it was when he spoke to any of them. "Soon, maybe another half-hour. No, don't worry about dinner for me, I'll just scrounge when I get home. Yes. Yes. No problem, I'll grab the recycling while I'm at it."

The office lapsed into silence as Detective Daggert hung up the phone.

"You know, you could wait for that call at home." Charles laced his fingers behind his head, his eyes still tightly shut.

"It's rude to eavesdrop," Todd called back, his usual baritone finding its way back into his voice. "And Serena and I have an arrangement. Nothing comes home with me. I leave work at work."

Charles nodded, opening his eyes when he heard the triple beep. Across the office, the 'Imperial March' played as Todd's phone rang again.

"Detective Daggert."

Charles rolled his shoulders back, stretching them as he fished his notebook out and tossed it on the desk.

"You're *kidding* me."

The corner of the notebook was damp and grimy, soaked through with sweat from his pocket. Charles frowned, gingerly flipping through the soggy pages.

"Well then what was it?"

Charles found the page from their interview with Sharon, laying it out beside his keyboard.

"What do you *mean* you have no idea? You're the expert, you tell me!"

Charles swung the mouse over, whistling tunelessly to himself as he double clicked the icon to open up a browser page.

"You're about as helpful as tits on a bull, you know that!"

Charles heard the clatter of a phone tossed contemptuously onto a particle-board desk.

"Chuck? That was the coroner, you're not gonna believe this."

Oh, I might. Charles waited patiently for the page to load on screen. The screen flashed white, the old desktop finally committing itself to the task of accessing the internet. "What's up, Todd?"

"That jogger—the one by the creek with the arm ripped off—coroner says it wasn't coyotes. Says the teeth-marks on the bones don't match. They're like nothing he recognizes. Weird, right?"

"*Weird*," Charles echoed back, typing 'X semi truck logo' into the search bar. The screen flashed again as the search results sprawled before him, the page filled with low-resolution cartoons of clipart trucks. Across the office, Charles heard drawers open and shut, mixed with the soft grunts of Detective Daggert struggling with the zipper on his coat.

"Stupid, piece of *shit*. Is *anything* gonna do its fucking job today?"

Charles frowned as he scrolled through the results, returning to the top to type in 'Red and Blue X truck.' There was a tap on his cubicle wall, drawing his attention from the screen.

"Well, this was fucking pointless. So glad I missed out on squash ravioli for this shit," said Todd, leaning against the grey plastic wall. He jerked a thumb towards the glass doors. "I'm heading out, Chuck. You want me to leave the lights on for you?"

"Yeah, thanks," mumbled Charles, turning back to the screen.

He heard Todd storm out of the office, muttering to himself about coyotes and coroners the whole way. Charles' frown deepened as he scrolled through another useless page filled with generic pictures of primary-colored trucks. He tried 'Semi truck logo,' 'Truck logo X,' and 'Red and Blue X logo,' his frown turning to a glower as he searched through pages and pages of results, with nothing coming close to matching Sharon's description.

Charles dragged his watery eyes away from the screen, rubbing the blurriness away with both hands. A glance at the computer's clock told him it was half-past midnight. He'd been searching for over four hours—and with nothing to show for it. Molten frustration bubbled up inside him, venting out in a long, sustained sigh. He reread the description scrawled on the waterlogged notebook page for the thirtieth time that evening, gaining no deeper insight into how to source it out.

Charles scratched the back of his head. He knew he should just go home, come back to the problem with fresh eyes in the morning. *Maybe Andrea could help too*. Charles scowled at the pictures of trucks lining the screen. His head was pounding, his back ached, his legs were sore. The smart decision would be to get some rest. But deep down, he knew that wasn't an option. He knew he'd just lie awake in bed before caving in and grabbing his laptop to continue searching.

Charles grit his teeth, snatching the mouse and highlighting the search bar at the top of the screen. His fingers slammed against the keys as he typed in another set of broad terms—'American Flag Semi Truck'—the keyboard bouncing on the desk with each stroke. The desktop whirred as the screen flashed white, pictures rolling down the page as it loaded. A stream of half-intelligible curses spilled out under his breath as he spun the mouse wheel, eyes darting across the screen as he searched the results.

He froze, cursor hovering over a single image among hundreds. A white, sleeper-cab semi, the trailer marked with a red-and-blue 'X,' billowing out into an American flag. Charles rubbed his eyes again, scarcely able to believe it. Double clicking the picture pulled up the image and its description.

Charles read the underlined text three times before it sank in. As the realization dawned on him, a hoarse, wheezing laugh spilled out past his dry lips.

'AAFES Delivery Truck,' the image description read. 'Army & Air Force Exchange Service.'

Chapter 11

Thursday

Morning thundered in with the blare of a digital alarm clock erupting from the bedside table. Weary brown eyes opened, then shut tight again, momentarily blinded by the glare of the morning light. Charles threw up a hand, blocking the audacious sun stabbing through the holes in the mangled blinds. He slapped at the bedside table, knocking over a half-empty of a Heineken from the night before as he silenced the chirping clock. The green bottle clattered to the floor, spilling its stale remains on the scuffed hardwood. Snorts and the clacking of short nails echoed down the hall as Petunia stormed in to investigate the disturbance.

"Nooo, get *back*," Charles groaned, shoving the inquisitive Frenchie aside as he leaned off the bed.

Setting the bottle upright on the nightstand, he mopped up the spilt beer with a lone sock he found by the bed. Charles stood up, tossing the wet sock onto the pile of dirty laundry in the corner. Petunia gave him rueful look, bat-ears wobbling as she snuffled at the drying spot. Charles covered a yawn as he stretched, sparing a glare for the digital clock as he shuffled off for the bathroom.

He was aware it wasn't the Timex's fault that he couldn't sleep—even the comforts of a cold beer and Instagram scrolling had failed to work their usual one-two punch on his anxious mind. It wasn't the clock's fault that every time he shut his eyes all he saw were rows and rows of needle-sharp teeth beneath a shiny green carapace—but he resented it just the same. He'd watched the hateful red numerals tick upwards in the wee hours of the morning, chipping away at the amount of time he had left to sleep. Turning on the shower, he envisioned a world free from the tyranny alarm clocks, or failing that, one in which it was socially acceptable to answer their grating chirp with a hollow-point bullet.

Charles felt twenty percent more human as he left the bathroom, skin still tingling on his face from a fresh shave. Forcing his body through the mundane rituals of getting ready, he emerged feeling slightly refreshed. He was almost ready to approach looking at the six email notifications he'd heard roll in while he was in the shower, but he stopped himself short as his stomach grumbled. He couldn't imagine another day as long or as grueling as the one before, but he wasn't about to chance it by starting this one on an empty stomach.

The kitchen was quiet, save for the soft clink of Savannah's spoon against the ceramic edges of her bowl.

"Out late last night," she observed as he entered the kitchen, her matted blue hair sticking up in the back.

Charles grunted in response, rifling through the cabinets for something instant and edible. Pushing aside the cherry PopTarts and the nearly empty family-size box of Cocoa Puffs, he snagged the box of organic quinoa bars. Pocketing two of them, he shook the last one free of the cardboard box, setting the empty carton on the counter next to the recycling bin. He wasn't sure if he was up for the commitment of purchasing another box, but he had to admit they were starting to grow on him.

"Coffee's on the table," Savannah said.

Charles offered her an appreciative grunt, sliding into the spindly oak chair behind the mug.

"Soooo, how's the case?" asked Savannah, chewing the words along with a mouthful of cereal.

Charles considered his response carefully, hiding the delay behind a long sip of coffee. *Fine, great*, he thought bitterly. *Found the subject, he's a ravenous, green, subterranean nightmare. Oh, you didn't know monsters are real? Well, they are. They live underground and feed on the homeless.* Charles shook his head, setting the mug down on the table.

"Busy," he replied instead, tearing the wrapper off the quinoa bar with his teeth. "Got a lead on the subject though."

"Goooood," nodded Savannah, chasing an errant puff with her spoon. "Description? I gotta know who to look out for."

About five-foot, fanged, mean, with six-legs, and red eyes.

"No description, maybe a link to the origin," Charles mumbled around a dry mouthful. Swallowing hard, he added, "We think he rode in on a government truck."

"Weird." Savannah twirled the spoon in the chocolate-dyed milk. "You chasing that down today?"

Charles nodded. "I'm meeting Andrea—Detective Morales—at the station. Going to try and track down that truck, trace its route."

Savannah raised an eyebrow. "*Andrea*, huh? New friend?"

Charles' eyes narrowed over the mug as he washed down a bite of dried bar. "What's it to you?"

"Nothing. I'm just glad you're actually getting along with a new *person*, even if it's just another cop." Savannah said, tilting the bowl up and drinking the leftover milk. She set the empty bowl back down, standing up from the table with a shrug. "It's good for you to broaden your world a little. Means less moping around here thumbing your way through the 'gram."

Charles scowled. "Isn't that your second bowl?"

"Third," she replied, fetching the box from the cabinet. "And don't crab at me. You need a better outlet—like a hobby or something."

"I'll add that to the list," muttered Charles, rising from the table. "First thing, right after I finish all of these *murder* investigations."

"It can be second," said Savannah, grabbing the jug of milk from the fridge. "As long as it's on the list."

"Uh-huh," grunted Charles, setting his empty mug in the sink.

Savannah *tut-tutted*, hands on her hips.

Charles grumbled to himself, snatching the mug up and rinsing it out.

Savannah sat down, picking up the cereal box and pouring another bowl. "Thank you. Otherwise, it stains."

Charles stomped his way to the door, fishing his keys out of his jacket pocket.

"Hey, wait," Savannah called out, looking up from her bowl. "Can you also add talking to your buddy to that long list of yours? About serving the TPO? I've got class again on Monday…"

Charles nodded, pulling the door open.

"I got it, no worries."

Charles pushed through the glass double-doors at the end of the hall, his holster catching on the edge of the door as he entered the investigations division. He paused mid-step, shifting his hip and separated the gun from the door. Most days he carried his sidearm without noticing, the M&P's weight familiar and comfortable as it rested on his belt. He'd cleared those double-doors day-in and day-out for years, and never once bumped them with his gun—that kind of thing was reserved for rookies fresh out of the academy. Charles felt a frown forming. *You're tired, yesterday was rough, you're just a little off your game.* Charles shook his head to clear it, stepping off in search of his desk.

Passing by Sergeant Briske's office, he heard the clatter of a phone dropping into its receiver.

"Is that Chuck?" the Sergeant's baritone rolled out of the office. "Chuck! In here, *now!*"

Charles didn't break his stride, pivoting sharply on his front foot. "Yes, Sarge?" he asked, stopping on the doorway's threshold.

"Chuck!" The wrinkles on the section chief's bald head furrowed in waves, his heavy hands sweeping through the air as he motioned for Charles to enter. "What *fortuitous* timing! I just got off the phone with Sergeant Gomez—you know, from the *State Police*."

Charles swallowed hard. "Yeah? How is he?"

Sergeant Briske's eyes glittered as his voice took on an air of loaded calm, like the tide rolling back from a beach before a tsunami hits. "Oh, he's good, his wife has a new book drive coming up and Cesar's rec center class filled up on Saturdays so he thinks he might start a second one on Wednesday nights."

Charles bobbed his head. "Good, sounds like he's doing well. I've got some leads to run down so I'll just be go—"

"He also asked me about how the investigation with Trooper Temmen is going," Sergeant Briske interrupted, dire tones creeping into his low voice. "Apparently, he'd just gotten off the phone with the DA, who was awfully curious about the state of the investigation. You know the DA, she asks a lot of questions, and apparently she wanted to make sure we were putting adequate resources into finding our suspect."

Must be an election year, Charles thought, shaking his head.

"And then, while I was in the middle of putting his mind to ease, explaining that I'd put my best detective on it, my top man for my top priority, I go to my *email*. I was all set, searching for the report, telling him I'd forward it both to his department and the DA to keep her out of his hair. You know, really ready to *highlight* your stellar work."

Sergeant Briske paused, eyebrows waggling as he made a show of squinting at his computer screen. "But then, much to my surprise, I couldn't. It seems that—*contrary to my unmistakably clear instructions*—I had no mid-week update on that case. I said to myself, 'Why, Sergeant Briske, that's impossible. No outstanding detective in your department could *possibly* forget to send in a report on *this* case. Not the incredibly important one, the one involving two departments—and a *murdered police officer*.'"

Charles winced. He should have known this was coming.

Sergeant Briske read the expression on the detective's face, and, sensing weakness, he pounced. "So, you recognize the problem here. *Good*. Now tell me, Chuck, where is your update?"

Charles backpedaled, struggling with his words. "I… Yes. The update, uh, it's in my—I wrote it out, but I—You see, there was a lead, and I—"

"Stop!" Sergeant Briske cut him off with a wave of his hand. "I misspoke. I meant to say, '*What* is your update?'"

Charles nodded, his mouth suddenly dry. *He* was still reeling from the shock of what they'd found yesterday, and was utterly unprepared to present those findings to his section chief. *Good news, Sarge, I found the killer. Bad news, he needs three sets of handcuffs and a muzzle. And maybe a SWAT team.* A bead of sweat rolled down the side of his face as the Sergeant's green eyes bored through him, waiting on his response. "I, uh…"

He was spared by the polite rapping of knuckles on oak. Relief flooded Charles as he looked over, catching sight of Andrea leaning against the doorframe.

"I hope I'm not interrupting," she said, her hand poised mid-knock. "I was looking for Charles. A guy up front said he was in here."

Sergeant Briske's eyes narrowed beneath the bushy brows. "He *is*. What do you need?"

"Detective Morales, Pueblo PD," Andrea announced as she strode up to the mahogany desk, a broad smile on her face as she stuck out her hand. "Were you guys discussing the Trooper Temmen case?"

"We were." Sergeant Briske's eyes narrowed further. He enveloped her hand in his, blinking with surprise at the strength of her grip. He released her hand, his voice taking on hint of wary respect. "What's *your* connection?"

"Same perp," She said matter of fact, curly hair bouncing from side to side as she spoke. "Slashed my victim at a gas station back in Pueblo. Charles called my office up earlier this week to link up, we've been working the cases in tandem for a couple of days."

Sergeant Briske's bushy brows furrowed, he waved a finger between the two detectives, connecting them with a line in the air. "You. You've been working a joint case. With *him*."

Hey! I'm not that *bad.* Charles opened his mouth to protest, but Andrea cut him off, stepping in quickly to save him from himself.

"Yessir, Charles has been a great partner, good eye for detail, couldn't do it without him. We've had some difficult witnesses and Charles really helped out with them. He's dedicated too—he was here late last night tracking down a lead we got off a witness. We think the perp's a trucker."

Charles cocked an eyebrow at Andrea, but let it slide. *Sure beats 'otherworldly hellbeast.'*

Sergeant Briske's mouth hung open as he processed what'd he

heard. Prior to today, he could count the number of times he'd been surprised on one hand. He blinked at the Pueblo detective, still struggling to comprehend a world in which *Chuck Davner* was a 'great partner' on a case.

Charles watch the initial shock turn into numb bewilderment on the Sergeant's face, and figured now was the best time to attempt his escape.

"So anyway, Sarge. Like I was saying, *we've* got this lead, and *we* need to go run it down…"

"Go," Sergeant Briske said quietly, his mouth still agape. He dragged a heavy hand across his face, massaging his eyes through closed lids. He used the other to shoo them out of the office. The section chief needed time to retrace every step he'd made that morning just to be sure he hadn't stumbled into a parallel dimension. "Just…send me an email at the end of the day. Give me what you guys find."

"Trucker, huh?" said Charles, as Sergeant Briske's door clicked shut behind them.

Andrea shrugged. "It was that or hitchhiker. I figured the truth wasn't going to fly just yet."

"Good thinking," Charles said, he waved a hand across the bullpen. "Shall we?"

Andrea performed a mock courtesy. "After you, Detective."

Charles wound his way through the maze of cubicles to his desk, pulling in the swivel chair from the empty desk next door. Andrea accepted it with a thanks, ignoring the puff of dust that welled up as she sank into its spongy embrace. Charles settled into his own chair, punching the desktop's 'on' button as he did.

Andrea laced her fingers behind her head as she leaned back against the swivel chair, the aging springs groaning as they flexed. "So, I got your two a.m. text, but fuck if I understood it. Whatdja find?"

"I found our truck," said Charles, eyes on the screen as the loading bar tracked to the right.

Andrea sat up straight in the chair. "Really?!"

Charles gave her a sideways glance. "Uh-huh."

"Well?" Andrea's hands were out, begging for more. "What was it?"

"It's better if I show you," Charles replied mysteriously.

The monitor flashed, the triple beep announcing the computer was done booting up. Charles panned the mouse over with a showman's flourish, double clicking the image file saved on the desktop. The screen flashed again, resolving itself into the picture of a white sleeper-cab semi, its trailer marked with a red-and-blue 'X' that billowed out into an American flag.

Andrea scanned the picture, brown eyes darting from left to right. She tapped the screen with an enthusiastic fingernail. "That's it, that's what Sharon described alright. What is it?"

Charles leaned in. "AAFES delivery truck."

Andrea nodded, curly hair bouncing with excitement. "No shit."

Charles dropped his voice in a conspiratorial whisper. "From a U.S. Air Force Base Exchange."

Andrea's eyes went wide as she looked back at Charles. "*No shit?!*"

Charles smirked. It wasn't often he had a case where he could pull off a dramatic reveal, and he was enjoying the hell out of this one. "*Mhmmm.*"

"I KNEW IT!" Andrea shouted, leaping up from the chair. "This is some straight-up *X-Files* SHIT!"

"*Shhhh*, keep your voice down!" said Charles, casting a wary eye across the office. He needn't have bothered. The only other occupant was Sam Marken, his spindly hornrims currently trained on a mountain of copies by the printer.

"I *knew* it," whispered Andrea, waving an excited finger beneath his nose as she settled back into her chair. "It's some government experiment that got loose. Some kinda bio-weapon bullshit!"

"Slow your roll," Charles said, putting up his hands. "We don't have evidence of *that*. All we've got is a truck that matches Sharon's description. We still need to trace its route and try and find the creature's origin."

Andrea waved away his procedural concerns. "And when we track that truck back to some shady weapons lab tucked away deep in the mountains?"

Charles rolled his eyes. "Then I guess we call them to collect their monster."

The phone whirred, filling the void of the empty line. There was a click, and the call connected.

"AAFES customer service, this is Linda, how may I help you?"

"Hello, Linda. This is Detective Davner, with the Colorado Springs Police Department.

"H-hello Detective Davner, how may I help you?"

"I'm looking for a truck."

"A truck?"

"Yes, a truck. For an investigation."

"An investigation?"

"Homicide."

"Like CSI?"

There was pause on the other side, followed by a heavy sigh.

"*Yes*, like CSI. Like I said, I'm looking for a truck."

"A truck?"

"A truck."

"What kind of truck?"

"An AAFES delivery truck. I'm looking for one that drove through Pueblo last Monday."

"Was that the thirteenth?"

"No, the eleventh."

"Oh, I had that day off."

"I didn't—I said I'm looking for a truck that was driving that day."

"March eleventh?"

"Yes."

"An AAFES delivery truck?"

"*Yes*."

"That drove through New Mexico?"

"What? No, Colorado. Pueblo, Colorado."

"Pueblo, Colorado?"

"*Yes!*"

"I'm sorry, sir, I can't help you with that. This is a customer complaint and service line. Do you have a problem with an AAFES related product or service?"

There was a sound on the other line, not unlike the flat smack of a palm against a forehead. It was followed by angry and muffled whispering. Linda could hear a woman's voice distinctly saying, *'No, no! let me!'* There was some shuffling, and then the woman's voice came over on the line.

"Hello? Hello, Linda?"

"AAFES customer service, this is Linda, how may I help you?"

"This is Detective Andrea Morales, is there a manager we could speak too."

"Certainly. And which AAFES related service or product is this related too?"

'Their service department!' bellowed a voice in the background. The woman's voice spoke quickly, trying to cover up whoever was yelling in the background.

"Shipping and inventory," she said sweetly.

"Thank you, please hold while I connect you to our service manager."

"Thank you."

"And have a great Air Force day!"

"…Thank you?"

The phone whirred, connecting over to the next line. Hold music filled the empty line, a horrid, whooshing electronic beat designed by market testers to be as inoffensive as possible, yet nevertheless delivering a sound experience more infuriating than empty silence. Minutes passed. Periodically, a message broke through the jingle to kindly suggest those staying on the line might be better served leaving a message and carrying on with their day.

Twenty minutes passed, then a click as the call picked up.

"Hello?" the woman's voice asked.

"Hello, this is AAFES Customer Service Manager Pierce, how may I assist you?"

'Fire Linda!' a man's voice shouted in the background.

"Shut up, Charles!—I'm sorry, this is Detective Morales, Pueblo PD."

"Hello Detective Morales, how may I assist you?"

"Hey, Pierce?"

"AAFES Customer Service Manager Pierce, yes."

"I'm looking to get ahold of someone in your shipping or delivery department. Can you help with that?"

"Delivery department?"

"Yes, I'm trying to track down the driver of one of your delivery trucks. It's part of an investigation."

"Oh, are you looking for a list of our drivers?"

There was a pause filled by muffled whispering back and forth. The woman's voice came back on the line.

"No, not yet. I need to speak to someone that tracks delivery and trucking routes. I'm trying to track down a specific truck that drove through Pueblo, Colorado last Monday."

"The ninth?"

"No, the eleventh."

"Oh. I'm sorry ma'am, but this is the customer service center. We don't handle delivery routes."

"I *know*, I'm asking you to connect me with the department that *does*."

"Oh."

There was another pause, this time on the corporate side of the line.

"Sooo, can you connect me with that department?" the woman asked.

"Uh, I think so. I think that would be our shipping department. This is a different center, though, so I can't speak for all of the other opera—"

"That's fine, just connect me with someone in ship—"

"You want to speak to someone in our shipping sect—"

"Yes, fine. Whoever in ship—"

"Will our Regional Shipping Manager work?"

"Yes, *please*, connect—"

"Okay, ma'am please hold while I connect you to our shipping section."

"Sounds good."

"Thank you, and have a great Air Force day!"

"You too," the woman muttered.

The phone whirred. The hold music returned, hollower, market-friendlier, and more terrible than before. Minutes passed, broken up by the periodic robotic interjection of '*Your call is important to us. Please, stay on the line.*'

A half-hour passed before the line picked up, a gruff man's voice cutting in over the seventh iteration of the robotic message.

"AAFES Central Shipping, this is Rob."

The woman's voice sounded relieved. "Hello, Rob? This is Detective Morales, Pueblo PD—"

"New Mexico?"

"No, Colorado."

"What can I do for you, Ms. Morales?"

"Detective."

"Pardon?"

"It's *Detective* Morales, Pueblo Police Department."

"Gotcha. What can I do for you, *Detective* Morales?"

"I'm running an investigation here in Colorado—"

"Makes sense so far."

"And I'm *trying* to track down one of your delivery trucks."

"One of our trucks?"

"Yes. For a homic—"

"An AAFES truck?"

"*Yes*. A semi-truck hauling a trailer through Pueblo, Colorado."

"So not a home delivery truck?"

"You have home delivery trucks?"

"No, that's why I asked. I wanted to make sure you weren't

confusing us with someone else."

"Why would I—never mind—I'm looking for a red semi-truck hauling a white trailer, with a big AAFES BX logo on the side last week."

"Can you be more specific?"

"About the truck? Or the timeframe?"

"Yes."

"No on the truck, just that description. But it was driving on Santa Fe drive in Pueblo, Colorado around six p.m. last Monday."

"1800 or 0600?"

"Uh, 1800."

"On Monday, the tenth?"

"No, the eleventh."

"So, Tuesday then?"

"No! *Monday*, the *eleventh*. Driving on Santa Fe drive. Around 1800."

"In Colorado?"

"*Yes!*"

"I'm sorry, Detective Morales, this is AAFES *Central* Shipping, I only handle shipping west of Memphis and east of Omaha."

There was an exasperated gasp followed by silence. When the woman spoke again, her voice carried a strained quality, as if forcing the words through tightly closed teeth.

"Am I right is assuming that someone in AAFES *West* Shipping might know about this truck?"

"Yeah, probably. If it happened in Colorado, that's covered by our Central-West division."

"Can you connect me with them? *Please?*"

"No, not directly. But I can give you their number. Do you want their num—"

"*YES!*"

"Okay. That'll be 719-266-2837."

"*Yes.*"

"Is that all?"

"Yes. Thank *you*."

"Okay, then have a grea—"

The line clicked, the woman's voice replaced by a chittering dial tone.

The phone whirred, filling the void of the empty line. There was a click, and the call connected. A man's voice spoke with the slight wariness and hesitation of someone picking up a call on a number they don't recognize.

"AAFES Central-West Shipping, this is Michael Norkin."

"Hey Michael, this is Detective Davner, Colorado Springs PD."

"Oh, how can I help you?"

"Real quick—I'm not trying to be rude but we've been on quite the run around here—do you handle AAFES trucking and delivery in Colorado?"

"AAFES shipping in Colorado? Yes, that's under me."

"Great, passed the first hurdle. What about trucking in Pueblo?"

"Pueblo is in Colorado, so, yes."

"So if we needed to find a truck that drove through Pueblo last week, you'd be the guy to help us?"

"If it's an AAFES truck, then yes. It's one of mine."

"Awesome, we're trying to track one down."

"Why, what happened?"

"It's part of an investigation, at this point I can't share too much beyond that."

"Does it involve one of my drivers though? I need to know if I should suspend someone's operating license and put them on leave."

"No, not the driver. It does involve a truck, more specifically something that fell off it."

"Like merchandise? 'Cause we have a Secure Loss Prevention team that might be better suited to answer that kind of question, I just manage routes and deliveries."

"Then it sounds like you're just the guy we've been looking for, Michael, I'm glad you picked up."

"Uhhh…alright. You said you're trying to find one of our trucks?"

"Yes."

"But not the driver."

"Correct."

"And this isn't about merchandise?"

"No."

A muffled exchange followed that statement. Michael Norkin had the distinct impression that another party on the line disputed that claim.

"No! We went over this. It's not *merchandise!* Now enough, you told me to handle this one—I'm sorry, Michael, where were we?"

"You were asking me about a truck?"

"Yes! We need to track down a truck's route, one that passed through Pueblo last Monday."

"The eleventh?"

"NO! Wait, *yes!*"

"Uh, alright. Let me pull up my shipping tracker. Can you give me plate on the truck?"

"No plate, but I can give you a time and a direction. Will that work?"

"Uhhhh, it *should*. It just might take me a little longer. Do you mind waiting a sec while I pull it up?"

"No problem, Michael."

The line was quiet, the soft clack of keystrokes fading away into silence.

"Okay, it's coming up. Sorry, this program always takes forever to load."

"No worries, Michael."

"Alright, it's open. Can you give me the time and location?"

"Northbound on Lincoln, around 1800 on Monday, March eleventh. It was a red semi, if that helps."

"We don't log truck color, but I should be able to sort through our trips that day and pick out the one with that route. It'll probably take a while though, do you want me to put you on hold?"

"*No!*"

"Oh, alright, then if you don't mind waiting…"

"I don't."

Silence lapsed between them, minutes passing. Every so often one of the men would cough, letting the other know they were still on the line. More time passed, before Michael Norkin broke the silence with a slight '*ahem.*'

"Detective Davner? Are you still there?"

"Yes. Got something, Michael?"

"I do. You're lucky, we don't run too many routes through Pueblo. There was only one truck that drove through in that direction at that time."

"Great! And you have a copy of its full route for that day? Can you email it to me?"

"I mean, sure, but it only ran two trips that day. Out from Peterson for a delivery run and then back up to Peterson."

"Cool, where was the delivery to?"

"Archambault Peak."

"Archambault Peak? I've never heard of that base."

"Oh, it's not a base. Archambault is a research lab in the mountains, between Fairview and Buelah Valley."

"Archambault Peak? Huh."

"It's pretty small, being just a research lab and all. I'm not surprised you haven't heard of it."

"And your driver was coming back from a delivery there?"

"An AAFES truck headed northbound on Santa Fe drive last Monday was. They've got a small shoppette we supply twice a month."

"Huh. Thanks Michael, that's very helpful. You don't happen to have a number we can contact for there?"

"For the shoppette?"

"No, the research lab."

"Sorry, 'fraid not."

"Ah, well, thanks anyway. This was a huge help to our investigation."

"And you're sure you don't need any information on the driver?"

"Well, actually, do you have some contact info?"

"Not in front of me, but I can track it down."

"Thanks. Now, if you can email that info and a copy of the truck route, that would be all we need."

"Sure thing. Email?"

"Charles.davner@cspd.city.org"

"Alright, I'll send it your way as soon as I find it."

"Thanks again, Michael, this was a huge help."

"No problem, Detective Davner, have a great—"

"Air Force Day! You too, buddy!"

The line clicked, empty again save for the beep of the dial tone.

"Research lab?!"

Andrea leapt up from her seat, drowning out the dusty creak of the swivel chair with excited squeaks of her own.

Charles shook his head. He knew this was coming as soon as he heard the word 'lab' on the other line. "Archambault Peak Research Laboratory. But! It's still coincidental at this point, we have to talk to the driver first to make sure he didn't make any other stops along the way."

"Whatever, Charles, I told you this would happen!" Andrea's whole body positively vibrated, toned arms twitching beneath the thin white fabric of her blouse as she danced in place. "I *told* you!"

Charles shoved her triumphant finger out of his face, turning his chair back towards the computer screen. "How about we look up the lab first, huh? We don't even know what they do there."

Andrea rolled her eyes, settling back into her chair. "You just don't want to admit I was right."

"You're *not* right, not yet anyway," Charles sighed, double-clicking the internet icon on the screen. "For all we know Archambault Lab is just a big telescope." He turned back to her as the page loaded, gesturing to the search engine behind him. "How about we, I dunno, do some cop work first and get some evidence together before jumping to wild conclusions?"

Andrea's eyes narrowed as she crossed her arms over her chest. "You know, with all this 'X-Files' shit going on, I finally figured something out."

Charles cocked an eyebrow. "Oh yeah? What's that?"

"That you're a fuckin' Scully."

Chapter 12

Friday

The Delta 88 wove along the mountain road, dappled sunlight glinting off its golden paint. A breeze whistled through the ponderosa pines, ruffling their stiff branches as they towered from the rocky slopes. A falcon soared above them, its lithe gray body silhouetted against the morning sky as it followed the road, patrolling for an unwary dove or squirrel. Fresh snow still capped the mountain edges past the tree line, deposited by the storms last week. As they drove, the chuffing of the Oldsmobile's 3800 series V6 mingled with the burbling of nuthatches and mountain bluebirds.

The tighter curves of the narrow, two-lane road were bordered on the outside edge by guardrails designed to keep those distracted by the breathtaking views from understeering and plummeting to their deaths. The thin ribbon of asphalt snaked its way up from highway 78, winding along through switchbacks and steep ascents as it climbed up the mountain. On each of these turns, the wide H-body frame of the Delta 88 pitched and rolled, like a steamer trapped in the embrace of a summer squall.

Andrea groaned inside the car, her normally tan face tinged green and pale as she death-gripped the handrail at the top of the cab. As they leaned through another turn, she summoned the last of her energy to glare at Charles.

"This is the last time I let you drive."

Charles kept his eyes on the road, keeping the Oldsmobile chugging as it straightened out. "I thought you didn't get carsick."

"Normally I don't ride in fuckin' *boats*," Andrea said through clenched teeth, gently massaging her stomach with her other hand. "Can we at least turn the air on?"

The road rose sharply up ahead in a series of pitched hills. Charles kept the gas pedal flat against the floor, spurring the shuddering engine to climb on. He looked over and shook his head. As stifling as it was inside the broad cab, they couldn't spare the power.

Andrea sighed, throwing her head back against the worn cloth seats.

Charles spared her a sympathetic glance. "Roll the window down?"

Andrea nodded with her eyes shut tight, her guts rearranging themselves at the top of each hill.

Charles tapped the buttons on the door, cold mountain wind rushing as the windows melted away into their frames. He sucked in a deep breath, crisp, thin air filling his lungs. Charles wasn't much of a hiker, or an outdoorsman in general, but every Coloradan loved the mountains.

Andrea groaned again, softer this time. The chill from outside working wonders on her nausea. As the car settled from bouncing over the last hill, her stomach quieted just enough for her to hazard conversation.

"So, what did our trucker say when you talked to him? Any details on the lab?"

"Just confirmed his route for the day. Left Peterson around ten that morning for a trip to Archambault with a half-full trailer. Unloaded to the shoppette, then back to Peterson. Normal delivery, no stops along the way."

"Nothing more?"

Charles shook his head. "Not the chatty type. I think it was his day off though, I heard a bunch of kids running around in the background."

Andrea's stomach lurched as they shuddered around another sharp curve in the mountain road. "Hard to believe someone takes a semi through this on the regular."

Charles shrugged, keeping his foot steady on the gas. "Practice makes perfect, I guess. It's probably why he only had the one stop, slow going there and back."

Andrea nodded, watching the road ahead. Their turn was on the right, a narrow offshoot of asphalt flanked on either side by towering pines. A small metal sign jutted from a post by the turn, blue paint marked with officious white lettering. 'Archambault Peak USAF Research Facility' read the stamped letters, 'No Outlet – Official Government Traffic Only.' Charles cranked the wheel, the Delta 88 trundling up the drive.

They drove on, the trees thinning around them and the ground outside fracturing into boulders pocketed with remnants of snow as they climbed in elevation. Passing the snow line, the sky opened up above them, crystal clear and impossibly high.

Andrea shivered, on the verge of suggesting they roll up the windows when she felt the car stop. She followed Charles' gaze as he looked out over the Delta 88's golden hood. The road abruptly widened in front of them, splitting into two lanes that curved around a small steel guard shack. The in-bound lane was blocked by a yellow steel barrier crisscrossed with red and white lines, while pop-up tire-shredders lined the other side. Razor wire topped a fence that jutted from the mountainside like a jagged crown as it fanned out from the guard shack.

Andrea pointed to the fence, noting the ominous red signs authorizing lethal force against trespassers that dotted its length at regular intervals. "Doesn't look like the type of place to welcome visitors."

Charles shrugged. "We're cops, should be official enough."

"*City* cops," Andrea said, rolling her eyes. "That doesn't mean much to the feds. Pretty sure you can't just roll-up, flash the badge, and get in."

Charles offered her a wan smile. "You'd be surprised how far that gets me most days."

They cruised up to the guard shack, stopping just short of the yellow swingarm. Charles caught a flicker of movement behind the heavily tinted ballistic glass. There was a click of a latch being disengaged. One of the windows sliding open to reveal a rotund man in his late fifties, the white stubble of his hair disappearing under a blue ballcap printed with the word 'Police' above the Air Force seal. Charles could see a half-eaten sandwich on the desk in front of him, next to supermarket-brand cola can and a portable TV tuned to the PGA tour. The guard leaned out window, black vinyl chair squeaking underneath him as he held out his hand to Charles.

"ID?"

Charles flashed his badge, sunlight glinting off the stamped steel. "Detective Davner, Co—"

"Thanks," the man grunted, slamming the window shut as he returned to his sandwich.

Charles blinked for a moment, before withdrawing his arm. He looked over to Andrea, who shrugged.

"Maybe we should call someone—"

She was interrupted by the creaking whir of gears as the metal arm swung up, clearing the lane for them. They exchanged another look before Charles eased the car past the gate, offering a wave to the shadowy guard behind the ballistic glass. Watching the swingarm fall behind them in the rearview mirror, they wove through a serpentine of concrete barriers and onto the installation's main road. There was a combination gas station and convenience store on the immediate the right, built into the side of the peak.

Charles pulled into one of the three spots out front, parking beneath an illuminated sign displaying 'AAFES Express.'

"Now what?" Andrea asked.

Charles peered over the dash and into the shoppette. "Looks like they're open. You need a RedBull or something?"

Andrea rolled her eyes. "I mean now that we're here. Are we just gonna drive around the hidden mountain laboratory until we find the building marked 'Secret Government Monster Factory—Keep Out?'"

Charles leaned out the window, squinting against the glare as he followed the asphalt line cutting its way up to the top of the peak.

"Looks like there's only one road up. Can't be room for more than a few buildings on top. Maybe it'll be that easy." Pulling his head back into the car, he looked over at her and shrugged. "But I'm the skeptic, *you're* the believer."

"Fine," Andrea sighed, tossing her head back against the tan seat rest. She waved her hand at him. "Lead on, MacDuff."

Charles pulled away from the gas station, winding up the narrow switchbacks carving around slabs of rock. As they crested the summit, they spotted a group of three buildings clustered along the edge of the peak—squat, drab squares of federal brick with flat grey roofs. The curve of a white geodesic dome rose from behind the central building, and a few cars dotted a parking lot stretched between them.

Charles guided the Delta 88 into the center lot, pulling into a space near the far end. He cocked an eyebrow at Andrea. "Which one do you want to start with?"

Andrea shrugged, looking out across the lot to read the pale brown lettering on the buildings' sides. "Your guess is as good as mine. Which one seems the most important?"

Charles squinted against the harsh sunlight, spotting a yellow sign marked with a black propeller on the side of the nearest building. 'Warning, Radiation Area,' the sign read in bold lettering, 'ONLY Authorized Personnel May Enter.'

"Dunno, but I vote we do *that* one last," Charles said, pointing out the yellow sign.

"Agreed," nodded Andrea. She eyed the building centered in front of the geodesic dome. "The one in front of the golf-ball thing says, 'Central Telemetry.' Wanna try there first?"

"Works for me," said Charles, stepping out of the sedan. "Same plan for getting in?"

"Why not?" Andrea wondered aloud as she shut the car door. "Let's see how far we can push our luck."

Up close, Archambault Peak's Central Telemetry building was just as plain and unassuming as the other two, its dusty brick faded under the unrelenting sun of the upper altitude. Gravel crunched underfoot as Charles and Andrea walked up to the unpainted steel door centered in the flat expanse of tan wall. Charles spied a RFID card reader by the doorknob, the grey square jutting out just below a beige telephone box mounted at chest height. Charles tried the door's knob, unsurprised to find it locked.

"Phone?" Andrea offered.

Charles nodded, undoing the spring latch and swinging the box's weathered lid open. Age and dirt lined the interior, almost obscuring the smudged sticker listing the office numbers on back of the lid. Charles lifted the phone from the receiver, dialing the first number listed. *So far, so good*, he thought as the dial tone whirred in his ear.

There was a click as the line picked up, a woman's voice speaking softly on the other end.

"Hello?" she asked, sounding slightly distracted. Charles could hear the clack of a keyboard in the background

"Hello, ma'am, this is Detective Davner. I'm looking for Dr. Weichel," he said confidently.

Andrea shot him a quizzical look at the mention of the name. Charles covered the mouthpiece, whispering to her, "Head researcher. I looked him up on the installation webpage."

'*Nice!*' Andrea mouthed silently, offering an admiring golf-clap.

Charles shot her a thumbs-up, mentally congratulating himself on his research and foresight.

"You're about two years late," the woman's voice answered icily. "Dr. Weichel retired in 2017. What is this about?"

Fucking website. Caught off-guard, he reached around for inspiration before settling on the simple truth. "Homicide investigation. I need to speak to the head researcher for Archambault Peak."

"*Oh*. Dr. Leventhal, speaking," she replied, the chill tone warming slightly. "Are you calling from the door? I can meet you out there and let you in."

"What're they saying?" whispered Andrea, leaning in to eavesdrop.

"She say's we're in. I told you, I've got this." he whispered back forcefully, pushing her away. Returning to the phone he said, "That would be great Dr. Leventhal, thank you."

Charles hung up the phone, fighting to close the lid against a sudden gust of mountain wind. Looking around as they waited by the steel door, Charles took a moment to appreciate the snow-capped ridges and green valleys stretching out all around them.

"Pretty view for monster factory," he muttered, kicking a rock out from under his shoe.

"Sure is," Andrea agreed, as she watched the clouds drift by on the eastern plains. "Really inspires you to put in your best work making nightmares come true."

They turned as the door opened behind them. A petite brunette stepped out—Dr. Leventhal he presumed—wearing thick spectacles and an orange sweater-dress over grey converse. Charles watched as she leaned her whole body against the door, thin frame shaking as she braced it open against another mountain gust.

"Good afternoon, Doctor," said Andrea, sticking her hand out. "I'm Detective Morales of the Pueblo PD, this is—"

"Detective Davner," Charles added, raising his hand. "Colorado Springs PD."

Dr. Leventhal's blue eyes, magnified several times by her lenses, narrowed as she took them both in.

"*You're* not OSI," she remarked, pointing an accusing finger at the two detectives. "How did you get in here?"

Charles shrugged. "Guard let us in."

"*Gawdamn DAF officers*," she muttered, ducking back in the building.

Andrea jumped forward, catching the door with her hand before it had a chance to swing shut. "Dr. Leventhal, ma'am, Like we said this is for an investi—"

"Homicide, I *heard*," the scientist replied, sweater-dress billowing as she strode down the hallway. "I've got four spectral tests to oversee today and a meeting with General Sinclair in an hour, but *sure* I'll take time to out of *my* day to tour some cops around. Follow me, we'll talk in my office."

Andrea looked at Charles, this was the last reaction she'd expected sneaking onto a classified military base.

Charles shrugged. "Guess we follow her."

It took a moment for their eyes to adjust to the mild fluorescents after the harsh brightness outside. They were greeted by a length of bare white hallway, dingy tile matched to the cheaply painted walls. Charles and Andrea stepped quickly to catch up with the head researcher, still muttering angrily to herself as she turned the corner on another hallway.

"And here I thought the knuckle-draggers Security Forces used to send us were bad, at least they had the presence of mind to check an ID. *Gawdamn* DAF can't even look up from his *gawdamn* TV," they heard her gripe as they made their way past office doors, conference rooms, and the occasional vending machine. Turning left down another hallway, the wall opened up into a full-length window revealing a central laboratory space. Charles could see scientists puttering away behind the window as they walked by—tweaking instruments, jotting notes down on some white boards.

"*I don't see anything with claws and teeth,*" he whispered to Andrea, watching the mundane display of intellectual busywork.

"*No kidding. They're not even wearing the white coats,*" she whispered back. She saw one of the scientists completely miss while tossing a piece of paper into a nearby recycling bin.

"So much for the monster factory," Charles snorted, moving on to keep pace with Dr. Leventhal.

Andrea shook her head, disappointed by the banal scene. "Maybe that's just what they *want* you to think?"

They caught up with the Dr. Leventhal in her office, jumping up and down to trigger the motion-sensitive light sensors in the ceiling. Andrea knocked politely on the hollow-framed plywood door as they entered.

"Come in, sit," the scientist ordered as the lights flickered on, gesturing to two short wooden chairs in front of her desk. "Trust the Air Force to go green in the dumbest possible fashion."

Charles was pretty sure he'd seen those same chairs in a kindergarten classroom, he opened his mouth to comment but a look from Andrea convinced him to keep it to himself. They took their seats, carefully tucking themselves into the narrow chairs. Still glaring at the lights, but satisfied they'd remain on, Dr. Leventhal stepped behind the cheap metal desk before hopping up into her high-backed office chair. A waterfall of university diplomas cascaded behind her on the back wall, and Charles spotted some 'Far Side' comics taped beside her computer keyboard.

"So," Dr. Leventhal said after a moment, sizing up the two detectives before her. "What brings a homicide investigation to my lab?"

Charles and Andrea shared a look, neither quite sure where to begin.

"There's been some deaths," Andrea said, piecing the words together as tactfully as she could.

"I gathered that when you said, 'homicide,' *Detective*," Dr. Leventhal scoffed.

"We believe there's a connection with your lab," Charles added, drawing out the words as he took out his notebook.

"I'm not missing any staff," she said, spectacles bouncing on her nose as her brow wrinkled. "So what's the connection?"

The detectives shared another look, sucking in a deep breath before wading back in.

"Alright, Doctor, these deaths we've been investigating are *unusual*. Covered in markings that suggest some kind of *animal*—"

"Odd lacerations, teeth marks on the bones—"

"And when we were examining one scene we found evidence of something in the sewers—"

"Storm drain—"

"*Whatever*. But when we found the *thing*, we lost it—"

"Good thing too, after it chased us about a mile—"

"And one our witnesses described it as originating from one of your trucks—"

"Not your truck specifically, an AAFES truck that came from this installation—"

"And so we believe one of your—"

"Experiments—"

"Yes, *experiments*, thank you, might have…*escaped*."

The detectives paused, words hanging in the air over the government scientist. Silence permeated the office for a few seconds as Dr. Leventhal processed what she'd heard.

"*What?*"

"One of your experiments," Charles explained calmly, flipping through the loose pages of his notebook. "We think it got out, hitched a ride on the AAFES truck, and killed a few folks in Colorado Springs."

"And Pueblo," added Andrea.

"Right—and Pueblo."

Dr. Leventhal leaned against her high-backed chair, two fingers pressed along her temple as her blue eyes darted between the two detectives. She settled on Charles, pinning him under a stare of irritated disbelief.

"What *the hell* are you both talking about?"

Charles opened his mouth to repeat himself, but she cut him off with a wave of her hand.

"I heard you just fine, what I mean to ask is, 'what kind of 'experiment' are you talking about?'"

"You know, some kind of *animal* experiments," Charles said, struggling to find the words.

"Animal experiments?" Dr. Leventhal's forehead knotted in on itself. She leaned forward, thin elbows propping her up on the metal desk. "What *exactly* do you think we *do* here?"

"Bioweapons?" offered Andrea, tenderly teasing out the word.

Dr. Leventhal gawped at her.

"We just thought," the detective added quietly, "I mean, since this is a military lab and all…"

"Yeah, a *communications* research laboratory," Dr. Leventhal replied, mouth hanging open in incredulity. She stood up to peer over the desk, doublechecking the badges she'd seen on their belts. "I thought you were *cops*. Did you do *any* research into who we are or what we do here? Or did you drive two hours up a mountain just to waste my time?"

Charles snorted. He'd skimmed the lab's description on the website, finding nothing but dense blocks of text describing 'parabolic dishes,' 'inferometers,'and 'aperture synthesis.' He crossed out several pages in his notebook, each filled with questions concerning what any of those terms meant. Looking up again, he hazarded another question. "Sooo, no genetic experimentation?"

"No! Of course not!" snapped Dr. Leventhal, throwing up her hands. "We do satellite uplink design! And deep-space signal research!"

Quiet fell over the office again as the detectives conferred in another shared look.

"Like a…telescope?" Charles asked after a moment.

Dr. Leventhal clapped a hand to her face. "Yes! What do you think that big dome outside is?"

"Told you," smirked Charles, tapping Andrea with his notebook. He leaned back in the chair as best he could, determined not to draw further attention to himself.

Andrea blinked for a few moments, fighting within herself to regain her footing in the conversation.

"Well, if you're not doing weapons research, then why are you in the middle of nowhere with all these 'shoot-on-sight' signs circling your perimeter?"

"The remote elevation gives us clearer telemetry without any backscatter," Dr. Leventhal explained, dragging the hand down her face. "There's over three million dollars' worth of finely calibrated sensor equipment in here, *of course* we put up a fence. And as for the signs, I think they come standard on any government facility." She swept a hand in the general direction of the guard shack outside. "But as you're well aware, security here isn't exactly at its tightest."

"Well, what about the other building? The one marked radioactive?" Andrea pressed. She hadn't spent ten years as a cop just to accept a coincidence at face value. "Maybe the radiation is our connection here? Could it've mutated some local wildlife?"

Dr. Leventhal shot her a withering glare.

"That's *not* how radiation works," she said tersely. "It's not some magic horror-ray churning out giant, killer beasts. If an animal came in contact with the radiation from *that* lab the only mutation you'd see is *cancer*."

Charles tried and failed to keep from snickering. *Being a Scully's not so bad now, huh?*

Andrea was crestfallen. She swatted him on the arm, pleading for him to take over.

Charles flipped through his notebook, looking for something of value to ask. "You said there's sensors here. Observe anything unusual in the last week?"

Dr. Leventhal rolled her eyes. "We're scientists, it's our *job* to observe the unusual."

"And?" asked Charles, waving her on with his pen. "Humor us. See anything *especially* weird in the last two weeks?"

The scientist sighed, exasperation rippling outwards like waves on the beach. "We had a large blip along the 770 gigahertz spectrum last week, but I'm *pretty sure* that's unrelated to a *homicide* in *Colorado Springs*."

It's actually several *homicides*, Charles corrected, but he kept it to himself. It seemed the wisest choice under the circumstances.

"On Monday, the eleventh?" Andrea asked, perking up from her chair.

"No," came the terse reply. "The day before. The tenth."

Charles watched Andrea's face fall, folding in on herself as she sunk into the tiny chair. *So much for theory,* he thought flipping the notebook closed. He rose from the short wooden chair. "Well, Doctor, I think that about does it for us, we want to thank you for your time in talking to us."

"The pleasure was all mine," Dr. Leventhal remarked bitterly, scowling as she turned towards her computer screen.

Charles looked back to Andrea. "Shall we, Detective?"

"I suppose," she conceded, gathering herself up to leave. Andrea fished a card out of her pocket, sliding it across the desk to the ill-tempered scientist. "Give us a call if you think of anything unusual or relevant that might be connected."

"Uh-huh," the researcher grumbled, stabbing away at her desktop keys. "How about this, next time you've got an animal problem—"

Andrea paused in the doorway, holding out hope for one last lead. "Yes?"

"Try a fucking zoologist."

Outside the lab, Charles squinted against the glaring sun, searching for the Delta 88 among the scattering of cars. The steel door opened and shut behind him, followed by the soft crunch of 5.11 boots on gravel.

"Looks like the 'X-Files' theory is bust," he said.

"I *wanted* to believe," Andrea sighed, kicking a rock out into the parking lot.

Charles patted her on the shoulder. "Want to sleep on it and regroup in the morning?"

Andrea nodded, pulling back her hair to keep her curls out of her face. "Yeah, I've got some filing to do for another case anyway. Might be good to get my mind off this shit for a little bit."

They walked over to the gold sedan, shivering as a cold wind picked up.

"Shoulda brought a coat," muttered Charles, stuffing his hands in his pockets to keep warm.

"I usually keep one in my car," said Andrea as she turned her collar up against the chill. "Helps with all these damn cold snaps at night. Aren't we supposed to get another one today?"

"That's what I heard," said Charles, teeth beginning to chatter as he dug his keys out of his pocket. Sliding onto the wide bench seat, he wrestled the door closed against the rushing wind. He closed his eyes, leaning back against the soft beige headrest. "I'll be glad when it's summer."

"Yeah?"

Charles nodded. "When it warms up, everything gets just a little quieter."

Chapter 13

Saturday

Twin chirps broke the warm stillness of Charles' room that morning.

The first text was from Andrea—*'ADA called me in for a strangulation deposition. Meet tomorrow?'*

The second was from Sam Marken. *'Another stabbing last night. Sergeant says all-call at 9. Sorry.'*

Charles eyed the clock on the nightstand—7:13. With a grumble he tapped out the same reply to both texts—*'cool'*—and dragged himself upright.

Leaning over on the side of the bed he thumbed his way over to a rainbow-colored icon of a camera shutter. A quick double-tap and the app opened, a wall of pictures from his feed filling up the diminutive screen. Idly swiping through, he rose from the bed and shuffled his way towards the kitchen. Helping himself to one of the mugs by the coffeepot, he poured a fresh cup while scrolling past images of dogs in sweaters, inspirational quotes misattributed to famous authors, stunningly expensive houses, and videos of workouts requiring a level of keen enthusiasm he would never achieve.

Charles stopped on the image of two men, hand in hand as they basked in the warm sunset of a Mexican beach. Tapping the picture, he felt his jaw tighten as it swelled to fill the screen. They were a good-looking couple—trim, tanned, and sporting a matching pair of pastel trunks as they stood on the warm, white sand. Charles' eyes narrowed— the look of pure, adoring happiness of James' smile burning its way through to back of his skull. He sized up the other man, scowl deepening at the sight of his immaculately styled blond coif.

"Sure makes Cabo look fun, doesn't he?"

Charles looked up sharply, catching Savannah leaning against the doorway to the kitchen.

"I. What? No. Shut up," he stuttered, hiding the naked jealousy stretched across his face behind his mug. "I was texting Sam. For *work*."

"*Mhmm,*" Savannah said, joining him at the counter. She filled her mug with the rest of Colombian blend, adding a few packets of raw sugar to the top. "You know, you could be happy too if you tried going out and actually *doing* things once in a while."

"Busy," grunted Charles. He took a sip of coffee, grimacing when he realized it'd gone cold. *When did that happen?* Charles shrugged. "No point in going out when I keep getting called into work the next morning."

"Another homicide? That's three in a week. Connected?"

Charles nodded. "And maybe more."

Savannah sipped thoughtfully. "I had plans to go with Tyler and La'shea up to Red Rock Canyon, should I cancel?"

Charles thought for a moment, then shook his head. "We haven't had any cases that far west, so just make sure you get back before dark. I've got an all-call to go over it at nine though, so I'll text you if there's any updates."

Savannah perked up. "Nine?"

"Yeah, why?" asked Charles, finishing the last of his coffee. He set the empty mug in the sink, careful to rinse out the dregs.

Savannah jerked her thumb to the wall clock mounted by the fridge. "Because it's 8:30 now."

Shit.

Charles stumbled through the door to Sergeant Briske's office at 9:05—unshowered, unshaved, his tangled blond hair still matted to one side. *But at least I'm in a clean shirt.* That's more than could be said for Detective Raines, the massive detective glowering from the corner in a rumpled blue oxford covered in mud and grass stains.

"Glad you could join us," gruffed Sergeant Briske from behind the wide, mahogany desk. "Now that everyone's here, we can begin."

Charles muttered an apology as he shuffled through the office, pushing past Detective Daggert to an open space. Even Detective Jimenez was there, enjoying her remaining maternity leave from one of the office's chintzy leather chairs.

Sergeant Briske looked out over the crowded office, his grim expression half-hidden behind steepled fingers.

"We had another homicide last night," he began at last, voice measured and low. "Another stabbing."

"Jogger?" asked Charles, speaking up from his spot on the wall.

"Dogwalker," grumbled Detective Raines, dirt-stained hands rubbing the bags out from under his eyes. "Half in the pond by Glen avenue."

Charles nodded, feeling an ounce of sympathy for the big man. He wasn't sure if it was Sam or Sergeant Briske looking out for him this time, but he was grateful either way that they skipped his name on the duty roster. Perry was a nice guy, but right now Charles couldn't handle another case. *Although I'd bet cash money they're connected...*

Sergeant Briske cleared his throat loudly, resuming control over the conversation. "As I said, we had another stabbing last night, in the same manner and form as six other preceding victims."

Perry started up from the corner, opening his mouth to protest, but Sergeant Briske cut him off.

"Yes, Perry, I said *six*. I'm including your case from last week. Looking at the coroner's report I'm not convinced by your knife-fight theory either. I need you to reopen it, have the coroner cross-reference the wounds with the other victims, and get with Todd about working out the links with his two joggers."

"Don't drag me into this," Detective Daggert muttered under his breath. "He can keep his shit attitude to himself."

Charles felt a twinge of guilt. It was his last update to Sergeant Briske that had put the section chief on notice about the connection between Perry's closed case and his own. *It's the right call*, he told himself as he watched the broad detective sink back against the corner, arms folded bitterly across his chest. *Just as long as Sarge doesn't mention my name.*

"*Six* victims in *five* cases in *two* weeks, all at the same time missing-persons reports double their usual filings," Sergeant Briske announced gravely, heavy hands sweeping through the air to underline the gravity of the situation. "After conferring with Chief Brosnan and the DA, we agreed that those facts exceed routine, vault over coincidence, and land us directly in the realm of deliberate design." Now the section chief became more animated, bushy eyebrows rising with his pitch and tone. "We believe there's a spree killer in Colorado Springs."

Sergeant Briske paused, allowing his hands and his words to hang in the air over the detective's heads. Quiet followed. Charles looked around, seeing a room full of nodding heads and stifled yawns. Settling back against the wall, he reminded himself that while *he* may have been ahead of the curve, it didn't take Sherlock Holmes to figure out where the Sergeant was going with all this.

Disappointed but undeterred, Sergeant Briske lowered his hands and pressed ahead. "The Chief and I talked through a few responses to this threat, but we both agreed that we need to get out in front of this. A spree killer active in our area demands that we be *proactive*, not *reactive.*"

"How the fuck are we supposed to do a proactive homicide investigation, Sergeant?" asked Detective Jimenez, exasperated indignation coloring her tone as she spoke up from the arm chair. "Track down vics *before* they're killed?"

Sergeant Briske's eyes narrowed to what Charles had termed 'dangerous slits.' He'd seen that look only once before, and afterwards the detective on the receiving end took a three month stint working the evidence locker. He marveled at Samantha's boldness. *Two months on maternity leave and she's lost her damn mind.* Charles watched the section chief open his mouth, wincing as he braced himself for her subsequent destruction.

But the moment never came.

Instead, Sergeant Briske said nothing, turning to the others with a disappointed shake of his head.

"Profiles and patrols," the sergeant said simply, eyeing each of the detectives in turn. "I know leads have been pretty light for the perpetrator in all this, so I want all of the metadata we have on our victims sent to Sam for cross-referencing."

Sam gave a thumbs up. "Got it, Sarge."

"I want any commonalities with current cases or any stabbings from the last three months highlighted and indexed. Allison, I know you're still on leave but I'd appreciate if you came in for a few days and give Sam a hand with the older files. I'll comp you time on the back end."

Detective Jimenez scowled from the leather chair, but accepted her assignment with a nod.

Charles was blown away, Sergeant Briske never comp'd time for *anyone. I've got to get me a kid…*

"Chuck, Perry, Todd, I need your case summaries and any subject descriptions sent to Sam so he knows what to look for in the older cases," Sergeant Briske continued, circling the three detectives with a pointed finger. "And I need that today, before anyone goes home."

Detective Raines crossed his arms tighter over the dirt-stained shirt, mumbling curses beneath his breath.

Sergeant Briske's eyes narrowed again, but he let it slide. He had enough experience to know grumbling helped soften the blow of bad news. He turned to Charles. "Chuck, I'm treating your CSP case as the start of all of this since it's had the most development, what can you tell us about it?"

Charles winced again. He knew that sooner or later it would come back to him, but he still wasn't sure how to frame this mess in a way that didn't deliberately send them out on a snipe hunt. He cleared his throat to buy more time.

"Uhhh," he began, feeling the weight of the room's attention. Looking up to the ceiling for inspiration, he sighed heavily, and opted for the truth. *Or, at least, a version of the truth.* "The first known incident with the killer started at a gas station in Pueblo. The subject slashed a man's throat, then hijacked a bystander's vehicle as she escaped, heading north out of the city. Following a traffic stop, the subject got the drop on Trooper Temmen, CSP, and fled the scene on top of the bystander's vehicle. She later crashed into a rockface along I-25, and presumably the subject fled from that scene up into the Springs. I've got nothing in the way of motive, origin, or a description solid enough for you to work with, but the main commonality is the murder weapon. The subject uses a thick-edged, jagged blade—something sturdy and sharp—with deep, powerful strikes to the victims' throats or body. It's unclear about the exact kind of weapon, but look for something heavy and sharp—like a serrated axe."

Sergeant Briske frowned. "A serrated *axe*?"

Charles shrugged, running an uneasy hand through his hair. "Or, you know, something weird—like a…banana knife."

The section chief's frown deepened but he said nothing, turning instead to face the other detectives. "Well, I suppose that's as good a starting point for a profile as any. Sam, do the best you can looking for any cases with odd, edged weapons."

Sergeant Briske paused, he knew the next part was going to sting. "Which brings me to the latter half of our strategy—patrols. Uniformed patrols are plussing up all around the city for additional cars and rounds at night. That's hefty strain on manpower, so to help ease the load, we've decided to pull in plain-clothes officers too—across *all* divisions."

For the second time that morning, the sergeant's words hung in the air over a silent office. Only this time, mere moments passed before it erupted into flurries of indignation.

Sergeant Briske silenced the grumbling resentment with a sweep of his heavy hand. "It's not a discussion, everyone is pulling in on this. I'll kick out a rotation schedule this afternoon, but I need a volunteer to take tonight."

Charles looked around an office full of shoegazing and studiously avoided eye contact. *What the hell, not like I had plans anyway…*

Charles raised his hand. "I'll take it, Sarge."

"Excellent, thanks," the section chief replied, accepting Charles' offer with a curt nod. "As for the rest of you, standby for your rotations and get that metadata to Sam. The quicker we catch this guy, the sooner we go back to normal."

Sergeant Briske surveyed the dissatisfied faces surrounding his office. Pissing and moaning was the primary response to most new things in a cop's life, and he readily accepted his role as the emissary of their frustration. In the end, they all had their part to play in this, and he trusted them to get the job done.

"Remember folks," the sergeant said, "*Proactive*, not *reactive*. Dismissed."

Charles filed out with the rest of the detectives, falling in step behind disgruntled mumbling and shuffled feet. As the group split off to their respective cubicles, Charles tapped Detective Raines on the shoulder.

"Hey Perry, got a minute?"

The big detective lumbered to a stop, turning towards Charles with doleful eyes. "What's up?"

"I need to call in that favor. Savannah's got a TPO filed on a creep from class and needs it served. I figured you wouldn't mind playing the tough guy?"

Perry looked down on his soiled shirt and stained khakis, then over to his cubicle to the mountain of paperwork stacked on the desk.

"Sure thing, Chuck," he replied, voice trailing off to match his gaze. "I'll add it to the list."

Charles hunched over the keyboard at his desk, typing the finishing touches on his email to Sam. In truth, it was the same update he'd sent Sergeant Briske earlier that week, minus the connection to the AAFES truck. *No use dredging up dead ends*, he thought as he clicked the send arrow.

Charles leaned back and stretched, the pops of his back echoing in the cubicle's silence. A glance at the computer's clock told him it was a quarter past eleven, and the rumble in his stomach reminded him he'd skipped breakfast. He fished around in his coat for a DexU bar—the last of the box from the cabinet—and was about to tear into the wrapper when his phone rang.

Buzzing violin strings split the quiet of the office as Charles snatched the phone out of his pocket, scowling all the way. He'd tried changing the ringtone last Thursday, only to find his settings had been locked. At this point, asking Savannah for the password was tantamount to admitting defeat, and he'd rather grit his teeth than swallow his pride.

Charles swiped a thumb across the screen. "Detective Davner."

"Hey Detective, it's Cynthia Baysere," said the cheerful voice on the line, "from the Risen Hearts shelter."

Recognition flashed through Charles, along with a sprinkle of guilt. He'd meant to call her after he'd found Celeste's body in the tunnel—even had it jotted down in his notebook—but as with most things of late, time had escaped him.

"Uh, yes," he replied, stalling for time. "How can I help you?"

"Well, I wanted to check in if you'd had any luck locating Celeste and Marcus yet?"

Sure did, all the bits it didn't like…

"Uh, no, not yet," Charles lied. "But we're working some strong leads."

"I understand," she replied, disappointment sanding off the chipper edges of her tone. "Thank you for trying though. I'm just glad *someone* is still looking for them."

Charles cringed, the sprinkling of guilt swelling to a downpour. "I'm sorry I don't have more for you right now. Is there anything else you needed?"

A few seconds passed on the line. There was a hitch in her voice when Cynthia spoke again.

"Yes. I—*we*—had some more residents go missing last night."

Holy shit, how fucking hungry is this thing?

"Who?" asked Charles, flipping open his notebook and grabbing a pen.

"Pax and Masi, they were two of our newer residents, both checked in last Wednesday. Martín—our night clerk—said that they were going for a walk up to the HAS garden."

Charles nodded, jotting the location down. "Can you describe them for me?"

"Pax is a big guy—I mean heavy, not tall—with blue eyes, a grey ponytail, and a tattoo of a palm tree on his neck. Masi's a stick—really slender and small—brown eyes and white hair—she's also missing her two front teeth."

"Ages? Ethnicity?" asked Charles.

"Both white, late forties? Early fifties? I can look them up on the intake sheet if you want me too."

"No, that's plenty to go off of," Charles said, scribbling furiously. "And you said they were headed north from the shelter?"

"Yes, towards the HAS garden."

"Then I'll start there," said Charles, setting the notebook down on the desk. "Anything else I should know?"

"No, that's it." Cynthia sounded relieved, like she was just happy someone cared enough to listen. "Thank you, Detective."

"No problem. Call me anytime," Charles replied, meaning every word. "But, with all that's going on, you might want to keep your residents indoors. Especially at night."

Quiet stretched on the other line.

"I mean, I can try," Cynthia said slowly, worry creeping back into her voice. "But I can't exactly lock them in. Freedom of movement is *extremely* important to our residents."

Charles sighed, weighing how much to share with her. "I understand, just…do what you can. We're putting some extra patrols out for the next few nights, I'll make sure we have some in that area as well. Help look after your folks."

"Really? You'd do that for us?"

"I'll see to it personally."

Charles' footsteps echoed off the concrete path, his corduroy collar turned up against the chill of the evening breeze. The creek burbled off to his left, flowing around rocks and sandbanks as he made his way south along the greenway trail. He'd left the office late, swinging by the apartment to check in on Petunia and Savannah before snagging a quick bite to eat as he ducked out the door. But a lukewarm Hot Pocket and half a can of flat RedBull could only sustain him for so long—his stomach had started growling almost as soon as he parked at the HAS Demonstration Garden.

The wind picked up again, long grasses waving furiously by the water's edge. Charles braced himself as it buffeted him, digging his hands deeper into his pockets as the wind tugged on the loose edges of his coat. He trudged on, scowling. Even the weather was against him today.

Predictably, he'd found no sign of Cynthia's missing residents at the garden. No blood stains on the concrete. No torn clothing. Just clean, well-tended horticulture starting its spring bloom.

Not that it feels much like spring. His teeth ground as the wind pushed on him again, icy currents flooding down from the mountains as the sun set behind them. Charles sighed. Searching the gardens had been a long shot. Logically, he knew that. But he'd held out hope that something would've turned up—that *anything* in this case might finally go his way.

He passed by some empty tennis courts, the nets still down from winter remodeling. Spotting an empty can, he occupied himself by kicking it along the concrete path. He chased the can almost half a block until he found one of the park's bins, depositing it neatly before carrying on.

"On your left!" came a shout behind him, a jogger in a grey hoodie whipping past as he stepped to the side.

Charles shook his head, moving back to the center and continuing his meandering patrol. *Haven't you heard, buddy? Jogging kills.* Still, he eyed the man as he sped off, appreciating the toned muscle rippling under his tight shorts.

A baseball diamond spread out to his right, the chalk lines fresh and clean against the dewy grass. Park District seasons wouldn't start for another few weeks, so they were likely to stay that way. Charles had never been one for team sports, but Savannah had played softball in pickup leagues from her elementary years up through high school. He'd whiled away plenty of afternoons with his butt numb on a creaking aluminum bench, watching her strikeout at bat again and again.

He turned left on the path, just past one of the creek's many small waterfalls. A footbridge spanned the water, connecting both sides of the greenway trail. Crossing the bridge, he slid his hand along the bare metal railing, the wind whistling in his ears as it rushed past him. Shadows lengthened ahead of him, drawing away from the steps of his black leather shoes.

Stepping off the bridge, he turned left again, heading north along the trail on the other side of the creek. After searching the garden, he'd planned on making a loop, walking the greenway's winding concrete for a couple of hours until he'd done enough patrolling to satisfy Sergeant Briske. *Who knows, might even find a clue if I'm lucky…*

The wind reasserted itself, sending a burger wrapper sailing past his ankles. Charles watched it tumble through the air, losing it in a nearby parking lot. He'd given half a thought to chasing it down before it blew under a red Subaru, but banished it with a shrug instead. His sense of environmental obligation only stretched so far.

Charles shivered a little as he walked, the silence of the park broken only by the solitary squawk of a nesting magpie. He regretted leaving his headphones in the car. Both Todd and Savannah had been raving about a new scifi podcast that had started the week prior. Charles hadn't given it a try yet, but tonight made a compelling argument to start. *Could've at least gotten through a few episodes by now,* he mused, *and it'd get them to shut up about how much I'm missing out.* The sun continued its descent behind the mountains, twilight deepening into dusk as he walked.

Charles spotted the jogger from before heading back towards him, arms pumping confidently, his grey hood up to block the chill. *Should I smile when he passes me again? Wave? Thumbs-up?* They were just far enough apart to give him several moments to consider his social options. *After all, might be the only other person I see tonight.* Charles debated with himself as the man drew near, locking eyes as the distance shrank between them. Inspiration flashed through him.

"On your left!" he called out as the runner passed, tacking on most of a smile.

The man returned the smile, jogging backwards a few steps to follow it up with a wave.

Charles smiled wider and waved back, watching him run off for a few more moments before turning back around. *See, Savannah, I do things. I meet people.* He had just picked up a foot to continue walking when he heard a rock skitter behind him, followed by a surprised shout and the dull thud of a body hitting concrete.

Charles whipped around, hustling over in the direction of the noise. Ahead of him, the jogger was in the process of unsprawling himself from the path, letting out a few groans along the way.

"You okay, buddy?" Charles asked.

"Yeah, I'm good," the man said, massaging his ankle as he sat. "Just rolled it on a loose rock."

"Happens to the best of us," Charles replied, extending a hand to help him up. Hood down and up close, Charles got a better look at him. He had olive skin and nice, curly black hair.

"Thanks." The man took Charles' hand, steadying himself on one leg as he tested the other. He grimaced as he put weight on it, sucking a breath in through clenched teeth.

"Sprained?" asked Charles, jerking a thumb in the general direction of the garden. "I've got a compression wrap in my car. I can run and grab it if you want."

"I'm good, my house isn't too far." The man looked up, flashing Charles another smile. "Thanks though. You're too kind."

Charles felt a swell of warmth inside. He tamped it down and shrugged. "I try."

Steadier now, the man tried the leg again, gingerly putting weight on the ball of his foot. He sucked in another terse breath but gave Charles a solid thumbs-up. "Good to go. I'm gonna head home now. Take care, man."

"You too," replied Charles, slinging some finger-guns his way.

The man chuckled, hobbling off down the concrete path.

Alone once again in the deepening gloom, Charles kicked himself as he watched him leave. *Smooth going, Charles. A hundred ways to play that and you chose finger-guns.* He sighed, scuffing his heel on the concrete. Looking back down the lane, he spotted the jogger stopped at the end of the bridge, leaning on the railing as he looked down.

Charles cupped a hand to his mouth and yelled, "Still good?"

The man straightened up from the railing and waved back. "Yeah, man. Just thought I saw something weird moving by the water."

Weird? Charles brow furrowed. *By the water?*

It took exactly one second for the words to sink in.

"*NO!* GET BACK! RUN!" Charles sprinted towards the bridge, heels pounding on the trail. "*RUN!*"

The man drew back from the railing. Charles could see confusion flash across his face as he got closer.

Charles opened his mouth to shout another warning, but he felt the words die in his throat. A wide, domed head rose behind the man, the waning light glinting green off its oily sheen. Clawed forelimbs gripped the railing, pulling the narrow body up and over with a metallic clink. Fully on the bridge, the creature rose on six, multi-jointed limbs. Staring down at the jogger, it seemed bigger than it was in the sewer—about the size of a horse.

It took a step forward as the man hopped backwards, ankle giving out underneath him. He tumbled out to the concrete, scooting backwards in desperation on his hands and feet.

Charles' hand found his pistol, thumbing the holster release as he ran. He was still too far to take a shot—not that the hollow-point rounds had done him much good before—but he took comfort as the M&P's stippled backstrap filled his hand.

He was in line with the bridge now, almost to the jogger. His gun was up, the glowing green dot of his front sight bouncing wildly ahead in his field of vision.

The creature took another step forward, easily catching up with the crawling man. Charles saw the toothy maw open, a spiky forelimb lifting off the ground in slow motion, raising up for the killing blow.

The flash of his muzzle split the night. 9mm rounds ripped out the barrel as the pistol barked in his hand. He was close now, still sprinting—one hand on his gun and the other outstretched.

The creature shuddered under the impact—a few of his shots found their place across its pale underside and on its flared skull. It reeled back from the noise, rearing up on its back four legs.

Charles kept shooting. He couldn't see any wounds, but he heard the bullets ricocheting off with a hollow *tink*. He'd reached the jogger now, his hand closing around the soft fabric hood.

He pulled, yanking the man back across the concrete as the first of the creature's forelimbs came down. Off balance from the shooting, it missed the jogger's chest, slicing deep along his side instead. The grey hoodie ripped open, blood pouring out onto the concrete as Charles dragged him up the path. The man cried in pain, his voice ringing out sudden and clear as the gun in Charles' hand went silent. Charles didn't waste time changing it out with a fresh magazine, he just stowed the spent pistol in a pocket and ran.

Out on the bridge, the creature recovered quickly, coming back to center with a few snaps of its toothy jaws. The broad head turned in their direction, and Charles could feel the hungry gaze of its many red eyes. Gravel and asphalt crunched underfoot as he made it to the parking lot.

The creature shrieked, six legs shaking in rage as it witnessed its prey being stolen away. It took a step off the bridge to give chase. Charles' mind raced, reconsidering if he should stop to reload. The man groaned loudly as he bumped along the pavement, answering Charles' internal dilemma. *Don't stop. PULL.*

The creature took another step forward off the bridge and onto the concrete trail. Idly, Charles wondered how fast it could run.

By now, he'd put a few cars between it and them, passing a red Subaru with a burger wrapper stuck inside the front wheel. Charles kept dragging, blocking everything out as he watched for the creature's next move. He was waiting for the thing to take another step. His lungs burned, heart thundering in his chest as he pulled. His heel clipped the concrete curb, sending him stumbling backwards as he pulled them out of the parking lot and into the street. Charles kept going, unwilling—*unable*—to stop. He eyed the monster through the sweat in his eyes, but it stayed put on the greenway, utterly motionless as it watched them flee.

It was so quiet, so eerily still as it stared back at them, that it gave Charles a second's pause.

What's it planning?

His world lit up in the blinding white of headlights.

And then there was nothing but darkness.

Chapter 14

Sunday

"Well, that was fucking stupid."

Charles cradled the icepack to his head, his other hand clutched tight to his bruised ribs. "What? Saving a guy's life? Or getting hit by a car? 'Cause it's not like I planned that last part, *Andrea*."

"*All of it!*" snapped Detective Morales, long black curls shaking in exasperation. "The car! The gunfight! Tracking down the monster *by yourself?!* It was ALL fuckin' *stupid!*"

Charles leaned against the hospital wall, the gurney underneath him letting out a small squeak. "In my defense, I didn't plan that last part either."

"I don't think you planned *any* of it!" Andrea cried out, throwing up her hands. "Just *bumble-fucked* your way in and were *just* lucky enough to skid out alive. *Again!*"

Charles squinted up at the furious detective, wincing as pain shot through the side of his head. "You know, I called you up here so we could plan out our next move. I didn't ask for the sass too."

"You called me up here because you needed *someone* to pick your busted ass up who wasn't gonna press you on the details about a ten-foot sewer-monster gutting joggers in the fuckin' park!" she said, wagging a finger in his face. "And you didn't have to ask. The sass comes complementary."

"Well as long as I'm not charged extra," grumbled Charles, shifting the icepack again. "Speaking of gutting, is the guy ok?"

"Alive, for now," Andrea grunted, straightening back up. "From what the doc told me, the laceration to his side was deep enough that they were worried about it nicking his intestine. He's still in the O.R., probably the rest of the day. Even when he does get out, they'll probably keep him under until Monday."

Charles nodded, instantly regretting it as needles of pain stabbed behind his eyes. "Saves me from paperwork for now at least. Any grand ideas on how to spin this?"

"You were on serial-killer patrol right? Plain clothes? Just say you saw him getting mugged and jumped in to intervene."

Spree killer, he corrected in his mind, just before realizing it didn't matter. The ache in his head died down to a dull throb. "What about the scene? That means I fired off fifteen rounds. All with no perp or body."

"Soooo, the mugger ran off, and you didn't get a good look at him. As for the rounds, chalk 'em up to you being a bad fuckin' shot. I dunno, man." Andrea shrugged. "But I think we've got bigger problems first."

"Like what?"

"Like our monster is bagging more people every day, and you said it was bigger than it was on Wednesday."

Charles nodded, slowly this time. "About the size of a horse this time."

"Exactly, and we've doubled our victim number in the same amount of time. It's ramping up its body count *and* growing larger. We've got to figure out how to stop it before it's the size of a house and snatching thirty people a night."

"I get what you're saying, but we've still got nothing in the way of understanding this thing. How it works, how to stop it—*nothing*. I put fifteen rounds into that thing without so much as a scratch." Charles flipped the icepack over to the cool side, transferring it from his head to his ribs. "We need information. And I don't know about you, but my rolodex is noticeably light on *monster experts*."

Andrea ran her hands through her hair, pulling the curls back with an elastic tie. "Doesn't your sister go to college around here? She know any scientists?"

"No, she's a history major," Charles said, grimacing as he reached an arm up and stretched his bruised side. He stopped suddenly, looking up at Andrea. "Wait! I forgot she's in a zoology class, maybe we can talk to her professor?"

Andrea's eyes flashed. "Perfect! Bitchy scientist said we should try a zoologist."

Bitchy scientist? Confusion crossed Charles' face but he shrugged it off, whipping out his phone instead. "Sure. I'll call Savannah, see if she can set up a meeting."

Andrea looked at the clock in the hall. "Right now? It's only four a.m."

"No, no, it's fine," said Charles, as the dial tone whirred in his ear. *About time I got her back...*

Clark Morrison wasn't in the habit of wearing a bowtie before nine on a Sunday morning. He greeted most Sunday mornings in a matched set of flannel pajamas, pressing start on his electric teapot before strolling down the driveway to pick up the paper. With the Gazette secured, he'd then make his rounds, checking in on each of the twenty-three glass-walled enclosures that filled the rooms of his modest home. Heat lamps were adjusted, misters engaged, food bowls refilled. The needs of his charges were many and varied—hailing as they did from biomes across the globe—but he saw them met every day before settling down at the kitchen table with his paper and a fresh cup of lemongrass tea. Clark Morrison was a creature of many habits and, like the menagerie of fish, reptiles, and invertebrates he cared for each day, he flourished best in a stable, sustainable environment.

But when one of his students calls him at seven a.m., requesting that he meet with her older brother—to assist in a murder investigation no less—habits bowed to the demands of duty and curiosity. And so, Clark found himself that morning in a freshly ironed poplin shirt and floral bowtie, offsetting his bright blue eyes and red goatee. He had no idea how one dresses for a criminal investigation, but there was a comforting familiarity in his standard teaching outfit.

The two detectives sat across from the professor in a pair of deep mauve armchairs, each holding a steaming mug of lemongrass tea. They were an unlikely duo, and a far cry from any of the detectives Clark had seen on TV. The one on the right—Savannah's older brother—wore a scuffed Carhartt jacket over a wrinkled button-up shirt and ripped jeans. There was an adhesive bandage on the side of his head and more than once Clark watched him wince and grab his ribs during a particularly large yawn. The one on the left—she'd introduced herself as Detective Morales—wore an expensive chic leather coat just tight enough to show off her broad shoulders, a simple white blouse, grey chinos, and shiny black combat boots. A matching set of heavy bags draped under both their eyes.

Clark set his own tea down on a sandstone coaster, smiling as he leaned back on the edge of a plain maple desk. "So, how can I help you two?"

Andrea sipped at her tea, sizing the professor up as her boots swung just above the hardwood floor. He certainly looked the part of a science geek, but this far into the investigation she was fast losing patience with all the false starts and dead ends. Looking over to Charles, she motioned with her mug for him to answer.

Charles suppressed another yawn, massaging his bruised ribs

with his free hand. "Uh, yeah, sorry to bother you like this but like Savannah mentioned, we're working some, uh, *unusual* homicides and hoped you might lend your expertise."

Clark nodded, long fingers tapping the rim of his floral-print mug. "How is Savannah, by the way? Was she able to get her protection order sorted out?"

"So it's a matter of—" Charles pause mid-answer, momentarily caught off guard by the question. *Most of the time you mention a homicide and that's all they want to talk about.* He searched the professor's face for hidden intentions, but all he saw was a pleasant smile and bright blue eyes tinged at the ends with concern.

"Her paperwork went through, and the other party is set to be served," Charles began again. "So, she's…managing. Why?"

Relief washed over the professor's face. "Wonderful, thank you for telling me. When she first came to me at the start of the semester and told me about her problems with Chris, I was so *worried* about her." He picked up the mug from the desk, clutching it tight in his hands. "I'm so glad she was able to get the protective order in place. I told her if she needed, I was more than happy to record the lectures for her or let her complete her assignments remotely so she didn't have to come on campus. Whatever she needed."

Charles softened, his earlier suspicions melting away at the emotion in the other man's voice. "That's very kind of you."

Clark sighed, inspecting the contents of the cup. "My classroom is supposed to be a safe space for *all* students, and for her to be harassed like that by a peer. I couldn't let that happen, not on my watch. It's just…it's *unconscionable*."

"I appreciate your concern, but she's managed to handle the whole thing pretty well." said Charles, offering a wry smile. "She told me you offered to testify for the TPO hearing. It wasn't needed, but I appreciate that too."

"That's good to hear," Clark said, looking up from his cup. He locked eyes with Charles, warm smile returning to his nebbish face. "I should've known she'd be fine. She's considerably self-reliant."

"That's a word for it," snorted Charles. Looking into those bright blue eyes, he couldn't help but smile a little wider.

Andrea coughed loudly into her hand.

She waved to them with her mug. "Gents. The case, *please*."

"Right, right." Charles shook his head, regretting it instantly after a moment of stabbing pain. "So, Professor Morrison—"

The blue eyes twinkled. "Please, call me Clark."

Charles felt warmth rising in cheeks *Focus. Murderous sewer monster. Focus.* "So—Clark—as I said earlier, we had some odd homicides recently and we're hoping you can help."

The professor chuckled. "Well, I haven't the faintest idea how herpetology intersects with forensics, but I'm more than willing to help."

Charles sucked in a deep breath, unsure exactly where to begin. He looked over to Andrea, then back to Clark. *Fuck it.* Setting the mug of tea on the floor, he began with the truth. "In the last two weeks we've had seven deaths. All of them violent, similar victims, same M.O., and all of them in Colorado Springs."

"My God," Clark whispered.

"*Mhmm,*" Andrea piped up from behind her mug. "Don't forget the attempted murder last night."

"Little hard for *that*," Charles said, rolling his eyes as he jerked a thumb towards his bandaged head. "But yeah, I guess that puts us at eight. The thing is, Clark, these aren't your usual homicides—mostly in that we know our suspect isn't, you know, *human.*"

Clark's eyes went wide, the floral-print mug gripped tightly in his hands. "What? Like a predatory *animal?* In the *Springs?*"

He looked over to Andrea, hoping for some kind of logical explanation.

Instead, the detective leaned back in her chair, smirking as she sipped her tea. She cocked an eyebrow at him. "Highly unlikely, perhaps, but surely not outside the realm of *extreme* possibility?"

Clark's mouth opened and closed several times without a sound. He looked back at Charles.

Charles shrugged. "Weird but true. We wouldn't be here otherwise."

Clark dragged a hand down across his face. "Wow. That's just...*wow.* I mean, I suppose a mountain lion is large enough to chance predation on a person. And it could have become desperate enough to expand its territory to encroach on city limits."

Andrea shook her head. "Sorry, *Professor*, it's not that easy. We don't know what it is exactly, but we know it's not a mountain lion. Or a bear. Or a fuckin' coyote. It's something *different*. And that's why we need you. We need you to help us figure out this thing—where it lives, what makes it tick, *yadda yadda.*"

Clark turned back to Charles. "So, you think some kind of animal is killing people?"

"Yep."

"And you don't know what kind of animal it is?"

"Nope."

"But you *do* know it's not a mountain lion, or any of the other native predators?"

"Yep."

"But you have *no* ideas on the species?"

"Ran into it twice. Like nothing I've ever seen before."

"Whoa."

"Yep."

"And so you want me to build some kind of profile—like a serial killer—to help you find it?"

"Pretty much."

Clark sucked in a deep breath, puffing out his cheeks as he exhaled. "That's a pretty tall order. Normally biologists observe the species first, *then* describe them."

Andrea circled the group with her mug. "Welcome to the party, pal. We're all in a little over our head."

Clark chewed this over, fingertips softly tapping the mug's rim. He looked back at Charles. "Is this going to be one of those situations where I help you but then quiet gentlemen in dark suits swear me to secrecy? Promise me I'm not going to disappear a few months from now in the back of a black helicopter?"

Charles shrugged, spreading his hands out in front of him. "All cards on the table, Clark, I have no idea how this all shakes out in the end. We've gotten by so far through playing this close to the chest, but without knowing what this thing is or where it came from, there's no telling what happens when we stop it. But right now, we need your help."

Clark nodded, responsibility settling over him like a heavy coat. The clock on the wall chimed softly, a gentle reminder that on any other Sunday, he'd have just finished with the paper and strapping on sneakers for his morning run. Clark Morrison was a creature of habit, and well aware of the consequences that followed imposing a radical stimulus on a stable ecosystem. He sighed, staring down into the lemongrass dregs clinging to the bottom of the floral-print mug.

"Before we begin, does anyone else need more tea?"

"There's so many unknown variables at work here. So, let's start with what you do know about it," said Clark, pulling a legal pad and pen out from a desk drawer. He drew two lines on the page, separating it out into quadrants. He marked each one, labeling them as 'description,' 'diet,' 'habitat,' and 'behavior,' before looking up at the two detectives leaning over him. "How big is it?"

"Pretty fuckin' big," snorted Andrea, stretching her hand up over her head to illustrate the creature's height.

Charles nodded, adding, "As of last night, about the size of a horse, height and width."

Clark mouthed the words 'as of last night' silently, befuddlement following on his face. He looked up at Charles, but shook his head and let it drop. Now was not the time. "Okay, so one to two meters tall, and about two meters long. What else? Body shape? Bipedal or quadrupedal? Scales, feathers, or fur?"

Andrea pointed to Charles. "That's all you, buddy. I only saw it when we were running in the dark."

"Right…"

Truth be told, Charles hadn't caught the clearest glimpse of it himself, what with all the running and shooting and more running. *Not to mention getting hit by a fucking car.* Still, he recognized his role as the one in the best position to describe it.

Charles closed his eyes, pulling his memories up through the dismal fog of his tired brain. "It's green. With red eyes—four of them actually—all lined up under a big, shield-shaped head. It's got one mouth—not sure if that matters—and a lot of teeth, just *so many* fucking teeth. Uh, body shape, it's got kind of a round body—tube-shaped—with tan underneath. No feathers or fur, maybe scales? I dunno, but it's got a thick shell—like some kind of giant, evil crab—that's really tough, especially the head. It shrugged off a few nine-mil rounds, even direct shots."

Clark nodded, furiously jotting notes on the legal pad. "Anything else?"

"Yes, it's got six legs, so that's uh," Charles pressed his fingertips against his closed eyes. "Sex-pedal?"

"Hexapedal, but close," Clark said, a wry smile on his face. "This is all rad, by the way. Incredibly bizarre, unlike anything I've ever heard of, but just…stinking *rad.*"

"As long as someone's having fun," Charles snorted. "Any ideas on what it is?"

"Absolutely none!" Clark replied, bobbing his head enthusiastically. "Some kind of enormous, arthropoid predator—in *Colorado* of all places? Just unreal. The closest terrestrial analogue I could think of would be a coconut crab—but they're not even a quarter of that size."

"Terrestrial?" asked Andrea, interest suddenly peaked. "You think it's some kind of alien? 'Cause if that's the case I've got some theories—"

Clark cut her off. "No, I meant terrestrial as in land-dwelling. Most arthropods are limited from growing too large on land because of their weight—a carapace that large would be too heavy for their muscles to move effectively—which is why the largest invertebrates are marine. But not even a Japanese Spider Crab gets as large as you described—and their legs are far too spindly to support their weight."

Undeterred, Andrea pressed on. "What if it was mutated? Like someone changed it to make it stronger or bigger?"

Clark chuckled and shook his head. "I'm afraid that'd be impossible. In spite of some just *amazing* movies, you really can't scale up an existing arthropod to wreak terror on Small Town, U.S.A. They'd never be strong enough to move on their own. Not to mention that without lungs they'd be utterly unable to pull in enough oxygen through their spiracles. It's part of the reason we haven't seen giant insects since the Carboniferous period."

Charles scratched the back of his head. "So it needs lungs, what's the big deal."

"It's not *just* the lungs," Clark assured him. "You described it as having some kind of outer-shell—one strong enough to repel bullets. A carapace that thick is unheard of on a larger animal because they already have issues dissipating heat due to their size—one of the reasons that elephants and other large mammals don't have thick fur."

Andrea crossed her arms, wholly unconvinced. "Yeah? What about woolly mammoths?"

"Excellent idea!" Clark replied, eyes flashing with excitement. "But, no. They, and the other Pleistocene megafauna, were specifically adapted for a frigid, glacial environment that doesn't exist anymore. That's what makes it so spectacularly preposterous that your creature is in Colorado Springs. Animals evolve to match a specific environmental condition, and they only thrive under similar conditions. And nothing in our front-range biome could give rise to something like this."

"But it's here now, Clark, that's the thing," Charles said, rubbing his tired eyes. Rather than clarifying, it felt like all of this scientific talk was leading them in circles. "Nobody here is suggesting that it's a native. And I don't know how you qualify thriving exactly, but seven bodies in a week with no sign of stopping is *probably* a good marker."

The professor's enthusiasm dimmed a bit at the reminder of the casualties. "Fair point, but that's a problem in and of itself. Any predator—even one that big—really shouldn't be feeding so much in so short a time. Humans might not be the most nutritiously satisfying diet, but we're certainly large. If it were, say, a lion instead we'd expect its predation to be much smaller, more in the realm of one or two kills a week."

"Could there be more than one?" Charles asked, the horrible

thought dawning on him.

Clark mulled it over, stroking his goatee. "More mouths to feed would make sense, but only if they're a social animal. Otherwise you'd expect territorial aggression to force them apart. Any evidence of pack hunting? Or a family unit?"

"Thankfully, no. Just the one," said Charles, suppressing a shudder as the events of the previous night flashed through his mind. "It's gotten bigger though, even just over the last few days."

Clark nodded. "It would certainly help explain an atypically aggressive feeding response. That, or if it was preparing for an energy-draining activity like hibernation…or reproduction."

Charles and Andrea exchanged horrified looks.

"We have to kill this thing before it lays eggs," she announced carefully, forcing a feigned calm into her voice. "How do we find it?"

"Well, assuming it operates like any other animal, you identify its territory and narrow the search within those confines for a burrow or a nest," the professor replied. "Most territories are limited by factors of geography, resources, and environmental conditions. I know you haven't interacted with it much, but any reference points on its behavior and the locations you encountered it can help narrow that down."

"Problem is we've only seen it twice, and both under vastly different conditions," Charles sighed, massaging away a spike of pain in his ribs with one hand.

"Not…ideal," admitted Clark, picking up his pen to jot more notes. "But it's a start. Tell me more about them?"

"Oh!" Andrea blurted, inspiration flashing through her. "The crime scenes, too! That gives us a few more to work with."

"Sure does," agreed Charles, fishing out his notebook. "We can plot them too, use that as a territory marker."

"I've got a topographical map of the Springs hanging on the wall," said Clark, pointing a finger down the hall. "We can use that." He turned back to Charles as Andrea left to retrieve it. "Now, the two times you saw it."

"The first was underground, around midday," Charles said. "by Monument Creek, just south of USA Judo."

"In the sewers!" Andrea called out from the hallway.

Clark shot Charles a quizzical look.

"She means the storm drains," he muttered, rolling his eyes. "But, yeah, it was in some kind of chamber in the drain. It'd stashed some bodies in there."

"Strong contender for a burrow," said Clark, writing in the appropriate quadrant. "But that will be more conclusive with more information. What was it like down there? Damp? Humid? Hot? Cold?"

"Damp, a little I guess, but not too humid. Muddy, like you'd expect." Charles scratched the back of his head, racking his memory. He recalled the goosebumps and wishing he'd brought a jacket. "Chilly."

Clark waved the pen in his direction. "And what about the second time you saw it? Were there any shared conditions with the tunnels?"

"It was night, so yeah, darkness," said Charles. "And by the creek, but not in it, so the same general muddy conditions."

Clark nodded, tongue pressed in his cheek as he wrote. "So not an aquatic predator per se, but it definitely enjoys moisture."

"The other ones were at night too," Andrea added, laying the map out on the plain wood desk. She looked pointedly at the professor. "Command strips? Really? Took forever to get this down."

"I didn't want to put holes in the wall," Clark admitted sheepishly.

Charles looked over the map, notebook in hand as he flipped back and forth between the various incidents. Clark offered him a pencil, and he used it to mark out the dates and locations of each of the scenes. He stepped back when he was done, letting the others lean in over his work.

Andrea let out a low whistle. "Looks like the creek is our center. All of the attacks are either on it or nearby."

"Large predator, probably needs the cover and brush around the creek to ambush its prey," said Clark, surveying the marks. "It might even use it for travel." He tapped the map with his finger. "Nocturnal attacks are another good detail, most predators take advantage of weaknesses in their prey, and it would make sense why no one's seen it before. What else is similar about those nights? Raining? Windy? Full moon?"

Charles thought for a moment, hands digging into the deep pockets of his coat. *The same coat I was wearing last night.*

"Cold!" he exclaimed suddenly. "They all happened on cold nights!"

"You sure?" asked Andrea. "You weren't there for most of them."

"No, but I heard enough bitching from Perry and Todd," he answered confidently. "All of the attacks were on chilly nights."

"Again, matching the conditions you found in the storm drain," noted Clark, underlining his notes. "Cooler temperatures would definitely fit with a large carapace too—helps dissipate heat. It probably retreats into its burrow during the day and only comes out at night to hunt."

"Sounds like the storm drain is our best bet to find it then,"

Charles said, looking over to Andrea. "Midday, when its hottest outside and we're sure it'll be down there."

"Man, I fucking *hate* sewers," Andrea shuddered. "But you're right. We need to hit this thing where we know it'll be."

"Alright, we know where and when, but we still need a *how*," said Charles, tapping his holster. "Hollow-points clearly ain't the answer."

"Bigger guns," Clark remarked suddenly, drawing their attention back to the seated professor. "I'm not surprised your pistol wasn't effective, it's a large animal *and* it has an outer shell. You need a heavy-caliber hunting rifle, or at least a shotgun with slugs. When I worked at the Denver Zoo, our response team was armed with both—slugs for the medium predators, rifles for the larger herbivores." He looked at the two detectives and shrugged. "You wouldn't hunt an elk with a handgun."

Charles cocked an eyebrow at Andrea. "I've never hunted elk. You?"

"*Pfffft*, not a lot of elk running around in Manhattan," she shot back. "But bigger guns, we can get. I can run back to Pueblo for our armory."

"It's almost noon now," Clark noted. "When were you guys planning this?"

Charles dragged a hand over his heavy eyelids, stifling a yawn. Being awake for the past twenty-four hours was exerting its merciless toll. He looked over at Andrea, spotting the same slow-blinking, hang-dog exhaustion mirrored on her face. "We can't today, neither of us are in shape right now to fight. If we're going to go after this thing, we need to be sharp. We need some sleep."

"Agreed," said Andrea, pulling out her phone. She thumbed over to the weather app, tapping it open. "Supposed to be warm tonight. Even better, it'll be hot tomorrow. Good chance it'll be down there then."

"Tomorrow works," Charles nodded, losing his struggle and giving in to a deep yawn. "We ride at dawn?"

"How about noon," replied Andrea, echoing with a yawn of her own. "More time to prep. We might even catch it sleeping."

"Deal," said Charles. He turned back to the professor. "Clark, you were an amazing help. I can't tell you how much we appreciate it."

"Of course, good hunting for both of you. Maybe when it's over we can meet up so you can tell me all about it," Clark said, flashing a smile as he picked up his tea. "As long as the men in black helicopters don't snatch me up first."

Charles couldn't help but return the smile.

"Don't worry, I'll put in a good word."

Chapter 15

Monday

Charles sat, eyes closed as he leaned back against the headrest. The sunshine filtering through the windshield was warm against his face and hands, and outside the car he heard a dove cooing in a nearby tree. He pulled a deep breath in through his nose, holding it in his chest for a moment. Stretching out his bruised ribs, he let it out slowly, massaging the tension out of his side with one hand.

Any moment now, he was going to summon the energy to reach out his hand and unlatch the door. He knew what needed to happen, he even pictured it in his mind—undoing his seatbelt, pulling the handle, rolling his body to one side as he left the comfort of the leather bolstering. Charles could visualize it perfectly, he just hadn't done it yet.

He knew that as soon as he left the quiet repose of the car this moment of gentle warmth would end. He would need to ready himself, keeping his nerves taut and focused. He would need to arm himself, hands wrapping around knurled foregrips and a rough steel trigger. He would need to leave the sunlight behind, traveling to a place of cold and dark. A place from which he was unlikely to return.

And so, he sat, waiting for strength to find him in the passenger seat of Andrea's squad car.

Had it been up to him, he would have preferred taking his own car. There was a soothing familiarity to the Delta 88. It didn't matter if it was ferrying him to the scene of a double-homicide or something as mundane as the library, he could always find comfort in the well-worn textures of the vinyl steering wheel.

Still, Andrea had raised two distinctly persuasive points. First, that her trunk was already loaded up with ammo, gear, and guns from the Pueblo precinct's armory. And second, that she's 'not starting off a monster hunt puking my guts out after riding in your stupid fuckin' *boat.*'

Charles' phone buzzed in his front pocket, dragging him from his thoughts and into the present.

'*Served the TPO,*' Perry's text read. '*S should be all set.*'

'*Any problems?*' Charles asked, thumbs tapping away.

'*Smooth delivery. Kid is fucking weird though.*'

'*No kidding.*' typed Charles. '*Thanks for handling it.*'

'*Anytime*'

Charles tabbed over in his phone, typing out a quick message to Savannah. '*Perry served the TPO. Says you're all set.*'

Three dots danced on the screen, disappearing and reappearing for several moments. Charles waited, he knew not to rush her. Finally, the dots resolved themselves into a single word.

'*Thanks*'

Charles nodded to himself, closing the screen as he slipped the phone back into his pocket. He considered texting Savannah a reminder to take care of Petunia, but he dismissed the thought. *They're fine. She'll take care of her. Always does.* Squinting out the windshield, he watched the sunlight sparkling off the asphalt lot. *So, that's it then*, he thought, sucking in another deep breath. *I guess everything's all set.* He let it out as one long sigh before reaching over to open the door.

Charles met up with Andrea behind the car, peering over her shoulder into the cruiser's open trunk. A half-dozen weapons greeted him from the carpeted floor, neatly arranged with spare magazines and boxes of ammo. He looked up and down the parking lot's empty lanes, suddenly grateful there weren't any onlookers.

"Alright then, whatcha got?"

"Two Remington 870s, two M&P-15s, a Remington 700, and a Colt .357," she replied, gesturing to each weapon in turn. "I also snagged some level III vests. They're a little chunky, but I figured the extra protection was worth it."

Charles agreed. The one-inch thick ballistic plates were heavy and cumbersome, but he'd seen firsthand what the creature's claws could do to bare flesh. The unbidden image of the jogger's torn side, blood spilling out onto the gray sidewalk, filled his mind. He suppressed a shudder, crossing his arms over his chest. He'd deal with the discomfort as long as it kept his insides *inside*.

Charles cleared his throat, focusing his thoughts back on the task at hand. "Good spread. And the armory was just cool with you taking all of this?"

"I told them I was taking a range day and wanted to practice for quarterly quals. Just like that, no more questions." Andrea shrugged. "Didn't even bat an eye when I asked to double up on the shotguns and rifles."

Charles snorted, but he wasn't about to question a good thing. He looked over the assortment of firearms, weighing each one in his mind. He dismissed the Remington 700 immediately, tight quarters and underground were no place for a scoped, bolt-action rifle. The snub-nose Colt was next, the last revolver he'd shot was a j-frame .357 on his uncle's farm in Golden. It'd been over ten years, but he remembered the long trigger and ferocious kick from the small handgun. *Now's not the time to play cowboy*, he mused, moving on to the M&Ps. Like most cops after September 11th, he was intimately familiar with the AR-15 pattern rifles. Easy to operate, maneuverable, and quick-shooting, the assault rifles were the go-to pick for most police officers in any tactical situation. Still, Charles had his doubts. The light, fast-moving .223 round the rifles were chambered for was well suited to controlled bursts in combat, but had a tendency to fragment on impact with dense objects. *Too risky*, he thought with a shake of his head. *I need something bigger*. That left the two shotguns. Slower to load, with significantly lower capacity than the rifles, but 12 gauge hit with a lot more force. Charles picked up one of the Remington 870s, checking the action as he racked the slide.

"My thoughts too," said Andrea, grabbing the other for herself. She picked up the box beside it, dumping the shells out in the open trunk. "I grabbed a box of slugs on the way over. Guy at the counter swore they'd stop a bear."

Charles nodded approvingly. Growing up near the mountains gave him a healthy respect for bears and anyone ballsy enough to hunt them. Leaning on the bumper, he snagged a handful of shells and started loading, forcing the red plastic cannisters into the tubular magazine with a soft *snikt*. Attention wandering as his thumbs worked, his eyes drifted over to a lumpy package wrapped in a garbage bag and tucked away on the side of the trunk.

"More ammo?" he asked, pointing to the package.

"No, *better*." Andrea's eyes flashed with excitement as she hopped off the bumper. She drew back the plastic bag with a magician's flourish, stepping back when she'd finished.

Charles frowned as he looked in the trunk, the distinct smell of benzene washing over him as he leaned over. He scratched his head, staring down at the neon barrel and bright green pump-action. It looked like she'd filled a squirt gun with gasoline.

"I filled a Super-Soaker with gasoline!"

Snatching the makeshift weapon up from the trunk floor, she spun it around in her hands, revealing an extendable butane lighter taped to the other side. "I strapped a lighter to it and a three-point sling. The box said with enough pumping it'll go fifty-feet!"

Charles cocked an eyebrow her way.

"*Nuh-uh*. Nope. Not a chance," Andrea said, warning him off with a wave of her finger. "You don't get to shit all over this. You heard Professor Bowtie, we're going into its lair, its *nest*. You know what *nest* means?"

Charles sighed, he could tell where this was going.

"*Eggs!*" Andrea cried out. "First, they hatch. Then, they're crawling. Then, they're implanting in your fuckin' *face*. I'm not taking that shit, man! The flamethrower stays and I won't hear fuck-all about it." Hugging the Super-Soaker to her chest, she ended her righteous tirade with her chin raised.

Charles rolled his eyes, resigning himself as he resumed loading. "*Fine*. But you're gonna look *real* stupid when you burn your eyebrows off."

Andrea stuck out her tongue in reply, slinging the squirt gun over her shoulder. They finished their loading in silence, cramming the last of the shotshells into the loose pockets of their vests. Charles picked up the plate carrier and inspected it, adjusting the Velcro shoulder straps to fit. He found some road-flares in an upper pocket, doublechecking the fuse caps before stowing them away. Shrugging the vest on, he rolled his shoulders a few times as he adjusted to the added weight.

"Good to go?" Andrea asked, throwing a fleecy jacket on before she picked up her vest.

Charles smirked. *What is it with women and always being cold?* He made a final test of his weapon's barrel-mounted flashlight, slinging it over a shoulder when he was done. He watched Andrea do the same, tucking her shotgun to one side and the ad-hoc flamethrower on the other. Grasping the edges of the trunk lid, she shot him a questioning look.

Charles did one last pat-down of his pockets before nodding. *I guess that's everything we need.*

Andrea closed the lid, the soft *thunk* echoing across the empty parking lot with an air of finality. Charles sucked a deep breath in through his nose, and they set off for the culvert.

Concrete flared out from either side of the drain's entrance like an open invitation to explore the tunnel beyond. The rusted edges of the grate had broken further, bent upwards as something large had pushed against them on its way out. Clicking their weapon lights on, they aimed past the grate and into the darkness beyond. As the stygian gloom swallowed up the pale circles of their flashlights, Charles looked to Andrea, her nose wrinkled in disgust.

"Man, I fucking *hate* sewers."

Charles opened his mouth his mouth to correct her but stopped short, his mind suddenly occupied by the growing buzz of rapid wingbeats. *Not now. Not here.*

"Weird. Usually you've got something snarky to add to that."

Charles tensed, his whole body suddenly rigid as yellow-and-black striped danger tumbled into view. Maybe, if he held still enough, it would be content to pass him by.

"Charles?" The disgust on Andrea's face faded first to confusion, then to concern.

The stinging menace approached, changing direction erratically to suit its dark, alien whims. Charles felt a cold sweat breaking out on the back of his neck.

"You alright, man? You've been quiet all morning."

Charles watched it blunder through the air, drawing closer to his face. The low drone grew louder, matching the blood rushing in his ears.

"It's okay to be scared, man. This whole case, bodies and monsters and shit? It's got me spooked too."

It buzzed by his face, and he could feel the rush of beaten air on his cheek as it passed. *No. Nonononononononono.*

"I'm here for you, but we have to work through this. Here and now. I can't have you freezing up in there."

Charles dared to breathe as the drone faded briefly, his throat catching as it suddenly swelled again.

"Charles?"

Another pass, this time from the other side. Charles' eyes darted right to left, tracking the furtive movements as it strafed by. It was close enough now for him to see the halo of coarse black fur enshrouding its hideous, bloated body.

"Charles?"

His nerves were at the breaking point, competing instincts warring within his body. *Hold still. Just hold still and you can get through this.* His heart sank as he watched it turn again to double back.

"CHARLES!"

His nerves broke as it headed right for him.

"Get that fucking thing away from me!" he shouted, dropping the shotgun as his hands swept up to protect his face.

Andrea was nonplussed. "What? The bee—"

"Yes, the fucking bee!" Charles snapped, eyes shut tight as he swung wildly, fending off his diminutive assailant.

Andrea said nothing, watching him blindly swat the air around his head.

A few moments passed before Charles stopped swinging, chest heaving as he dropped his arms. "I…I think it's gone."

Andrea rolled her eyes. "Yeah, man. I think you got it."

Charles picked his shotgun up from the culvert muck, wiping it clean on the thighs of his pants. He forced himself to breathe through his nose, slowing his pounding heart. "Alright. I'm ready. You ready? Let's go."

Andrea stared at him. "Soooo…We not gonna talk about this?"

"Nope," Charles said brusquely, clicking his flashlight back on. He ignored her look, walking deliberately to the mouth of the drain.

"We're not gonna discuss that little freakout then?"

"Nothing to talk about."

"You sure? 'Cause I—"

"Yup!"

"But maybe we should—"

"No need!"

Charles ducked under the rusty grate, squinting into the gloom of the tunnel. He looked back at Andrea. "You want to kill this thing or not?"

"Well, yeah. I just thought you might want—"

"I *don't*."

Andrea shrugged. "Alright then, let's fucking go."

Charles and Andrea stomped through the murky tunnel, the crisscrossing beams of their flashlights fading away as they trailed off into the distance.

"Should've brought night-vision goggles," grumbled Charles. They had a general idea of the way forward, but with miles of drainage underlying the city he would have given anything at the moment to be able to see clearly.

"I thought about it, but our armory didn't have 'em," replied Andrea, carefully stepping over the lip of a pipe junction. "Best I could do was the road flares."

The tunnel ended in T-intersection, splitting left and right. Charles paused, sweeping his flashlight across the silt-stained bottom. White bone glinted back as Charles traced the outline of a dismembered hand jutting out from the muck.

"Good to know we're still on track," he mumbled, panning his flashlight to the right. "This way."

Andrea nodded, following Charles through the hushed gloom. The thud of their footsteps echoed softly down the tunnel length, mixing with the sounds of dripping water and the faint scurrying of rats.

"So, how long have you been afraid of bees?"

Charles sighed, he'd been enjoying the quiet. It helped him focus on what lay ahead. "I thought we agreed to drop that."

"I know, I know," said Andrea, flashlight bobbing as she fought to keep up with his long strides. "I just think it's funny that we're on our way to fight a man-eating, ravenous hell-beast and the thing you're most afraid of is a little *bug*."

"Not a bug. A *bee*," corrected Charles, stopping as the tunnel forked again. *Was it all right turns? Or all lefts?* He deliberated for a moment before making up his mind to go right. He waved for Andrea to follow. "Besides, everybody's got their thing. *You're* afraid of sewers."

"I'm not afraid of sewers, I just find them disgusting," Andrea said, sidestepping something slime-covered dripping from the ceiling. "And, as we've established, they're also home to flesh-ripping monsters."

Charles said nothing, stepping over a deep pocket of mud as he turned at another intersection.

Andrea was not so lucky. There was a wet squelch and the sounds of a struggle behind him, followed by a string of cursing as her boot finally pulled free.

"But bees, man. What's so bad about bees?"

"They sting you," Charles said dully, shrugging his shoulders as he slogged ahead. He wasn't sure which was more tiring, carrying the tactical plates or this conversation.

"Noooo, bees are nice," Andrea replied, dragging her heel on the concrete as she scraped off the excess mud. "They just bumble around some flowers and make honey. You're thinking of wasps. Now *those* guys, they're the assholes."

"They're *all* assholes," Charles corrected, peering through the murky shadows. "Bees, wasps, hornets, no difference. They fly. They sting. They're awful."

"C'mon man, don't be like that. They're not *that* bad."

Charles snorted, suppressing a shiver as they walked. He'd forgotten how chilly it got this far into the tunnels, the damp cold setting in the further they went. He wasn't about to admit it to her, but he was beginning to wish he'd brought a jacket as well.

"Besides, it's pretty easy to avoid getting stung."

"Don't say it," Charles muttered under his breath as he slogged ahead. "Don't you fucking *dare*."

"Just don't bother them, and they won't bother you."

"Gawdamnit."

They reached another intersection, this time the right side

terminated about twenty feet on. Charles nodded to himself, remembering this section from before. *Shouldn't be too much further*, he thought as they turned to the right. He kept his flashlight low as they walked, searching the muddy ground ahead.

He spotted it just as the tunnel began another jog left, the silver shine of two quarters at the edge of the turn. Turning back to Andrea, he put his finger to his lips to let her know they were close. She nodded, tucking the shotgun's buttstock tight to her shoulder. Charles gave his a last once-over, pulling back on the action to check the round seated in the chamber. Satisfied, he shouldered his as well, and stepped off down the last stretch.

The first thing Charles noticed was the smell of blood. It saturated the still, underground air, the sharp notes of copper permeating throughout the tunnel. They moved together in silence, heels rolling to keep their footsteps light on the concrete floor. Flashlights aimed low, they could just make out the entrance to the chamber up ahead, a shade lighter than the surrounding gloom. Straining his eyes, Charles could barely see by the dim sunlight filtering around manhole covers in the chamber's ceiling. He slowed his pace, mindful of kicking any errant rocks or debris. This close, they couldn't risk losing the element of surprise.

Tension filled the atmosphere underground as they neared, a palpable pressure like the building of a storm on the great plains. As they closed in, the damp chill became more pronounced. Goosebumps rose up and down his arms, and Charles felt the faintest of breezes brushing past his hair.

The tunnel widened up ahead, the curved walls of the cistern spreading out before them. Charles held up a hand as they reached it, pausing on the threshold of the tunnel's end. Holding his breath, he listened closely for the tell-tale scrape of claws. A moment passed, filled with nothing but the staccato beating of his heart. Charles looked back at Andrea, nodding once. They shouldered their weapons, flashlights crisscrossing as they took their first step into the creature's lair.

Charles let his breath out slow and quiet, panning the light around the wide room. Blood clung to the wall in drips and swathes amid the pockmarked holes of drainage inlets. Most of it was dry, but here and there a patch reflected wetly in the thin circle of light. A fat red drop fell and splattered on his shoulder. Looking up, he saw clumps of gore and offal spread across the ceiling.

Charles shuddered in disgust, stepping out of the way of another falling drop. He felt his foot connect with something soft and squishy. Lip curling as he glanced down, he realized he'd kicked over the soft something's shredded remains, its intestines spilling out among matted black and grey fur. *Should've figured people weren't the only thing on the menu…* He shuddered again but forced himself to keep moving. A quick pivot and his section of the chamber was finished—one of the perks of searching an open room for a creature so large. Easily ruling out avenues of approach was another. After seeing it on the bridge, he knew it was safe to ignore the smaller inlets in the walls, focusing instead on two tunnels the same size as the one they'd entered from.

"Clear," he whispered to Andrea.

"No monster," she whispered back, "but I'm gonna need you to take a look at this."

Charles backed up towards the middle of the room, keeping a wary eye on the tunnels leading out. "What? Are there eggs?"

"No?" she replied, her tone stilted and hushed. "I…I honestly don't know what the fuck I'm looking at."

Charles felt a faint breeze brush past his ears, raising hairs on the back of his neck as it went by. The back of his vest butted up against hers, and he chanced a look over his shoulder.

A section of the chamber wall stretched before them, smooth and bare of the usual bevvy of inlets and holes. Patches of dried blood stained the pale concrete, but unlike the haphazard globs coating the rest of the chamber, these were arranged in a clear, unbroken pattern outlining a triangle stretching from floor to ceiling. Strange, looping markings dotted the outline in clusters, etched into the concrete by a broad, sharp edge.

Charles turned fully, taking up a spot beside Andrea to get a better look. The marks were like nothing he'd ever seen before, the gouges deep and thickly drawn like runes on an ancient temple. They were undoubtedly deliberate, the wall scored with purpose and precision. Charles felt a prickly unease creeping over the back of his neck. Pushing it aside, he found his attention drawn sharply away from the bizarre markings as another faint breeze whistled by, pulling his focus to what occupied the triangle's center.

A void hung in the center of the wall, an amorphous absence of matter roughly six inches across. Energy pulsed and crackled along its outer edge, emitting a faint glow of iridescent purple and a low, malevolent humming. He felt the cold breeze on his face again, emanating from the void's depths. Charles stared, jaw hanging slightly open.

"Yeah," Andrea muttered quietly. "*That's* what I was talking about."

Staring at the formless nullity before them, Charles felt the swelling of atmospheric pressure in the base of his skull. The iridescent glow of the edges surged brighter, the indistinct hum growing. They watched as the glow and the hum steadily built, radiating out in waves. Then a line of energy arced suddenly across the void's surface, the chamber momentarily backlit with a purple flash. Charles shut his eyes tight, feeling his ears pop as the mounting pressure suddenly released. When he opened them again the iridescence around the edges had faded, the low hum dimming to its previous, nearly indistinct level. The void still hung in the center of the bloody triangle, now more than a foot across.

"Fuck me," he murmured, hands tight on the shotgun's textured grips.

"*Mmhmmm*," Andrea said beside him. "And we just watched it get bigger, right?"

Charles nodded. "Yup."

"And whatever the fuck that is, we're in agreement that it's no good?"

"Oh yeah," replied Charles, eyeing void's malignant glow. "Might even be worse than eggs."

"Right, okay then." Andrea slung her shotgun over her shoulder, snatching the Super-Soaker from the other side in one swift move. She worked the charging handle back and forth, pressurizing the chamber with a few quick pumps.

Charles' eyes went wide. "What are you *doing?*"

"Scientific method, Charles," she answered calmly, tucking the plastic stock to her shoulder as she continued pumping. "We need to stop it, and don't know how, so I'm gonna try everything on the list until something sticks. Starting with *fire*."

"Just be careful with that thing," Charles said as he took a step back, putting ample space between them. "But you're on your own if you catch on fire. I'm not stomping you ou—"

Claws scraped concrete on the far side of the room, cutting off his last word. Charles whipped around, aiming his flashlight down the further of the darkened tunnels. The edge of an oily green carapace glinted in the thin circle of light, moving past as the creature emerged from amid the swirl of shadows. Stepping out from the tunnel's edge, it rose to its full height on multi-jointed limbs. Still roughly the size of a horse, the tip of the wide, domed head reached just below the cistern's ceiling, dwarfing the two detectives in the chamber's narrow confines.

Charles froze, the closer of the two, but the only one with hands on a gun. He took a cautious step towards the middle, buying Andrea a second of reaction time while he centered himself in front of her. He kept the shotgun trained on the beast's pale, yellow underside, knuckles white against the textured grip.

The great head turned back and forth, red eyes blinking at them as it surveyed these intruders to its lair. The toothy maw clacked open and shut, clearly puzzled by the wanton boldness of its prey. Charles took another step towards the center. The four red eyes shifted, focusing entirely on him. He could feel the weight of its gaze, the predatory hunger lurking within its feral mind as it sized him up.

He decided to take the initiative.

The Remington roared in his hands, a fireball erupting from the smooth barrel to sling an ounce of lead-alloy into creature's belly. The thunderous boom echoed off the walls as he racked the fore-end, ejecting the spent plastic shell out the side and chambering another round. He fired off another shot, just clipping the creature's shoulder high and to the right.

Out of the corner of his eye he saw Andrea stepping off to the side, swinging her shotgun up to her shoulder as she dropped to one knee. He felt the cacophonous heat and pressure bloom from her barrel as she stroked the trigger, forcing him to shut one eye.

The creature trembled under the sledgehammer force of the slugs' impact, its spiky forelegs leaving the ground as it reeled back. The sharp-toothed mouth opened in a hellish scream, barely audible over the ringing in Charles' ears. As it raised up, he spotted a silver glint on its underside—the flattened remains of the first slug. He made a matching streak with another pull of the trigger.

"It's too tough!" he shouted to Andrea, stepping off to the side.

"WHAT?" she shouted back, cycling the action on her gun.

It has to have a soft spot somewhere, he thought grimly, yanking back on the slide. He had the sudden image of a cajun crab dinner he'd shared with James pop into his head, the two of them laughing as they pulled the boiled legs apart at the joints.

Charles cupped his hand to his mouth, bellowing to be heard above the din. "BODY'S TOO TOUGH! AIM FOR THE LEGS!"

The creature screeched again, lowering the wide, shield-like head. It launched forward at them, six legs blurring together in a burst of speed. Charles fired again, slug glancing off the chitinous shell as it charged. The flat expanse of green filled his vision, coming for him at blistering speed.

Charles hopped backward on one foot, narrowly stepping out of the way. He could feel the *whoosh* of air as it rushed past, slamming into curved cement wall. Purple light flashed behind him, momentarily lighting up the dim chamber.

The creature recovered quickly, six legs scuttling as it turned to face them both. Andrea was still on one knee, firing as fast as she could. Charles swung the shotgun back up, centering the front sight's white bead on the nearest leg.

White flame blossomed from the end of the barrel, the recoil rocking him backwards. His back foot come down on the remains of something soft and squishy, thick rubber heel slipping out from underneath him. As Charles felt himself sliding, he pinwheeled his arms desperately as he fought for balance. He lost the struggle, and found himself tipping backwards.

Headfirst into the crackling void.

Chapter 16:

An icy wind whipped across the barren plains, carrying snow and the deep groans of shifting glaciers. Charles opened his eyes, squinting against the sudden brightness of the harsh, blue sunlight. Miles of tundra lay beneath him, permafrost and snow-capped dunes stretching out towards an uncertain horizon. Charles' head and shoulders hung suspended in space above this glacial world, even as he felt firm ground beneath his feet and the rasp of concrete under his hands. His shoulders tingled as the amethyst edges of the void crackled around them, pressing in on him in a tight embrace.

A rumbling cry echoed across the land, like the twisting shriek of metal shearing free. Charles saw towering figures in the distance, lumbering towards him as they dragged their heavy, spiked limbs through a veil of frigid mist. Sunlight sparkled off the dark green domed heads and the icy shards thrown up from the impact of their thundering steps. He shivered as the arctic wind whipped by again, ruffling his hair. The figures' keening cry sounded again, drawing closer. Pushing hard against the concrete under his hands, Charles pulled himself free from the void, the alien world disappearing before him with an audible *pop*.

Back in the cistern chamber, he stumbled away from the wall, frost rimming his eyebrows. The slick concrete floor rose to meet him as he pitched back, catching himself with his hands just before he hit the ground. Charles' world spun around him as his eyes readjusted to the dim light. A haze of cordite smoke hung across room, and he heard the sound of someone screaming in the distance. As he caught his bearings, it took a moment to realize that it was him.

"Charles!"

Andrea's cry cut through the surrounding fog, snapping him back to the here and now. She was crouched on the far side, a line of blood seeping from a cut on her forehead. Aiming up at the beast, she jammed the butt of her shotgun against the wall for stability. The creature was advancing, its unnatural gait hobbled slightly by the shredded flesh surrounding the joint of a spiky forelimb. He saw her jerk the trigger but nothing happened, the firing pin falling on an empty chamber.

Purple light flashed behind him, the chill breeze swelling as the void widened. Charles felt around for his shotgun, unwilling to take his eyes off them. The cold wind howled at his back. He watched Andrea, her fingertips fumbling as she jammed a fresh shell into the open action of her shotgun.

His heart fluttered as he brushed against the coarse nylon sling, snatching the Remington up off the blood-soaked ground. He jammed the heavy stock into his shoulder, redrawing a bead on the creature's wounded leg. He had to be careful with the angle, any miss could hit Andrea. The creature took another step towards forward, the tattered leg joint shuddering under its immense weight. Charles held his breath, fingertip caressing the curved trigger.

Fire and lead belched from the barrel, the thunderous boom echoing off the concrete walls. An alloy slug tore through the injured leg, severing it in half. The creature shrieked in pain, rearing back as sky-blue blood sprayed in a fountain from the ragged stump.

Andrea ducked as the monster spun around, hitting the ground hard as she tucked and rolled out of the way. Chips of concrete showered her as she rolled again, a claw stabbing down in the space her head used to be. Andrea swung her gun up, firing off a glancing shot as she jumped back.

The void flashed again, a white hole opening up in its center as it grew larger. Tufts of snow piled up at the foot of the grimy wall, carried in by the glacial wind. Charles mashed his cheek into the shotgun's stock, fingers tight on the knurled foregrip as he chambered another round. He knew they had to stop it, figure out some way of closing the void up. *No telling how big it'll get, might even swallow the whole city from underneath. Or worse,* he shuddered, *allow something other than snow to get through.*

He took aim at the creature again, barrel bouncing around as he tried to line up a shot on its other leg. He fired and missed, the slug burying itself in the far wall.

Across the room, Andrea took another step back, Super-Soaker knocking softly against the wall at the end of its sling. Charles glanced over, momentarily taking his eyes off the front sight. Between them lay the void, its edges pulsing with malevolent will. Goosebumps rose on his neck, and for the briefest moment he thought he saw a glint of dark green obscure the white center. Whatever that thing was, they needed to stop it. Fast. *Try everything in the book if we have to.*

Charles stood up suddenly, a glimmer of an idea sparking in him. He slung the empty shotgun over his shoulder, frantically patting the top of his vest. *There.* He felt them, three solid tubes jammed in the upper pocket. He pulled out the road flare, a half-smile crossing his face.

One of them was pretty good at trying new things. But trying things took time. And for that they needed space. *Breathing room.*

He gave one last look across the void to Andrea, curly hair hanging in her face as she jammed fresh shells into the tubular magazine.

They needed a distraction.

Charles struck the end of the flare, red flame erupting brightly as it ignited.

"Hey!" He swung the flare in front of him, casting long shadows across the cistern. "Hey you!"

The creature paused, cocking its head as it studied the flickering light.

Got its attention at least, he thought grimly, waving the road flare aggressively. *Now I need its interest.*

Charles stopped waving, turning the flare over slowly and deliberately as he held it out. He stared into the multitude of eyes lining the underside of the domed head, he needed them focused entirely on the bright red flame.

As he jammed the flare's lit end into the crackling edge of the void.

The reaction was immediate, the purple energy surrounding the void arcing away from the flame with a sizzling *crack*, the white center momentarily flickering out of existence.

The creature reeled back, a panicked shriek bursting out of the toothy maw. It turned and barreled towards him, eyes alight with murderous rage.

That did it.

Charles turned sharply, sprinting for the furthest tunnel. The monster roared again, sharp claws digging in as it scrambled across the concrete.

"What are you doing?!" Andrea shouted, her voice barely audible over the creature's enraged bellowing.

"Scientific method!" he yelled back, holding the flare high over his head. "We have to close the void!"

"What about *you?*"

"It's okay!" Charles' heart pounded in his chest as he leapt over the threshold and into the dark tunnel beyond. "I have a plan!"

Charles did not have a plan. He just ran, the smack of his rubber bootheels on the concrete jolting up his legs as he tore down the tunnel. His empty shotgun smacked against the back of his vest, one hand still carrying the road flare high. He could hear the cacophonous scraping of the creature behind him, and at any moment he expected to feel the searing pain of a hundred needle-like teeth ripping through his flesh.

He saw an intersection up ahead, the shadows cast by the flare jumping wildly around him as he turned right. He didn't have the faintest idea where he was going, he just kept turning in the hopes of making a larger loop around. The thought of hitting a dead end crept into his mind, but he pushed it aside. Right now it was either run, or die.

He felt a whoosh of air behind him as the creature crashed into a wall at the turn. Big as it was, it was having a harder time negotiating the narrow confines of the drainage tunnels, hampered still further by the loss of one leg. *I might actually be able to stay ahead of this thing*, he thought, arms pumping wildly at his sides. Needles lanced through his bruised side, the muscles of his chest seizing up in protest.

Charles took another turn, boots kicking up silt and mud behind him. Sweat poured down the side of his face, mingling with the frothy spit collecting in the corner of his mouth. His shirt clung to his back, thoroughly drenched under the tactical vest. His thighs burned, heart hammering in his ears as his breath rushed out in gasps. *God, if you let me live, I promise I'll do more cardio…*

Corridors of tunnels split off left and right off the main line. Charles picked one at random and ducked right, grabbing ahold of the wall's edge and swinging to keep his momentum. Caught off guard, the creature rushed past, scrabbling to a stop before doubling back. It bought Charles an extra hundred feet of distance between them, and he needed every inch he could get.

Keep going. Faster.

Shadows danced ahead of him in the flare's flickering red light. Something cold and wet dripped from the ceiling, soaking into the shoulder of his shirt. He pressed on, lowering the torch as he pumped his arms for momentum.

Faster. Must go faster.

His bootheel came down on the wrong side of a loose stone, his ankle buckling and rolling underneath him. There was an audible pop, his leg shuddering as a wave of pain arced up from his calf. Charles slowed, but kept going, driving hard with his good leg. He could hear the creature scurrying behind him, sharp claws clicking against the slimy concrete. Gritting his teeth, he pushed himself forward, forcing the breath in and out of his lungs.

The tunnel split again, the right end looked like the longer path but he could see the faintest glimmer of purple light shining from the left. His ankle throbbed, his foot numb below it, and he could feel himself losing steam as he hobbled along. *I don't know how much time that bought, but it's gonna have to be enough.* As Charles angled left, he tossed the flare hard down the tunnel to the right.

"COMING IN HOT!" Charles bellowed as he cleared the threshold the chamber. He stumbled as he hit the rough pavement, momentum carrying him forward the last few feet.

"I hope…you…figured it…out," he gasped, one hand pressed to his aching side.

"Almost," Andrea replied calmly, stepping back from the wall. She extended a hand, helping Charles off the ground. "I at least got it to stop growing."

"Better than nothing," grimaced Charles, taking her hand and rising on his good leg.

Glancing at the wall, she'd managed to scrub at least half of the symbols from the around the triangle, chunks of concrete and twisted lead littering the floor in piles. The void still remained, hanging in space with a white hole at its center nearly a foot across. Cold wind howled forth from it, depositing snow and frost onto the cistern floor. He'd hoped for more at this point, but he was encouraged by the dimmed purple glow around the void's edges.

"Whatever the fuck this thing is, it's resilient. Half the stuff I tried only made it flicker, and come back bigger. It wasn't until I got some of the etchings off I made *any* kind of progress. But now I'm all outta slugs, dropped my flashlight in the damn hole, bent my multitool, cracked my buttstock, and chipped away sixty dollars in dip powder," Andrea sighed, ruefully surveying her broken fingernails. She shot him a weary look, the flushed outline of a fresh bruise rising on her cheek. "Only got one thing left to try, after that…"

She shrugged.

Charles nodded, shoulders slumping as grim reality settled in on him. Scuttling echoed out from the tunnel behind them, sharp claws clinking off the concrete like the ticking of a clock. He'd hoped his ruse with the flare would buy them a few more seconds, but it was not to be.

Charles sucked in a deep breath, unslinging his shotgun and digging a few shells out of his cargo pocket. He pushed the slugs in, the loading gate snapping shut with an air of finality. "That last idea of yours…Better make it quick."

"No shit," she muttered, bending over to retrieve the Super Soaker leaning against the wall. She pumped the neon green handle, filling the chamber with compressed air.

Charles shouldered the Remington as he hobbled into the center of the room. He exhaled through his nose, wheezing softly as he tried to calm his beating heart. A single claw extended from the shadows of the tunnel, oily chitin glinting in the dull purple light.

No use waiting. Charles pulled the trigger, illuminating the cistern in a flash of burning powder and a clap of thunder. His first shot was high and left, the slug leaving a crater in the crumbling concrete wall. He was quick with the second, two ounces of lead leaving the barrel with the first shot still ringing in his ears.

The leg withdrew sharply, a spray of sky-blue arcing out as it pulled back into the cover of darkness. Charles was already moving, hopping on one foot to get a better angle. *If I can just keep it in there*, he thought, knuckles white as he pumped the foregrip. *Hold it off with a few good shots…*

The creature roared out of the tunnel, dagger-teeth bared wide. Its back four claws dug long gouges into the blood-stained floor, wounded forelimbs tucked up underneath it like a praying mantis. It spied Charles as he hurried to the side, shaking with anger and unleashing its unholy screech as he retreated.

Charles cracked off another shot, dust and debris raining down from the low ceiling as he stumbled away. His shoulder hit the far wall and he rolled, pressing his back against it for support. He cycled the shotgun with one hand, gasping for breath as pain erupted from his ankle.

The great domed head lowered, and the creature launched itself at him. Charles dropped flat, the air leaving his chest as he bounced off the ground. The wide, shield head crashed against the wall above him, cracks radiating out from the point of impact. Charles braced the stock on the ground, drawing a wheezy breath as he aimed. He pulled the trigger, the slug boring in under the creature's bony chin.

He felt the warm spray of blue blood showering down on him. Rolling to the side, he dodged a downward slash as the beast reared back. It shook its wide head, scattering fat drops of blood and a few shattered teeth across the room.

Charles used the gun to push himself up, dragging his bad leg under him as he shuffled back. Chambering his last round, he shouldered the Remington and squinted down the barrel. The creature turned on him, torn jaw clicking as it worked it side to side. It drew itself up to its full height, filling the small space as it stared down at him. Cold hatred emanated from the four red eyes. Charles planted his feet firm, a snarl on his face as he aligned the bead of the front sight with one of the four red eyes.

Bright orange flared up from across the room, bathing the two of them in a warm glow. The creature paused, domed head turning suddenly towards the light's source. Charles took his eye off the front sight, glancing over as well.

Andrea let out a wordless cry of righteous fury, the plastic stock tight against her shoulder as she unleashed a jet of liquid fire.

Time passed slowly as the flaming stream burst from the squirt gun's barrel, sailed through the air, and collided with the void.

At the first touch of flame the crackling edges sizzled and smoked, before flaring up in a ring of purple fire. She swung the barrel side to side, coating the wall and the void in burning gasoline. Charles could feel the heat from across the room, thick smoke pouring forth as she set the void ablaze. Amid the conflagration, the white hole in the center blinked twice and disappeared.

A mournful wail erupted from the creature's throat, a high, undulating note that poured out from amid the gnashing teeth. It turned away from Charles, ignoring him entirely as it rushed toward the burning void.

The purple flames grew larger, forcing Andrea to jump back. In her hands, the Super Soaker's stream petered to a dribble as the plastic barrel melted down. She threw it against the wall, the reservoir of gasoline cracking and igniting as it hit the bloody triangle.

Still wailing, the creature stepped between her and the void, the domed head bobbing amid the abundant smoke. It reached out a ruined forelimb, caressing what remained of the ruined symbols and empty spot where the void used to be. Charles watched the four eyes close as it rested its head against the flaming wall. A sharp, keening note trailed out from the toothy jaws, as if in mourning.

Then the oily claw lit up in purple flame.

Chalres lowered the shotgun, Andrea rushing to meet him in the center of the chamber. They looked on as the purple fire spread across the creature's back, the chitinous edges curling into black ash as flames grew larger. The creature shuddered, but remained against the wall, the mournful sound just audible above the hisses and pops of oily fire.

Charles jerked a thumb towards the tunnel behind them. "I, uh, think we should leave now."

The blaze surged higher, roaring as it engulfed the creature entirely. The wailing had stopped, replaced only with the crackling of the flames and a low, ominous hum.

"Agreed. No part of that is good," she said, tipping her head towards the flames. "You gonna make it on your own?"

Charles tested his weight on his bad leg, a sharp hiss escaping him as it folded beneath him. He looked at her and shook his head. "Only if we go slow."

The low hum grew louder, ebbing and flowing in ever quicker waves. Andrea looked from the tunnel, to the fire, to Charles.

"Slow might not be an option." She pulled his arm over her shoulder, taking the weight off his ankle. "Not too proud, right?"

Charles snorted, slinging his shotgun as he leaned on her fully. He pointed to the tunnel they'd first entered. "That one. Let's make like a tree."

Andrea nodded. "And get the fuck outta here."

The humming rose behind them as the shuffled down the tunnel, moving as fast as they could on three legs. The sound was no longer low, the register escalating further and further upwards. At last they reached the turn marked by the two coins, hobbling around the corner and throwing themselves against the near wall.

"Think we're far enough?" Andrea panted, legs shaking from the effort of carrying them both.

Charles wiped the sweat from his eyes with the back of a muddy hand. "Let's hope."

The hum had reached a fevered pitch, the waves too fast to distinguish as they echoed off the concrete walls. It rose and rose, until they could feel it reverberating inside their skulls. Charles closed his eyes, gritting his teeth as the onslaught grew.

There was a burst of heat and flash of purple light, cutting through the darkness so fiercely he could see it through his closed eyelids. The light disappeared as suddenly as it came, flicking off like a switch, and taking the hum with it.

Silence filled the tunnels in its wake.

Charles and Andrea waited, neither willing to draw a breath. Moments passed, but at last he forced himself to open his eyes. Green spots danced in front of his vision as they looked at each other.

"Think that's it?" Andrea asked

Charles stood up from the wall, shining his flashlight back around the corner of the intersection. Scorched walls stretched forth, coated in soot and ash. He followed the thin beam, tracing the tunnel ahead as he hobbled back to the cistern. Andrea followed him without a word, ears perked up for the tell-tale rasp of claw on stone.

But only charred silence greeted them as the tunnel widened up ahead. Charles stood in the mouth of the opening, panning his flashlight across an empty room. The light reflected dimly off waves of muddy brown glass, the silica mixed in dingy concrete of the cistern fusing and melting in the fierce heat. Andrea joined him, passing her beam over the far wall, seeing nothing of the former etchings and malevolent symbols. The bloody lines were gone, the void vanished, with only dirty ceramic left behind. Charles took a step forward, a stifling warmth prickling his exposed skin as it emanated from the walls—like reaching a hand inside an oven. He stepped over a black silhouette of ash on floor, one of the incinerated bodies of the creature's prey.

He took a few more steps, grit crunching under his boots, the ground slick in spots with new ceramic. His eyes watered from the heat of the wall where the void used to be. A low whistle escaped him as the thin flashlight beam illuminated a massive pile of oily ash, dwarfing the previous silhouettes. Nudging it with the toe of his boot, he watched it flake and collapse in on itself.

"Yeah," he muttered, "I think that's it."

"So what do you think they were? Some kinda inter-dimensional travelers?"

Charles sighed, bracing one hand against the wall for support as he hopped. He regretted telling her about his experience inside the void. There'd been nothing but questions for the last ten minutes.

"Cause that's what you saw in the portal, right? Some big-ass ones in the distance? On the ice planet?"

"I don't know what I saw," grumbled Charles, his right boot sinking into a deep patch of mud. "And I'm not calling it a *portal*."

Andrea threw up her arms in disbelief. "C'mon man! We just stopped an *alien invasion* back there and you don't even what to guess what it was about? Could you quit being fuckin' *Scully* for five minutes already?"

"Let's get one thing perfectly straight," snapped Charles. He turned on her suddenly, waving his finger under her nose and mustering up as much solemn dignity as he could on one leg. "We have absolutely no *fucking* idea what was going on in that chamber. And thanks to that flash, we've got no evidence either. No void. No strange marks on the wall. No creature. *Nothing*. Just soot and ash and melted concrete. Now I don't know about your department, but mine was expecting some kind of resolution on over six homicides involving a machete-wielding spree-killer, and instead *all* I have is *ash*. So maybe instead of wasting time on wild speculation, we can start guessing about how to fix that!"

Silence followed his outburst, and for a moment Charles worried that he'd carried it too far.

Nice job, idiot. Sergeant Briske was right, you ARE an asshole.

Then Andrea began to giggle, curly hair bouncing as it progressed into a full-blown laugh. Charles stood perfectly still as she doubled over, cackling, unwilling to say anything else for fear of breaking the moment.

"No shit! Of *course* we're gonna plan a cover story, you, you *dumbass*." She reeled back, wiping a tear from each eye. "I was just spitballing ideas between the two of us. You really think I'm gonna type 'Regarding the death of Will Springsley… A fucking monster did it, the end.' and then hit submit on my report? C'mon *Chuck*."

Charles opened and closed his mouth without a word. He watched her double over again, sides heaving with her hands on her knees. And, in spite of himself, he joined in as well.

"I'm sorry, I should have known better," he admitted, face red from laughing. "But it's my first X-File."

"Apology accepted," Andrea said, an ear-to-ear grin as she straightened back up. "The way I see it, we've got about twenty-four hours to get our heads together and make some kinda coherent narrative. But I'm not worrying about that now. Priority one is getting out of this sewer and into a fucking *shower*."

Charles chuckled, turning his back on her and hobbling down the drain. There was light up ahead, the rusted edges of the broken grate just visible around the tunnel's entrance. He took another few steps before stopping, his pocket buzzing loudly.

Fishing around for his phone, he turned it over to see the newly cracked screen light up as it downloaded a text from Savannah. *No reception underground*, he thought, swiping across on the fractured screen. It buzzed again as another text from Savannah came on screen. *Must be all downloading at once.*

Charles tapped the message app, his smile evaporating as he read the messages.

"Charles?" Andrea caught up with him. "What's up?"

His phone buzzed a third time. Charles read the message before breaking into a run, limping his way towards the sunlight.

"Charles! What's going on?"

'Can you come get me? La'shea said she saw him walk into the building. I thought Perry served the TPO?!'

'He's here. He's Mad. I heard him shouting for me.'

'He's got a gun.'

Chapter 17

Monday

Red and blue lights flashed in sync with a howling siren, blurring together as it sped by. Andrea's squad car tore across the asphalt, afternoon traffic parting before it like the Red Sea. Charles kept his right foot planted to the floor, the 5.7-liter V8 roaring to the redline as he wove in and out lanes.

Death-grip on the ceiling handle, Andrea spoke up from the passenger seat. "What's the plan?"

"Get Savannah," Charles grunted, cutting off a breadvan as he made a sharp left. Horns blared over screeching brakes.

Andrea crossed herself with her free hand. "Fuck's sake, man. *Slow the fuck down!*"

Charles ignored her, hammering the throttle as he shot through the narrow gap between a lifted F-150 and a beaten down Volvo.

"Charles."

He said nothing, concentrating on turning into the slide as his back wheels kicked out on a hard right.

"Charles!"

Tires squealed, rubber tread fighting a losing battle against the counterforce of angular momentum. He hung tight to the steering wheel, snapping the pursuit sedan back in line.

"CHUCK!"

"WHAT?!"

"The *PLAN?!*"

Charles sped around a UPS truck, inches between their bumpers as he cut into the lane. "I told you, go there, sweep the building, bag the guy, secure Savannah."

He hadn't told her, but she let that slide.

"What building? What floor? Who's the fucker we're snagging? What does Savannah even *look* like?" Andrea shouted, bouncing in her seat as he clipped a curb. "Details, man! I need fuckin' *details!*"

"Oh. Right," Charles winced, easing off the gas as they pulled into the community college parking lot. "Building 280. The one in the middle. Her class is on the third or fourth floor, no idea on room. Creep's name is Chris. Only saw him once, pale, chubby guy with curly hair and a beard. Savannah's easier, short girl with freckles and bright blue hair." He stomped on the brakes, the black Charger slamming to a stop at the edge of the sidewalk. He threw it in park, turning to Andrea as he unclipped his belt. "We split up after entry, clearing floors front to back and then leap frogging in the stair well. You take floors one and three, I'll take two and four."

"Thank you. Not so hard, huh?" carped Andrea, checking the pistol holstered on her side. "What's he armed with?"

"Dunno," replied Charles, throwing open the door and rolling out. "Be ready for anything."

Andrea nodded, muttering to herself. "Ain't that the moral of the fuckin' day…"

The aluminum front doors of the building were wide open, the tinny squawk of the fire alarm resounding in the empty halls. Charles stood on the threshold of the concrete stoop, hands tight on his pistol's stippled grip.

Andrea shot him a sideways glance. "You ready?"

Charles doublechecked that the volume was up on his handheld radio. He met her look and nodded.

"Wait!" Andrea leaned in, swiping her hand up and down the front of his vest. "You got blood and shit all over you, couldn't even see the 'POLICE' tag." She leaned back, offering him a half smile while she wiped her hand on the side of her pants. "There, not such a hot mess now."

"Thanks," grunted Charles, mustering up a small smile in return. He took in a deep breath, gave her another quick nod and stepped through the door.

Muddy boots squeaked on the checkered linoleum, the amber flash of the alarm lights reflecting off the dull waxed floor. Charles pealed right, pushing in on the stairwell door while Andrea continued straight down the first hall. He'd been in here only once before—dropping off Savannah's laptop for class—but the blocky, C-shaped structure was easy to navigate. *Four floors, two stairwells. Front to back, then move up.* His gun was out and in front, the back of his vest brushing against the far wall as he took his first step up the winding staircase. *Easy. Smooth. No sweat.* He continued up, cutting a wide angle to sweep the next level up as he ascended the rubber-lined steps. He ignored the twinge in his ankle, working his way to the start of the second floor and pausing at the door to the hallway.

Charles crept around at the edge of the wall, pieing around the corner until he was sure it was clear. The ardent squall of the alarm clanged out of red boxes along the wall.

No screaming. No gunshots… yet.

A row of classrooms lined the right side, some with open doors. Poking his head in each one, he tried to remember his training. *Slow is smooth, smooth is fast*, he reminded himself, his instructor's words echoing through his head. *Quick insert, sweep the corners, and back out. No people? Move on.*

He cleared each of the fourteen rooms methodically as he passed down the hall, each filled with rows of long, curved desks, but otherwise empty. *Students must've run out with the alarm*, he mused, shutting the door on the last room. He wondered if Savannah had done the same, or if he'd find her tucked away under one of the long desks. Or find *him*.

Charles had never shot someone before. In fact, outside of the last two weeks, he'd gone seven years as a cop only drawing his gun once—serving a high-risk warrant on a mid-level drug dealer. Even then, it was more out of procedural obligation than tactical necessity. The suspect had opened the door, took in the twelve, heavily-armed officers surrounding his doorstep, and surrendered immediately. Holding out his hands for the cuffs, his only response had been a shrug and a resigned 'Aight then.'

Charles paused for a breather when he reached the back stairwell. The twinge in his ankle had swelled to a dull throb, his shoulders ached from tensing up under the weight of the tactical vest, and he noticed a slight twitch in his right hand. Charles took his hand off the pistol, raising it to eye level as the twitch progressed to a tremor. He glared at the hand, making a fist to force it still. *She needs you, pull yourself together!* He shook himself, pushing aside his discomfort and nerves as he pressed through the stairwell door.

"Blue coming through!" he called down.

"Blue coming up!" came the reply, Andrea jogging up to meet him.

"See anyone yet?" he asked as she drew alongside.

"Nothing but empty rooms."

Charles nodded, "Same."

They climbed the wide rubber-lined stairs together, covering each other until they reached the third floor. Charles tapped Andrea on the shoulder as he passed her, leaving her behind to wait as he crept up the last two flights. He paused again at the stairwell door, looking through the narrow rectangle of the wire glass window.

He counted down to Andrea. "Three…two…one!"

They thrust through their respective doors, rolling their heels to keep quiet. Charles stopped at the first corner, holding his breath as he pied around.

The scene in the hallway was empty, but chaotic. Books and scattered papers littered the ground, pages fluttering in the breeze of an open window. Charles passed a forgotten backpack and an upturned trash can, their contents spread out across the tile floor. Stepping around a half-empty water bottle, he moved purposefully to the door of the first room.

Charles nudged his way past the hollow-core door, pressing to the far wall as he turned to clear the three corners. Reaching the last row of desks, he skirted along the edge of the back wall, splitting his attention between watching the two doors and searching underneath the desks. Satisfied the room was empty, he swallowed hard and stepped back out into the corridor.

As the door shut behind him, he heard the unmistakable rasp and click of another door opening at the far end of the hallway. Flattening himself against the wall, Charles peered down the hall in the direction of the sound, just as a figure slunk out of one of the last classrooms.

He was dressed in a oversized black hoody, draping down loosely over lumpy black cargo pants. His hood was down, revealing a head of curly brown hair, and as he turned, Charles spotted a matted beard to match. He couldn't see anything in the man's hands, but the long-barreled rifle slung across his back was clear under the fluorescent lights.

Charles sucked in a deep breath, stepping off from the wall and leveling his pistol on the stalker. Distantly, he realized that the fire alarm had stopped.

"Police!" he barked, heart thudding in his chest as he moved down the hall. "Show me your hands!"

Chris froze in place, turning slowly to face him.

"Hands!" shouted Charles, blood roaring in his ears. "Hands NOW!"

Closer now, Charles could see the shock spread across the bearded face, even as Chris kept his hands down by his waist.

"*HANDS!*" he bellowed, his voice hoarse and ragged.

His finger slipped down, finding its place on the trigger.

Don't make me do this…

"TASER, TASER, TASER!"

Two darts sailed through the air, thin conductive wires trailing out behind them. They sank into Chris' back, hazel eyes widening in surprise. Then the circuit completed, and the still hallway was split with the crackling of fifty-thousand volts pouring into the man's body.

Charles skidded to a stop, lowering his gun as Chris twitched and fell face-first on the floor, every volitional muscle in his body locking up.

The hulking form of Detective Raines stepped out from around the corner, the black and yellow grip of the TASER clutched in his hands. "Chuck?"

Relief flooded over Charles. "Perry! Savannah called you?"

"Sure did, said ol' boy was armed and lookin' for her."

The TASER chirped as the voltage timed out. Chris let out a soft moan from the floor.

"Fucker," the Detective spat, pulling the trigger and unleashing another round of electricity into the stalker. He pointed to the weapon slung across his back. "Rifle or cuffs?"

"Cuffs," replied Charles, a shiver of post-adrenaline fatigue coming over him.

Perry pulled on a pair of neoprene gloves, grabbing the barrel of the gun and sliding it over the man's head as roughly as he could. Charles pulled the steel cuffs from his vest's back pocket, clicking them over Chris' wrists and double-locking them in place.

He stepped back, looking over to see Perry squinting suspiciously as he fiddled with the rifle.

"Shit's plastic," the big man grunted, before sliding open a hatch in the stock. "No fucking way…"

Charles' brow furrowed. "What?"

Perry turned the gun over, dozens of plastic pellets spilling out onto the tile floor. Leaning over, he bent down to scold the man directly. "You wanna blow in here, cause all this fuckin' trouble, and all you brought was a fuckin' BB gun? What is this? *Gawdamn amateur hour?!*"

Charles couldn't help but laugh. From his pocket, he heard the chirp of the radio.

"Chuck? I heard yelling. You alright?"

Charles plucked the radio from his vest. "Yeah, Andrea. S'all good. Perry tased him and we got him cuffed."

"Good deal. I found Savannah, she barricaded herself with Professor Bowtie in his office. We'll be up to meet you as soon as they finish moving the desk back."

Charles leaned back against the wall, watching as Perry continued searching Chris. Perry stepped back as he finished the search, discovering pepper spray, zip ties, and an orange ball-gag tucked away in the many cargo pockets.

"You want the honors?" he grunted, stripping off the gloves.

Charles shook his head. "S'all you, man."

Perry yanked the stalker onto his knees with one hand, fishing a card out of his wallet to read him his rights. Charles closed his eyes, slap-happy weariness settling over him like a thick blanket.

"Chuck?"

Charles' bleary eyes snapped open, taking in the welcome sight of Andrea walking with Savannah and Clark in tow. Pushing himself off the wall with his elbows, he hobbled over, sweeping his sister into a crushing hug.

"I was so worried," he whispered in her ear. "I'm so glad you're safe."

"It's ok. I'm fine." Savannah mumbled, struggling to breathe in the tight embrace. "But you're squishing me."

"I'm sorry." Charles released her, eye watering a little as regret cast long shadows across his face. "I'm so sorry. I didn't answer."

"It's alright. You did everything you could. And, look, I'm fine. I survived," Savannah said, reassuring him with a wan smile. "I called Perry when I couldn't get ahold of you. And Professor Morrison helped me barricade in his office."

Charles looked over to Clark.

"Don't mention it," the Professor said, waving him off before he could begin. "Full credit goes to Savannah. It was her idea to take shelter. And to pull the fire alarm to evacuate the building. And to call your friend. I just provided the office."

Charles nodded. "Still…thanks."

Clark offered a wry smile. "Of course."

"*Gents*," Andrea said, coughing loudly into her hand. "If we're finished here…"

"Right! The slasher!" piped Savannah, pushing out of her brother's arms before he could smother her again. "Andrea said you guys were chasing him. What happened? Did you catch him? What are you covered in? Is that your blood or his? And why you smell like shit?"

Charles shot Andrea a look. "Sooo, we're settled on slasher then?"

"With a banana knife," she smirked, crossing her arms over her chest.

"Now that's a story I'd like to hear some time," replied Professor Morrison drolly, blue eyes twinkling. "Provided, of course, the men in black helicopters approve."

"Sure thing, but later," Charles laughed, starting his hobbling path towards the stairs. "First I need a shower, a beer, and a fuck-ton of ibuprofen."

Chapter 18

Saturday

Sharon Kruschek stretched out on the worn leather couch, phone in hand and a blue throw pillow tucked behind her head. Sydney sprawled on the carpet below, markers in hand and tongue sticking out. The rain outside tapped a gentle staccato on the front window, mingling with the soft clink of a wooden spoon against a pan in the kitchen.

"Lunch is almost done," Gregory announced from the other room. "Hope you're ready for spaghetti!"

It was the fourth time they'd had spaghetti that week, but Gregory had insisted on taking care of the cooking ever since her discharge from the hospital. Not that she was complaining, she still got splitting headaches any time she stood for more than an hour. Sharon sighed to herself, nestling deeper into the warm confines of the couch. Her eyes had just drifted closed, when a knock at the door sent them fluttering open. Rising to her elbows, she paused for a moment to let the world stop spinning.

"I got it!" yelled Gregory, pasta fork in hand as he bustled in from the kitchen. He set a fresh cup of peppermint tea for her down by the couch. "Don't move, honey. I got it."

Sharon smiled, laying her head back down and shutting her eyes.

"What do these guys want now?" she heard him mutter by the door, followed by the click of the latch and the rasp of its opening.

"Who is it, Greg?" she murmured from the couch, giving serious consideration to simply napping through lunch.

"It's the cops, the ones from last week," he called back. "They want to know if you can speak with them."

"Oh, sure," she sighed, forcing her eyes back open. Louder, she replied, "Invite them in, Greg. It's raining."

"Afternoon, Mrs. Kruschek," Detective Morales said warmly, an expensive-looking leather coat draped over her arm as she walked in with Detective Davner.

Sharon eyed them both coolly, sipping at her tea. Detective

Morales had a touch too much foundation over the fading bruise under her right eye, and Sharon spotted a double-line of stitches along her temple that disappeared behind the tangled black curls. Detective Davner looked far worse, sporting a half-healed split lip, a fat purple knot rising from the side of his head, and an enormous blue brace strapped around one ankle.

"Afternoon, Detectives," replied Sharon, taking another sip of her tea.

"Hey Sharon," said Detective Davner, offering a friendly wave. "Hey Sydney, whatcha drawing today?"

"P'lice car going fast," she said, scrutinizing the page before exchanging her yellow marker for royal blue.

Sharon rolled her eyes. "All she's been drawing for the past two days. *Somebody* let her watch *Hot Fuzz*."

"Great movie," said Andrea. She crouched down beside the little girl, her voice lilting up with encouragement. "Sydney, do you want to be a police officer when you grow up?"

"No. P'lice don't drive dump trucks," Sydney stated matter-of-factly, capping off the blue marker. She picked up her latest masterpiece, calling over her shoulder as she ran off to place it on the fridge. "*I* wanna drive a dump truck."

Andrea sighed, standing up from the floor. She looked over at Charles for support.

He chuckled. "She's not wrong…"

The room fell quiet as he trailed off, a long pause stretching between the three adults.

Sharon broke the silence with a polite cough. "Sooooo, what brings Colorado's finest by on a rainy Saturday afternoon?"

Andrea eyed the kitchen, her tone officious and calm. "We came to inform you we concluded our investigation."

Sharon raised an eyebrow at Charles.

He nodded. "We got it."

"Dead? You're sure?"

"Crime techs spent the last three days canvassing the drains," Charles assured her. "Nothing but ash."

"And was that the only one?" Sharon sat up suddenly, ignoring the ensuing wave of lightheadedness. "It didn't lay eggs somewhere, did it?"

"See!" Andrea cried, smacking Charles on the arm. "I'm not the only one worried about eggs."

"Hey! Careful with the wounded." Charles winced, dramatically rubbing his arm. He turned back to Sharon, reassuring her with a shake of his head. "Techs cleared through over eight miles of tunnels, took them all week too. All they found was ash and some parts of other victims. No eggs."

"Good. Thank you," said Sharon, leaning back against the blue throw pillow. "So, is this the part where you make me promise not to tell anyone what I saw?"

Charles shrugged. "Our official report lists the subject as an unknown drifter on a killing spree—armed with a banana knife—who hitched a ride on the roof of your vehicle after murdering William Springsley. After killing Trooper Temmen during the traffic stop, he continued his spree in Colorado Springs."

Sharon frowned. "A drifter?"

"Yep."

"With a banana knife?"

"Uh-huh."

"Hitched a ride on my car for twenty-miles just to kill people in the Springs?"

"Sure did."

"And *that's* the story we're going with?"

"Fine! You tell people what you fuckin' want!" Andrea squawked, throwing up her hands.

"Bad word, p'lice lady," Sydney called out from the kitchen.

Andrea sighed, pinching the bridge of her nose with two fingers as she forced herself back into a level tone. "We're just letting you know the officially reported story just in case you wanted to make sure it all jives when you're recounting *your* part of the events. As a *courtesy*."

"World famous spaghetti, coming up!" Gregory chimed in, a heaping plate of spaghetti in each hand as he swung into the living room. He paused mid-step, sizing up the two detectives. "What about you two, staying for lunch?"

Charles side-eyed Sharon. She replied with the smallest shake of her head.

"Uh, No. Thanks!" Charles blurted, fumbling for a good excuse. "We…have…other appointments."

Enthusiasm undiminished, Gregory shook the plate at Andrea. "You sure? The sauce is authentically Italian…"

Sharon caught Andrea's eye, shaking her head and silently mouthing the word 'Ragu.'

"So, very, very kind of you," grimaced Andrea. She threw on her leather coat, motioning to Charles and the door. "But we really were just leaving."

Gregory gave Sharon a questioning look.

"You heard them, Greg. Appointments. Cases. Important stuff," she said bemusedly. She gestured towards the dining room with her mug. "Why don't you go set the table? I'll be there in a minute."

Gregory shrugged, whistling *'Tarantella Napoletana'* to himself while he strolled out of the room.

Charles shook his head, zipping up his coat as he limped to the door. He turned back to wave. "Bye Sydney. Bye Sharon."

"Bye P'liceman!" Sydney shouted from the kitchen.

Sharon caught Andrea's eye again, circling the air with her mug. "So this is it then. No more…"

"No ma'am, all done." Andrea confirmed, making her own way to the door. "And with the official reports submitted, this is probably the last you'll see of us."

"Good. Good," replied Sharon, leaning back and closing her eyes. "I sincerely fucking hope so."

Sergeant Briske rested an elbow on the vast expanse of the mahogany desk, a thick finger pressed to his temple as he scrutinized the reports before him. His pale green eyes darted back and forth, skimming the dense text of the investigation summary. Reaching the end of the final page, he leaned back against the tall, leather chair. Sergeant Briske took a deep breath, holding it in his chest for a moment before exhaling in a long, slow, exasperated sigh.

Charles cleared his throat, hands in his pockets as he stood across the room. "Soooo, Sarge—"

The Section Chief silenced him with a sharp look. He skimmed the report a second time before turning it over, dragging a heavy hand down his face as he considered his response. In true cop fashion, the entirety of the investigative report was a formulaic homologation of boilerplate 'official phrases' strung together in compact typeface. The events it described were extraordinary—dismembered victims, a pitched gunfight with the subject, a sewer lair rigged with incendiaries—but retold in the same flattened, un-ceremonial tone of a DMV pamphlet. Sergeant Briske had read reports like this before, usually from internal affairs, but never from Charles. He eyed the detective standing before him carefully, not quite sure what to make of it. Or the report from a Pueblo PD detective sitting in the top drawer of his desk, the text of the two identical—right down to the typo in the second line.

"When did you believe our suspect was hiding in the drainage tunnels?" the Sergeant asked, fingers steepling as he looked out over the wide, wood desk.

"After Detective Morales and I mapped out the victims," Charles answered, his face studiously neutral to match his tone. "Monument Creek seemed like the common denominator, so we started canvassing the area between the scenes. That's when we found a piece of a victim's clothing snagged on the broken grate."

Sergeant Brisked nodded. "And that led you to search the tunnels."

"Yes, sir."

"Why didn't you call for back-up?"

Charles shrugged. "Didn't think we'd need it at the time. We found the subject during the evidence survey. Pure accident."

Sergeant Briske frowned, forehead wrinkles massing up over the shiny bald head. Charles and the PPD detective had both been outfitted in body armor and carrying shotguns. None of that squared up with happenstance.

"*Hmmmmmm.*" The Section Chief's eyes narrowed over his fingertips. "So you found one victim's arm, decided to press on and search a few of the surrounding tunnels until you located the subject?"

"More like stumbled across him. Like I said, we were looking for evidence related to the victims when we found the two bodies."

"The folks from the homeless shelter."

"Risen Hearts, yes."

"And that's when the subject walked in. How did you recognize him?"

Charles shrugged again. "We didn't, he was just a scraggly-looking guy dressed in green. But he started shooting as soon as he saw us, so we figured it out."

"And that's when you returned fire," the Section Chief nodded, checking the story in the report. He cast a sideways glance at Charles. "No call for backup then either?"

"No time," The detective said, crossing his arms over his chest. "It all happened too fast. We walk in, he comes up on us, starts shooting, we take cover and return fire, then he detonated."

"Right, right," Sergeant Briske noted, turning the report back over. "The incendiary device. You said the device ignited and the other detective pulled you out of the way of the flames?"

"Sure did, that's when I rolled my ankle," said Charles, patting the blue boot around his foot. "Detective Andrea Morales, by the way."

"Right," Sergeant Briske grunted, eyes narrowing further. "Pretty quick thinking on the subject's part. Sees you two, starts shooting, then gives up and triggers a series of preplaced explosives."

"Guess he figured the game was up."

"Figured the game was up," Sergeant Briske echoed back, letting the words hang in the air. "You know it's funny, the crime lab spent all week analyzing the trace residue from the explosion. They still haven't pinned down the accelerant used or the method of ignition."

Silence stretched between them as he studied the younger detective, trying to read the thoughts lurking just behind the pat answers.

"No telling what that guy's background was. Could've been a high-school chemistry teacher for all we know" Charles replied, breaking the silence with a forced laugh. "Or a government scientist."

The Section Chief said nothing, bushy eyebrows tightly knit as he stared Charles down. None of it was adding up, and he didn't need fifteen years on the force to know it. Sergeant Briske hated a lot of things in this world—secrets most of all—but he also knew the value of letting some things stay buried. He watched the detective shift in place, crossing and uncrossing his arms a few times before simply jamming his hands in his pockets again. Still, in a single day, Charles had tracked down a spree killer responsible for eight open homicide cases across two counties *and* responded to an active shooter at Colorado College. Not to mention intervening in a mugging and saving a jogger's life the night before. Sergeant Briske took in another deep breath, holding it in his chest before letting it out slow. Whatever he was hiding, he'd probably earned a bit of grace.

"Well, thank you for coming in here and walking me through all of it," the Sergeant said at last, puncturing the tension with a gentle smile. "I'm sorry to have dragged you down here and interrupted your convalescent leave."

Relief washed over Charles' face. "No problem, Sarge. I was just on my way to lunch with a friend."

Sergeant Briske's eyes narrowed again as the detective beat a retreat for the door. Self-detonating sewer killers were one thing, but Charles with *friends* stretched the limits of credulity. He sighed as the door shut, contemplating the inscrutable absurdities of his present reality while drawing a bottle of Four Roses out of the bottom drawer. Picking up the phone with one heavy hand, he popped the cork on the bourbon with the other. As the connection whirred in his ear, Sergeant Briske took a long, long pull from the bottle. Some way or another, he was going to have to explain all of this to Sergeant Gomez.

Charles opened the door to the Delta 88, sliding in behind the wide, tan wheel.

"Did he buy it?"

"I dunno. He's hard to read sometimes." Charles rolled his head back and forth, working the tension out of his shoulders. "Did yours?"

Andrea shrugged. "Mostly. My Section Chief was righteously pissed about the busted shotguns. If we hadn't wrapped up the case and busted that punk at the school, I'd probably be facing suspension. As it is, they gave me a week of admin leave—best outcome all things considered."

Charles nodded, rubbing the back of his neck. "I guess that balances out."

"S'pose so." Andrea watched the clouds pass, reflected on the vast, golden hood. "Lunch?"

"Sure," said Charles, buckling himself in. He gave her a half-smile. "I know a pub around here with decent sandwiches."

"I could go for sandwiches," she said, returning the smile as she leaned against the worn cloth seats. "And as I recall, you owe me a beer."

Quiet hung over the apartment of Charles Davner, the darkness of the room broken up by long fingers of amber streetlight filtering through the tattered blinds. Petunia stretched out on her bed in the far corner of the room, snoring mightily on a full stomach. The digital clock on the bedside table projected 11:03 in bright red numerals from behind a few empty green bottles.

Charles sat up in bed, leaning against the plain wooden headboard. His face was lit with the blue glow of the laptop resting on his knees, a half empty Heineken tucked in the crook of his elbow as he scrolled past pictures of sunlit waterfalls, kittens nestled in baskets, auto-playing videos of vegan recipes, and advertisements for multi-level marketing schemes. Charles sighed, alone in the apartment and in his thoughts.

A chirp came from the bedside table, jerking him out of his doldrums. Charles picked up his phone, swiping across as the name 'Clark Morrison' flashed on screen.

'Hi there! Sorry to bother you so late.'

'No worries, still up.'

'Exciting night?'

Charles looked down at the laptop and half empty bottle. Petunia belched from the corner.

"Extremely," he muttered, before typing, *'Nope. Still on convalescent leave.'*

'Oh, right. How're you feeling?'

Charles stretched his leg, ignoring the pop in his ankle as he

wiggled his toes. *'Pretty good. Should have the brace off by Monday.'*
'Glad to hear it.'

Charles smiled a little. *'What about you? Back in class yet?'*

'No, thankfully. Still a little shaky about going back in after everything on Monday. But, I've got the next week off. Spring break.'

Charles nodded to himself. *'Right. Got any fun plans?'*

Waiting for a response, the quiet weighed in on him from all around the dark room. He took a nervous sip of his beer, wild, speculative thoughts rampaging through his head as the seconds passed. Setting the phone down on the bed, he snatched it back up when it chirped.

'As a matter of fact, yes! I'm heading out to hike near Cave of the Winds on Wednesday. One of my students insists she spotted a Boreal Toad out there and now I HAVE to check it out.'

Charles chuckled, setting aside the beer in his hand. Halfway through typing, his screen flashed again.

'You're welcome to join me.'

Charles' chewed his lower lip. In spite of the many attempts by those around him to change his mind over the years, he still considered hiking and the outdoors as things to endure, rather than enjoy. Savannah, in particular, was always nagging him to get outside and experience the wonders of the Coloradan wilderness. She'd even given him three-hundred dollar insulated boots for his last birthday, splitting the cost with James.

Charles looked over at the boots as they sat in his closet, still wrapped in tissue paper and nestled inside the speckled carboard box. He ran a hand through his tousled hair, a dozen excuses popping in his mind for why he shouldn't go. Muttering to himself, his eyes settled on the bedside table, the picture on the laptop screen reflected back in the many empty bottles. Charles stared hard at the sunset beach distorted in the curved green glass, before reaching over and closing the laptop screen. Setting it aside, he picked up his phone again, anxious thumbs finding their place on the narrow keyboard.

He tapped out a brief reply and closed his eyes, leaning back against the plain headboard.

'I'd like that.'

Epilogue

Monday
One month later

Dr. Leventhal hunched over the keyboard at her cheap, government desk, the latest laboratory financials from General Sinclair reflected in her thick spectacles. As she scrolled through shortfall projections and stricken budgetary items, she felt an ache growing behind her eyes. She let her glasses dangle by her neck, driving the stress away by pressing hard against her closed eyelids. She opened them to near darkness, the motion-sensitive lighting having once again failed to register the existence of the petite scientist. Dr. Leventhal scowled, hopping out of the high-backed chair.

"I bet *Jerry Ostriker* never has to deal with this shit," she grumbled, yellow converse sneakers squeaking off the dingy tile as she jumped up and down.

There was a knock at the door, the fluorescent bulbs flaring to life as her JTRS supervisor, Adam Klausten, poked his head in the office. "Dr. Leventhal, ma'am."

She stopped jumping, arms dropping by her side to smooth out the bunching in her oversized sweater dress. "Yes, Adam? What is it?"

"SDR transceiver just picked up another of those weird blips again."

"770 gigahertz?" Dr. Leventhal sighed, replacing the glasses on her face.

Klausten nodded. "Yep, just like last month, and the one December."

The ache behind her eyes returned, matching the vein throbbing in her temple.

"Do…do you want to come see?" Klausten asked, jerking a thumb down the hall.

Dr. Leventhal took another look at the projections on the screen, scowl deepening as she weighed it against the thirty-two other tasks she ahead of her that day.

Klausten waited in silence, inching his body back from the doorway.

"Fine! Fuck it!" she barked at last, yanking her ID card out of the computer terminal and storming out the door.

Klausten flattened himself against the wall, giving her space as she passed. Coffee sloshed out of his mug and onto his khakis.

"But you call AnthCom and get one of their techs on their way *now!*" she demanded, jabbing Klausten with a reedy finger as she whipped by. "We didn't spend one-hundred-and-seven-thousand *gawdamn* dollars for that transceiver to crap out two months after the warranty expires!"

Klausten watched two interns duck into a spare closet, clearing a path as she stomped down the narrow hall. He let her go, the billowing, purple knit dress disappearing around a corner while he rubbed the sore spot on his chest. He knew he should follow her, if for no other reason than to shield the junior techs from having to work with her looming over their shoulders. Looking down at the half-empty mug, he waited a moment, listening as her disgruntled muttering faded down the hall. Then he sucked in a deep breath, counted down from ten, and set off as well.

Miles away from the Archambault Peak Research Facility, tucked away on the western slopes of a snowy peak, two bighorns clashed. The dry crack of their horns reverberated across the rocky ground, echoing throughout the snowline and in the windy ravines. Again and again the rams came together, their primal skirmish a witness to the coming spring. A cold wind whistled down the mountainside, ruffling their thick wool as it passed.

Several yards down, a marmot dozed on a granite boulder, watching the spectacle of the two sheep. Plump body spread to catch the sun, its thick fur obscuring some of the strange, looping markings etched into the smooth stone. A line of dried blood dripped down the boulder's southern edge, the triangle it formed loosely connecting the patches of clustered markings.

A sharp whistle cut through the air—a warning cry from the colony's sentinel—and the marmot was off, scrabbling down the nearest burrow.

Behind it, a low hum came from the boulder's side, a gathering thrum like the slow beat of an ancient heart.

The hum grew, the disquieting buzz becoming loud enough to distract the rams from their petty quarrel. They stopped their jousting, nervously stamping their hooves. Atmospheric pressure swelled on the mountain slope, building in waves timed to the steady hum.

The hum deepened, pressure escalating with terrible foreboding. It released in a flash of purple light, a line of energy arcing between the scattered markings with an audible pop. Thoroughly spooked, the rams took off, narrow hooves kicking up loose stones as they ran.

They left behind a small, purple void hanging in the center of the rock face, encircled by a thin edge of crackling energy. The humming swelled again, the void widening in another flash of purple iridescence.

And out of the void stepped a shiny green claw.

ENJOY OTHER STORIES FROM THE AUTHOR!

For the troopers of AZH-01, life is an exercise in routines.

Wake up, respond to alarms, stand in formation—slack off in between. Get your gear, don't break scram-time, and stay out of Sergeant's crosshairs. Securing the edges of populated space isn't the glory and excitement they were promised, but these aren't the Inter-Stellar Coalition Force's best and brightest.

Rania doesn't mind routines. Routines give her something to hold on to, they guide her as she finds her niche in the sweaty locker room of military life. Just like the other troopers, all she wants is to do her job, stay out of trouble, and get one day closer to getting out. That routine is shattered when something claws its way through the station's doors. Something swift. Vicious. *Hungry*. With the chain of command shredded and the power knocked out, it's a race against time for Rania and the other troopers of AZH-01.

They were just trying to get through the day, now they're fighting to survive the night.

ABSOLUTE ZEROS

BRITTLE
SYSTEMS
XANDER
FRANKLIN

Ian Bernard is very far from home.

Newly promoted, and possessed with a healthy fear of the outdoors, he's left his wife and son for the first time on a deployment to the sun-scorched dunes of Anius. Dust-storms, sand-worms, and black mold — Buck-Sergeant Bernard is fighting just to keep his head above the shifting sands.

But a simple workplace accident uncovers a conspiracy implicating the ICF's elite special operations unit—the Commando Raiders. Caught in the crossfire, he'll face murderous commandos, military bureaucrats, and a particularly tenacious safety investigator.

Up against a ticking clock and the galaxy's finest warriors, it'll take luck, wits, and guts if he hopes to clear his name.

Unfortunately, time isn't the only thing in short supply.

Brittle Systems

www.ingramcontent.com/pod-product-compliance
Lightning Source LLC
Chambersburg PA
CBHW070350200726
48294CB00003B/830